THE MUSTANGERS

This Large Print Book carries the
Seal of Approval of N.A.V.H.

THE MUSTANGERS

ANDREW J. FENADY

WHEELER PUBLISHING
A part of Gale, a Cengage Company

Farmington Hills, Mich • San Francisco • New York • Waterville, Maine
Meriden, Conn • Mason, Ohio • Chicago

GALE
A Cengage Company

Copyright © 2019 by Andrew J. Fenady.
Wheeler Publishing, a part of Gale, a Cengage Company.

ALL RIGHTS RESERVED
Wheeler Publishing Large Print Western.
The text of this Large Print edition is unabridged.
Other aspects of the book may vary from the original edition.
Set in 16 pt. Plantin.

LIBRARY OF CONGRESS CIP DATA ON FILE.
CATALOGUING IN PUBLICATION FOR THIS BOOK
IS AVAILABLE FROM THE LIBRARY OF CONGRESS

ISBN-13: 978-1-4328-6773-7 (softcover alk. paper)

Published in 2019 by arrangement with Pinnacle Books, an imprint of Kensington Publishing Corp.

Printed in the United States of America
1 2 3 4 5 6 7 23 22 21 20 19

For

BEN JOHNSON
  Champion Rodeo Cowboy
  Academy Award Actor
  Unflappable Friend
  All-'Round "Nicer Feller"

DUKE FENADY
  With a Beholden
  Tip of the Stetson

And, of course
MARY FRANCES

Prelude: Out of the Past

The land changes. Sometimes it takes years. It takes centuries. Hundreds, sometimes thousands of centuries, during the journey of ages immemorial. At other times, the land shudders, cracks, and abrupt peaks protrude to pierce the skin of soil and steeple over the still-restless earth. And with the infinite turning of the earth, vast oceans waste and dry into sand and desert.

The sea, sporadically dotted with islands, at times is calm, a liquid horizon. But the sea at other times is fierce, with scolding winds, upturned trees, and stark destruction, leaving naked islands sinking to a watery tomb of an exhausted deep.

But the sky is eternal. Ever changing, yet ever the same. Sun and clouds and mist. Even through thunder, lightning, and rain. Then, after the curtain of night falls and rises, the sky is ever the same. Sun and clouds and mist.

Where, a hundred years ago, in the mid-1870s, through the same western sky, only eagles flew, on this day a lone jet streaks between towering spires to fulfill a promise . . . a promise made when the West was old . . . but younger.

CHAPTER ONE

Flying over the rugged crests of the western countryside, the silver Gulfstream jet streamed through protruding peaks.

Patrick Merrill walked out of the pilot's cabin and closed the door, then paused. There were those who said he had a striking resemblance to the actor Tony Curtis. Merrill didn't mind, didn't mind at all. In fact, he agreed.

He smiled and looked down at the leggy, blue-eyed, freckled, blond attendant sitting in a front chair, reading *Life* magazine. The small metal plate pinned to her tunic identified her as Trudy Ryan.

Merrill pointed back to the pilot's cabin.

"Just checked the compass. You can relax, Tru; we're right on course."

She glanced up, semi-smiled, and went back to *Life.*

Unfazed. Patrick Merrill continued to smile. He smiled a lot, like he was kidding the whole world, including himself — but not his boss, Senator Jimmy Deegan.

Senator Jimmy Deegan sat at a small desk making notes on a yellow legal pad, with a slim open briefcase on the desk. Near the briefcase, a framed photograph of a handsome redheaded woman and two young sons.

In his midforties, Senator Deegan, shirt-sleeved, with a rugged face, muscled build, and a few needles of gray at the temples, looked up at his approaching assistant.

"Senator, the pilot says that we just crossed the state line. Your state, Senator. Be landing within the hour."

"Thanks, Patrick."

"Can I have the attendant get you some coffee?"

"No, thanks." He nodded toward the photograph. "Mary Frances says I drink too much coffee."

"I *know* I do. I'll pass, too." Merrill turned and started to walk toward the attendant.

"But I do have the time and inclination for an overdue Montecristo. Why don't you sit down, Patrick?"

"Don't want to interrupt you, Senator."

"All done, m'boy, take a seat." An unlit cigar rested in an unused ashtray. Senator Deegan lit the Montecristo, placed the legal pad into the briefcase, then lifted and looked at the photograph.

"You know, Patrick, next month will be our tenth anniversary."

"Congratulations, Senator. Too bad she couldn't come along."

"With two young ones and expecting a third, Dr. Davies prescribed no flying. We're hoping for a girl this time. Even got a name picked out . . . Shannon. Mary Frances is Irish, you know."

"You're a lucky man, sir. It isn't easy to find a girl like her."

"You bet."

"Me, I'm waiting for a girl like that to find me . . . in the meanwhile . . ." Merrill looked up front toward the attendant.

Senator Deegan chuckled, puffed on the Montecristo, put the photograph into the briefcase, and looked down out the window.

"You were born around here, weren't you, Senator?"

"No, born in the East, but I used to spend the summers here on my father's ranch, the Big Brawny. In those days it was on the rim of the Dust Bowl."

"Dust Bowl?"

"Yep. And you, Patrick, where were you born?"

"In the East," he smiled. "The *far* East.

11

New Jersey. Passaic. But seems I heard about the Dust Bowl . . . saw a movie about it once on television. Can't remember the name . . ."

"*The Grapes of Wrath.*"

"Yeah. All that happened a long time ago, didn't it?"

"Well." The senator shook his head and smiled. "It wasn't all that long ago, at least it doesn't seem like it, during the thirties."

"Still, I guess that things have changed a lot since then."

"In a movie, John Wayne once said, 'Things usually change for the better.' I'd like to think he was right."

The senator looked out of the window again. The plane was flying lower now. He pointed below.

Patrick Merrill leaned and looked down.

A herd of horses galloping across the terrain. The speeding shadow of the jet approached . . . crossed . . . and passed by the herd running wild and free.

"Horses." Merrill smiled. "I guess there'll always be horses."

"Those aren't horses. Not just horses."

"They're not?"

"No. You city fellas can't be blamed for not knowing the difference, but those are mustangs. And in a way that's why I'm making this trip."

"I don't understand."

"No reason why you should unless I tell you." The senator looked at his wristwatch. "We've got some time yet. You want to hear?"

"You bet. Yes, sir."

"Well, then, light up one of your coffin spikes and I'll bend your ear."

Patrick Merrill reached inside his suit coat jacket, pulled out a half-empty — or half-full — pack of Pall Mall cigarettes, lit one, and leaned back to listen.

"It started when I met a cowboy named Ben Smith."

The senator thought a moment, then proceeded.

"No, I guess it started before." He took a draw from the Montecristo. "I'll tell it like a story I might write about him someday when I'm through with politics — and vice versa."

A rodeo arena in Globe, Arizona — band music — the stands overflowing with spectators — men, women, and children. Flags, balloons, streamers. Rodeo clowns performing in the arena, prelude to the next event.

Beer flowed and was swallowed from the bottle, the can, and paper cup. There were hip flasks left over from Prohibition and the early thirties, when hard cash was rare in the cities, states, and country. But there was prize money to be won during the Depression of the midthirties.

Ben Smith had ridden thousands of broncos at hundreds of rodeos. He was no stranger to Globe, where he broke some of Tom Horn's records that people said would last hundreds of years.

But this time it was different.

There's an old saying "There never was a horse that couldn't be rode — there never was a cowboy that couldn't be thrown."

Ben Smith made his way toward the chutes.

Three of the most interested spectators stood watching while he walked closer to one of the gates.

Two friends. One, the opposite.

The friends, Quirt Dawson and Stretch Monahan.

Quirt, lanky, nearly six and a half feet tall, almost a couple of decades past his rodeoing days, with a broken beak that had been struck by fists and the ground. And even in these lean days, there were scattered few ranchers, racehorse owners, and speculators in this area who didn't pay for Quirt Dawson's appraisal before shelling out hard cash for horseflesh.

Stretch Monahan, former jockey, and a good one, until he started spending prize money on booze, broads, and betting on the bangtails. He got the nickname years ago when he enlisted in the Fighting 69th during the War to End All Wars. The recruiting sergeant asked, "Weight?"

"One hundred twenty . . . more or less."

"Height?"

"Five foot two . . . when I stretch."

From then on, Danny became Stretch Monahan. Now, instead of riding racehorses, Stretch Monahan groomed and timed them.

Spud Tatum, the third interested party, was a young cowboy contestant full of himself, and himself only. He could sit a bronc well enough, but the size of his Stetson kept swelling in order to keep up with his hubris.

The announcer's voice gusted through the speakers.

"Ladies and gentlemen . . . and cowboys and cowgirls, the next rider is number thirteen, Ben Smith, riding that dreaded terror of the circuit, Basher."

Ben Smith was in the chute and saddled. Tall, lean, broad of shoulders, with a creased face, clear, narrow blue eyes, and a chiseled chin line, leaning forward on Basher.

The announcer's voice heightened dramatically.

"You all know Ben is a three-time All-'Round Champion Cowboy . . . a living legend of the rodeo circuit."

"More like 'ancient history,' " Spud snorted. "Ol' bones was lucky to step up on that horse."

"And you, flannelmouth," Stretch looked up at him, "are a horse's ass."

"Yeah, button up, tinhorn." Quirt looked down at him. "You couldn't carry Ben's spurs."

Spud Tatum grinned.

"We'll just see who carries home the prize money."

The announcer was now at full steam on the public-address system.

"Ben Smith in the saddle, now ready to ride on Basher!"

Ben Smith nodded toward the gateman.

"Outside!" Ben declared.

The gate swung open — the animal leaped into the arena as the crowd roared. Hooves springing into the air, pounding, forward, scraping against the fence, snorting, sunfishing . . .

. . . all in less than five seconds. Ben was thrown off.

Ben's head crashed hard, too hard, through the fence rail — spectators stood — some screamed — some turned away — then stunned silence.

Rodeo clowns and other cowboys rushed to the aid of the unconscious man.

There never was a cowboy that couldn't be throwed.

CHAPTER TWO

In the first aid room, Ben was conscious, barely, and still disoriented, as they all came into focus.

Dr. Blake Lewis, a big man with a gentle touch and a bedside smile, who had been through it all too many times, for better or worse.

Deek Evans, the rodeo owner, friend and foster father to Ben since Ben won his first contest at his first ride at this same arena in the early postwar years.

And, of course, Quirt Dawson and Stretch Monahan.

Ben looked around and did his best to raise his bandaged head from the bed. It was not easy.

Dr. Lewis placed his hand on his patient's shoulder.

"How you doing, Ben?"

His patient managed a smile.

"You tell me, Doc."

"You were sent for, but you didn't go. You're all together, but that fence isn't."

"That hammerhead . . ." Ben coughed. ". . . lived up to his name."

"You gave him a ride, son," Deek Evans said.

"Yeah," Ben replied. "A short one."

Night at the Appaloosa Saloon, the bar was populated with men and women in western attire at the counter and at tables — drinking, playing cards, pinball machines — smoke crawled upward toward the tin ceiling to the tune of western music from the blinking jukebox near one of the circulating fans suspended from above. Some of the jukebox lyrics were audible, some were lost due to the cacophony of conversation, laughter, and alcoholic intake of the customers.

At a table not far from the entrance, Ben, Deek Evans, Quirt Dawson, and Stretch Monahan were drinking beer. Ben's head was still bandaged but it didn't prevent him from wearing his Stetson.

Irene Swinderski, one of the waitresses, strawberry blond, hazel-eyed, a wee mite thick, but fetching, dressed in jeans cut off above the knees, pink boots, and tight-fitting denim shirt, was weaving her way around tables and customers. Not coincidentally, the lyric refrain from the jukebox accompanied her tour . . . "Good night, Irene, good night . . ."

"Hey, Irene," one of the customers stood up from a table and shouted, "they're playing our song!"

"Not *our* song, bub, *my* song," Irene Swinderski shot back, and kept on traveling toward her destination.

"How's the beer supply, boys?"

Quirt lifted a near-empty mug.

"Close to desperate, Miss Irene."

"Well, that's my department. I can do something about that." She pointed to Ben's bandaged head. "Would you want me to toss a couple of aspirin in that beer, cowboy?"

"Shot of bourbon might be better," Stretch suggested.

"No, thanks," Ben smiled. "Just a straight mug of Lucky Lager, if you please."

"I try to." Irene Swinderski nodded and walked away.

"Some try, she succeeds," Stretch snorted. "Or so I'm told."

There was applause from the area near the entrance as Spud Tatum strode in, one hand full of money and the other arm wrapped around the upper body of a voluptuous Valkyrie who could start or stop a human stampede.

Spud Tatum nodded and smiled at the hand clappers, then smiled even broader as he approached, then paused at the table where Ben Smith and his friends sat.

"Evenin', gents," then at the rodeo owner, "Mr. Deek Evans, you run the best rodeo west of the hundredth meridian, yeah-bo, most prize money I won this year — or any year," then waved the money toward Quirt. "I told you, didn't I, Quirt, ol' dirt?"

Quirt, ol' dirt didn't respond, and Spud continued and squeezed the Valkyrie's bare shoulder.

"Hey, you fellas all know Wanda, here?"

All the fellas nodded.

Wanda nodded back.

"Sure, I know the fellas."

Spud grinned toward Ben Smith.

"How you doin', ol'-timer?"

"Still tickin'."

The winner winked at his companion, said, "Yeah," more than a little too loud, "but windin' down, I'd say," and laughed.

Quirt rose in a quick, aggressive move, but Ben took hold of Quirt's arm for just a beat.

Spud stopped laughing and turned toward Wanda.

"Come on, you sweet bag o' sugar. We got some celebratin' to do."

He commenced to guide her across the room. The way she walked was an anatomical marvel.

"She knows what she's got, all right," Stretch noted, "and how to use it."

"I knew a filly like that in Wichita." Quirt rubbed his chin. "Sexy, but not romantic."

Spud Tatum's voice roared at the bartender.

"Drinks for the house on the big winner!"

At Ben's table, Deek Evans shook his head in disgust.

"Stupid loudmouth."

"Diarrhea of the jawbone," Stretch added.

"He's young," Ben smiled.

"He won't always be young," Quirt said, "but he'll always be stupid. That's something he'll never outgrow," and finished his beer.

Irene Swinderski approached with a tray loaded with mugs of beer.

"Here you be, gents. You heard what the bronc squeezer said. This round's on him. Drink up, anyhow."

After the mugs were distributed, Deek Evans lifted his and nodded.

"Well, Ben, good health and good fortune." They drank.

"Yep," Ben said, "and speaking of health . . . Deek, I thank you for everything, but I'm hanging 'em up. Through rodeoing."

"Say it isn't so, Ben," from Quirt.

"Pay no 'tention to that two-bit tinhorn," from Stretch.

"You sure, Ben?" from Deek Evans.

"Won my first prize money from you, Deek, but I been through for some time. Gonna quit while I'm still in one piece and can look back with a little pride."

"Ben, some of your records'll never be broke," from Quirt.

"But some of my bones will be."

"Ben," Evans countered, "just 'cause you're not going to ride . . . well, your name's still a draw, a big draw. I can give you a job, a good job . . . be pleased to . . . you've earned it."

"Thanks, but I don't want you to give me anything. Going home."

"Home," Quirt said. "For some of us 'home' is just another word for 'saddle.' "

"Not for me. Not anymore."

"Where, then?" from Stretch.

"The Little Brawny. Fair-sized ranch. Just enough land. Just enough challenge."

"And family, Ben?" Deek Evans asked.

"No."

"Well, you got more friends than there are fiddlers in hell," Deek Evans smiled. "Need a stake, Ben?"

Ben Smith shook his head and took a swallow of beer.

"Thanks, no, Deek. I'm fine."

As Tatum and Wanda approached, it was hard to determine which of the two was laughing louder.

"Whoa, Nellie!" Tatum pulled Wanda to an abrupt stop at Ben's table. "I wanna bid adios to these here hoot owls." He made a mock bow to the table. "Well, good seein' you old cabin robbers, but Wanda and me got to make a couple more stops . . ." he glanced at smiling Wanda ". . . before we turn in and mate."

Silence from the cabin robbers.

A well-seasoned, white-bearded westerner hesitatingly approached the table, looking at Ben Smith. The stranger carried a slim autograph book and fountain pen.

"Excuse me, all. But Mr. Smith, sir, they told me you were in here. Missed you at a couple of other rodeos. Come all the way from Casper, Wyoming, to add your autograph to my collection before it's too late . . . for me, not for you. Would you do me the honor, sir?"

Ben nodded.

"My honor, Mr. . . . ?"

"Bailey, Austin Bailey."

Ben took the book and wrote across a page, while the others watched, then he handed the pen and the still-open book to Austin Bailey.

"There you are, Mr. Bailey."

Mr. Bailey's hand shook slightly as he gazed at the page, then at Ben.

"Thank you, Mr. Smith . . . and thanks for the sentiment that you wrote. I surely appreciate . . ."

Spud Tatum cleared his throat and smiled.

"I s'pose you want my autograph. I'm Spud Tatum, you know."

"Yes, I know," Bailey nodded, "but I only collect signatures from All-'Round Champion Cowboys. Thanks again, Mr. Smith." He turned and slowly walked toward the entrance.

"Strange ol' coot," Tatum shrugged, then turned to Wanda. "Well, come on, sweet bag o' sugar, time's a-wastin'." Then one parting look at Ben Smith.

"By the way, ol' Ben, I just put another nickel in the jukebox for a song that'll be comin' on about now, dedicated to you."

As Spud and Wanda made their way toward the door, Tatum looked back and smiled.

Young Gene Autry's voice swelled through the jukebox.

. . . Git along, little doggie, get along, git along.
I'm heading for the last roundup.

CHAPTER THREE

The wonder of it all.

Ben Smith was on a journey of a little less than a thousand miles and a lifetime of a little more than forty years.

After a quarter of a century, weary, bone bruised, now without the bandage, but wearing his Stetson, the three-time All-'Round Champion Cowboy, instead of on a horse, sat behind a steering wheel.

He had slipped into his already loaded pickup in Globe before first light at four a.m., so as to avoid good-intentioned friends and strangers with a volley of "farewells" and "amens," "till we meet agains" — as if he ever would with most of them again.

Times change. People change. And when you're traveling, the land changes. Especially in the West.

And Ben had time to think while he found out all over again what a big country this is — and no two places are exactly alike.

27

The wonder of it all.

How they survived their journeys, just over a hundred years ago — those who survived — on horseback, on mules, on wagon trains. On foot.

This same terrain that Ben was crossing from south to north, but a hundred years ago the varied voyagers were compassing east to west.

Westward from the Mississippi across the open plains where buffalo had ranged and were commissary for Indians — then slaughtered by invaders — by the army, railroaders, hunters, sportsmen — for the delicacy of tongue, the fashion of robe, the ornament of horn on walls of easterners who had never seen a live buffalo.

Until the Indian commissary was empty, as were the Indian bellies.

Through the white-hot heat of scorched desert sands — the winter frost and blinding snow of sky sierras — the deep and cavernous canyons — across raging rivers and bleak horizons.

With desperate hope ahead and wooden crosses on lonely mounds to mark, for more than a few, journey's end.

And for the descendants of some of those pilgrims who were making another journey even now — "Okies" moving west toward

California . . . on rattling Fords, creaking Chevy pickups, on bicycles, and on foot, leaving behind them abandoned skeletal houses leaning windward, along with thin needling dust that had savaged once-fertile land, leaving behind the Dust Bowl.

Ben Smith crisscrossed some of these vagrant caravans crawling west while he drove north through that devastated Dust Bowl.

During the so-called Great War, he had seen and been a bloody part of men in opposing trenches doing their damnedest to destroy one another. But they had weapons — guns and grenades and cannon — and a cause — to end all wars.

But these were men, women, and children, babies, ragged and half-starved with no weapons, except the will to move on — and to survive.

If Ben had ever felt sorry for himself, now, at the sight of these poor, oppressed migrants, he realized how sorrow was spelled.

He had suffered his share of lumps, but unlike those vagrants, he had some idea of what was ahead — the Little Brawny — "Fair-sized ranch. Just enough land. Just enough challenge."

One door closes. Another door opens.

Even though he didn't know the extent of

the "challenge" part, compared to those Okies, he was one damn lucky cowboy.

That's right, he told himself, one damn
lucky cowboy driving in the comparative
comfort of a 1934 Chevy pickup, equipped
even with a radio that had been accompanying him with dozens and dozens of country-
western songs. Words and music that all
seemed to blend together — until he crossed
his state's border.

Then there came a song with words and
music he had never heard before, titled,
"You Can't Ever Go Home Again."

A man'll come home
to the place of his youth
in search of the things left behind.
He looks for a place,
for a smile on a face.
But the last mile's the hardest to find.

I've known the high country
where lone eagles fly,
the desolate no-path terrain.
And now that my years
are all winters, I try
to call back the summers in vain.

So don't you know,
don't you know, my friend.

Know the hollow cry
of the lonesome man.
You can't ever go home again, again.
You can't ever go home again.

Ben turned off the radio.

After listening to that, he didn't want to hear any more songs for a while, and he thought to himself.

Two of the most unpredictable, uncertain times in your life are when you leave home and when you come back.

CHAPTER FOUR

The terrain was different now, gentler, greener, and more hospitable.

The front of Ben's pickup was different, too, and less hospitable.

Steam from the radiator curled above the fore of the hood, and vaporous clouds drifted toward the windshield.

The good news was evidence of civilization.

Still steaming, the pickup pulled into a gas station at a crossroad, RANDY'S INDEPENDENT GAS.

"Great thunderin' hallelujah," Randy shouted as he approached and almost instantly recognized his customer. Randy, a born westerner, tall, bowlegged, and booted. He wore a Stetson-style hat except it was fashioned out of straw and made him look more like Huckleberry Finn than Billy the Kid. His smile broadened into a gaping grin. "You're Ben Smith, himself, ain't you?"

"Have our trails crossed, pardner?"

"No, sir," Randy shook his head and tilted the brim of his straw Stetson. "But I seen your pictures and read all about you!" The young man with the crooked smile gushed. "I'm Randy Rawlins at your service, sir."

"Well, Mr. Rawlins." Ben pointed to the hood. "Can you do anything about that?"

"Can I? Watch this!"

"I'll do more than that, Randy. I'll give you a hand."

"Not on your tintype, sir. This is my specialty. Happens all the time."

A few minutes later, with the hood lifted and steam still spouting, Ben stood watching while Randy held the radiator cap in one gloved hand, poured a stream of water from a hose into the radiator with the other.

"That's the sunny side of ownin' this business; you never know who's liable to show up. I wouldn't be surprised to see Shirley Temple drive in some day . . . or . . ." Randy was still smiling, ". . . Boris Karloff."

"Well, it's good to see that a young fella like you actually owns a business like this."

Ben pointed to the sign. RANDY'S INDEPENDENT GAS.

"Well, I'm actually buying it from my daddy. Old sign used to say 'Randolph's

Independent Gas.' Might take the rest of my life — or his'n — to pay Daddy off. Just a short while and you'll be on your way."

" 'Preciate it."

"Nothin's too good for the best cowboy ever come out of these parts, Mr. Smith."

"Ben."

"You back to visit, or stay, Mr. . . . Ben?"

"Stay."

"Wahoo!"

"Yeah . . . wahoo. Might as well fill 'er up when you're done, son."

"You bet . . . well, lookee there, Mr. Lofty Lofty, himself."

A custom-designed Chrysler woody station wagon drove in and braked next to one of the two pumps. Mounted on the hood of the wagon, a pair of long horns.

The driver and passenger stepped out. James Deegan, in his forties, dressed in custom-made boots, tailored pants, and western shirt. Near him, his son, Jimmy, eight, taller and thinner than most his age.

"Be right with you, Mr. Deegan, soon as I . . ."

"Go ahead and take care of him," Ben said. "I'm in no hurry."

"Yes, sir."

The young boy proceeded toward a drinking fountain as his father popped the Chrysler hood and moved toward Randy, who was filling the tank.

Ben removed a lariat from his pickup and was idling with it as the boy finished at the fountain, then noticed Ben with the lasso. The next minute the youngster began to tentatively approach, eyes on the lariat.

"Hi . . . uh, my name's Jimmy Deegan."

"Howdy. Ben Smith."

"I . . . I guess you're a cowboy." Jimmy pointed to the lariat.

"I guess."

"So's my dad. He owns a lot of cows. Got a great big ranch. I'm staying there all summer."

"Sounds good . . . and healthy."

"Yeah . . . I guess. Uh . . . I wonder . . ."

"What?"

"That rope . . ."

"This is a lasso, son," Ben smiled.

"Well . . . uh . . . could you lasso something with it?"

"What?"

"Anything," Jimmy Deegan shrugged.

Ben looked around.

Effortlessly, he circled the lariat, threw, and looped it around the horns of the Chrysler about fifteen feet away.

"Neat!" Jimmy exclaimed.

Just as effortlessly, Ben loosened the noose

of the lariat and flipped it off the horns. As he started to draw it back, Jimmy's father approached and held out his hand. James Deegan looked like a man of the West. But only when he spent time in the West. Tall, athletic, impressive. But Deegan also spent time, just as much or even more time, on the East Coast, and was just as impressive and comfortable in a Savile Row suit and homburg. A man of many successful enterprises. A man of all seasons — and all regions.

"Jim Deegan."

They shook.

"Ben Smith."

"Pretty handy with that lariat, Mr. Smith. Haven't seen you around here before." Deegan pointed at the pickup. "Passing through?"

"No," Ben smiled, "my passin' days are over."

"Looking for work, Mr. Smith? I could use some help. Own the Big Brawny Ranch."

"That's a coincidence. So could I. Own the Little Brawny."

There was a slight pause.

"Yeah, I guess you could. That place is somewhat out of shape."

"Well, so am I. But I hope to do something

36

about that . . . about the Little Brawny, I mean . . ."

"Good idea."

". . . now that I'm off the circuit."

"Oh, *the* Ben Smith. Now I recognize you. You're the rodeo rider, aren't you?"

"Was." Ben glanced at the young boy. "Now, if I had me a son like that, he could . . ."

James Deegan's voice was flat.

"Jimmy has diabetes."

"So does Duke Morton."

"Who's Duke Morton?"

"Last year's All-'Round Champion Cowboy."

No comment from Mr. Deegan, who turned and started to walk away, then over his shoulder.

"We better be getting along, Jimmy boy."

Jimmy's attention was still on Ben Smith.

"I'm learning to ride. Dad gave me a pony for my birthday."

"That's fine. You got the makin's of a real wrangler."

"But could you teach me how to lasso?"

"Jimmy!" James Deegan's voice from a distance.

"Better get goin', son," Ben said. "Your mom'll be waitin' . . ."

"Mom's not with us."

"Oh, I'm sorry . . ."

"She's not dead or anything. They're what they call 'separated.' It's custody for the summer."

"Jimmy!" The voice more imperative.

Ben nodded toward Deegan, then looked at Jimmy.

Jimmy turned and walked toward his father but waved back to Ben.

"So long."

"Adios, cowboy," Ben lifted the lariat.

The Chrysler turned onto the road and headed toward the Big Brawny.

Ben moved to the pickup where Randy had just finished filling the gas tank.

"Fifteen cents a gallon, ten gallons even; that'll be a green sheet and a half, sir."

"Here's two green sheets. Keep the hard part."

"Much obliged, Mr. . . . Ben, and I was wonderin' . . ."

"What?"

"Do you mind if I call Skinny Dugan over at the *Beacon* and tell him that Ben Smith's back to stay? He writes about you most every week. Keeps printin' that same picture of you as the three-time All-'Round Champion —"

"You mean Skinny Dugan, *Junior*?"

"No, sir, the original, only he's not as

skinny anymore. Must tip a hundred seventy pounds."

"— The same Skinny Dugan who charged up San Juan Hill with Teddy Roosevelt?"

"The same. I'd appreciate it, so would he."

"Well, go ahead if you want to, but I was a mite thinner in that picture, too."

"Thanks! And, hell's fire, I hope I'm in as good a shape when I'm your age."

"Thanks . . . I think," Ben smiled.

The closer he drove toward the Little Brawny and away from the Dust Bowl the more the land changed. What had been a barren behind was melding into fertile ground. The stripped brown land had given way to darker, richer soil and green grass that bent with the summer wind, and still damp from the recent drizzle of rain and crowned with splashes of wildflowers scattered from the level valley platform upward along the rising flanks of the pitted hills.

The land changed for the better, but the vision in his mind changed, too.

It was one thing to sit at the Appaloosa with aches, bruises, broken bones, and scars on his body, his expression and voice putting on a calm front, and announcing to close friends that he was quitting the life, times, and triumphs he had experienced most of his adult life and was going home

— it was altogether another to face the reality of doing just that.

In the past, he had sometimes gone into a strange, new place and had the feeling that he had seen it, or been there before.

But now he was doing the opposite — going to a place where he had spent his youth, among family and friends — and wondering what it would look, and feel, and actually be like.

Yes, one door closes, and another opens. But what lies behind that new door?

After years of championships, cheering crowds, applause, prize money, adoration, and more money, the rodeos in small towns and big cities from Globe, Lubbock, Hattiesburg, Pueblo, to Abilene, Wichita, Kansas City, Chicago, New York, and even Hollywood, where he met and made friends with some of the most famous people in movies, and the world.

But how much can the human body endure? How many aches, bruised, broken bones, and scars?

He had known a battalion of rodeo riders who took one more ride and ended stove-up cowboys on Gower Gulch or worse, much worse, on crutches, wheelchairs, pathetic and penniless in this decade of the Great Depression — with no home to go back to.

Ben Smith had escaped from all that. He was going home to the Little Brawny.

He was practically on the last mile.

The song said, "The last mile's the hardest to find."

Would it look familiar?

Or like a place he had never been to before?

Was Ben Smith trying to "call back the summers in vain?"

CHAPTER FIVE

On the main street of the town of Sheridan, the sign on the window in broad, faded yellow letters read:

THE SHERIDAN BEACON
Published Every Thursday
SKINNY DUGAN
Publisher, Editor and Scribbler

Inside — vintage everything, rolltop desk, battered furniture, celling fan, Ben Franklin heating stove, printing press, and clutter of years of use and abuse. On the scarred walls, dusty framed portraits of Ulysses S. Grant, Theodore Roosevelt, and Franklin D. Roosevelt.

At the rolltop, on the candle phone, Skinny Dugan listened.

"Yeah, yeah! I'll be a son of a horny toad . . . yeah! He was? . . . He did?! When? Hell, yes! Anything else? You sure? . . .

Damn well told . . . next edition . . . you bet . . . sure . . . your this week's advertisement is no charge."

Skinny Dugan hung up, swiveled on his chair, and called out.

"Ty-Roan!"

"Yes, Mr. Skinny," came the usual response.

"How you doin' with tomorrow's edition?"

"All done."

"Well, tear out the front page."

Skinny Dugan rose, strode up to his assistant.

Tyrone Roan, some said he looked like a scarecrow, only thinner, and there were those, kinder, who said he favored that character actor Slim Summerville. Ty-Roan had been Skinny Dugan's assistant since Woodrow Wilson was president.

"Say again, Mr. Skinny?!"

"We're reprinting the front page . . . make it an Extra!"

"Make what an Extra?"

"The story . . . exclusive . . ."

"Somebody shoot the president?"

"Hell, no. This is the biggest story since Prohibition was repealed."

"From one of our usuals?"

For years, Skinny Dugan's three unpaid

43

roving reporter staff consisted of Louie Martini, the barber; Clay Sykes, the postmaster; and young Randy Rawlins.

"Good ol' Randy . . . looks like we're gonna work all night."

"*We* are?"

"Yes, we are."

"Why this time?"

" 'Cause somebody's come to town . . . and dig out that picture of Ben Smith."

Ben Smith was on his own land again. He had driven off a main road, onto a side road, then on what was little more than a dirt path toward the Little Brawny headquarters and subsidiary structures, small bunkhouse, corral, barn.

"Out of shape" was an apt description. Headquarters in the early days was a two-story, twelve-room timber dwelling with three stone fireplaces and wraparound porch.

When the headquarters burned to the ground after the big war and Ben came back, he had replaced it with a cabinlike structure, then left ranching for another unpredictable profession . . . rodeo riding.

Ben got out of the pickup's cab, and out of habit took the lariat with him. He walked up the two steps onto the small porch, then turned around for another look at the remnants of a once vast, proud, and thriving enterprise.

Was this now Ben Smith's "last mile?"

He had expected to be met by someone, someone named Alexander Brown, the old caretaker/house sitter who had lived here since Ben left. But Zander Brown was nowhere in sight.

Ben had no key, but he walked to the front door, turned the knob, and the unlocked door creaked open.

He went in.

Looked around.

Ben Smith was home.

He had been in better places, much better. But also, in worse, much worse.

He noticed a sheet of paper on the table. He sat at one of the Douglas chairs, put his hat and lariat on the table, picked up the paper, which had been weighted down with a heavy cup, smiled, and read the uneven print on the page.

Deer My Friend Mr. Ben.

So sorry I had to leeve earlier than we expected but my younger sister by 6 years Eliza come all the way from Messula to take me to the old folks home where she works that I told you about

45

and she had some car trouble she had to buy a used tire and spark plugs thanks to part of that $500 that you sent me as a bonus for the little work I been able to do around here.

I don't know what I would have done without what you been payin me for doin practicaly nothing around here.

I left the front door unlocked since nobodys come around for a long time anyhow.

Mr. Ben please turn this paper over to the other side

The electric is on and the new telephone works for you.

Excuse the poor printin and grama but you know I only got thro the middle of the 6 grade before I had to go to share croppin with my daddy to help out the family.

I tried to call you and tell you all this but you had gone from Globe by then.

God bles you and keep you for all your goodness all your life. Mr. Ben you're the best man I ever met.

My arthuritis has really got worser to where I can hardly get around.

Your truly

Zander Brown

P.S.

Theres some eats in the icebox — air tites on the shelf and a can of coffee on the shelf.

Ben took a pack of Lucky Strikes out of his shirt pocket, lifted and lighted a cigarette, and inhaled.

During his rodeo years, he had received hundreds of what they called fan letters.

But this was the first time his eyes were moist.

Ben was not a heavy smoker, in fact he was trying to quit. But not cold turkey. He had a plan. Put a pack of Lucky Strikes in your shirt pocket, smoke nothing else, let it get stale. Every once in a while, when the urge mounts, light one of the stale sticks. Inhale a few bitter puffs and usually you'll want to snuff it out.

Usually.

But not this time.

Instead, Ben rose and walked out of the open door to get a breath of fresh air along with the stale intake.

He just got to the porch when he heard it, and reacted to the sound — faint at first, but not for long.

It grew louder. The staccato beat of a distant drum. Then closer, louder, like a hundred drums.

He dropped the butt of the Lucky onto the porch, then squashed it with his boot. Took another step to get a better view.

A view he hadn't seen in too many years.

They were all the colors of the West — dun, sorrel, red, black, mouse gray, dappled, creamy palomino — and black stallion.

Mustangs.

Ben Smith watched, smiling.

The thundering herd — wild-eyed and snorting — their flanks billowing — dust curling up from the ground and clouding up in their wake.

With Ben, still smiling and absorbing the fading sight and sound.

The mustangs streaked toward the foothills and disappeared.

But the sound of the horses' hoofbeats had segued into a vibrating sputter.

Ben squinted as he looked toward the horizon and the pursuing aircraft, a Ryan M-2 mail and passenger plane left over from the early 1920s, now flying so low that Ben could make out the pilot's resolute face.

Ben was no longer smiling.

From any angle or even high in the sky, only part, a small part of it could be viewed. It would take a rider on a good horse days, weeks, even longer, to cover all of it.

At the entrance, a huge stone arch with deep, carved letters:

THE BIG BRAWNY

The plane was flying over the varied landscape — an empire.

Line shacks, water holes, even a small lake and runway, barns, corrals, and cattle, cattle, cattle.

The headquarters, a sprawling mansion surrounded by smaller edifices.

A single calf was isolated in a pen with about a twenty-foot circumference. The calf stood on unsteady legs, and its head drooped.

But the calf was not alone.

Dr. Amanda Reese, an altogether attractive veterinarian in her early thirties, carrying a medical bag, started to walk away from the calf toward the gate.

Waiting just outside, James Deegan, his son, Jimmy, along with Pepper, late fifties with a more-than-slight limp — an unmistakable range veteran with a Bull Durham paper badge hanging by a string out of his shirt pocket. Pepper had remarked more than once, "When I got to where I could afford tailor-mades, it just didn't seem like

49

smoking — course, my thumb and forefinger ain't what they used to be, so it takes me longer to roll 'em."

Standing next to Pepper, Joe Higgins, Big Brawny foreman, who resembled Wallace Beery, the actor.

The look on all of the adults' faces was serious, more than serious, concerned, while waiting for the doctor's diagnosis.

"Dad," Jimmy broke the silence, "what was the lady doing out there with . . ."

"She's called a veterinarian, Jimmy — an animal doctor."

"What was the veter . . . animal doctor doing?"

"Making some tests, son."

"How come?"

"Well, uh . . . to see if the calf is sick."

Jimmy looked toward the unsteady calf.

"Is the calf . . . gonna die?"

"Let's hear what Dr. Reese has to say." Deegan opened the gate and Dr. Reese came through.

Joe Higgins moved up and closed the gate behind her.

Not only was Amanda Reese as attractive as any actress her age, she could play a real-life scene for all it was worth.

She looked from Pepper to Higgins and settled on James Deegan without a hint of judgment.

"Dr. Reese," James Deegan's voice was shallow, "just tell me it's not contagious."

Dr. Reese knew when to smile.

"Not if you find the snake that bit it."

"Great balls of fire!" Pepper exuded.

"We were afraid," Higgins sighed, "it might be cattle plague or rinderpest."

"Some of the symptoms are the same, swelling, discoloration, but it's a snakebite, all right. I gave her a shot. She'll recover . . . and so will you, Mr. Deegan," she added.

"I have to take shots every day," Jimmy said.

Dr. Reese tousled the boy's hair.

"You do?"

"Jimmy's diabetic." Deegan nodded. "He's . . ."

Deegan's voice was drowned out by the sound, then the sight of the light plane above. The plane flew lower and the wings dipped and flew toward the small runway.

"You have an air force, too, Mr. Deegan?"

"Not exactly, Doctor," Deegan smiled. "That's Al Norkey. He's going to do a job for me."

"I've heard about Mr. Norkey . . . and his jobs."

They started to walk toward headquarters.

"Dr. Reese, would you like to stay for dinner? Pepper here is a three-star chef."

"Thanks, but I've got to make another call over at the Connor ranch. Not many of my patients come to my office."

"Or tell you," Deegan grinned, "what's wrong with them. About your fee . . ."

"That can wait until my patient recovers. But I would like to take a rain check on Pepper's three-star dinner."

"I'll fix you up one of my Parisian dee-lights."

"Sounds good, Pepper."

"Smells good, too . . . and tastes better . . . with one of my secret ingredients . . . cow grease."

"What's that?"

"Plenty of butter."

The sun had not yet dipped behind the western ridge, but after a long day, Ben sat at the table having supper out of a cold can of beans.

As he dined a fly buzzed close to his face. He waved it off with a fork. But the fly persisted. It circled and made another pass.

Ben set his fork on the table, looked up, studied the pesky insect's flight, and waited.

He didn't have to wait long.

With a swift, sure movement, his hand captured the intruder in midair.

For a moment he looked at his gently closed fist, smiled, and serenaded with an old tune.

"Mosquito, you fly high,
Mosquito, you fly low.
Mosquito, you done land
on me,
You ain't a gonna fly
No mo."

Then talked to his prisoner.

"But you ain't no mosquito — so go about your business — and I'll go back to my beans."

Ben opened his fist and the fly fled.

At other times in other places, Ben had won many bets, and many beers, doing what he just did.

But here, at home in his cabin, there was no one to bet with.

And there was no beer.

At the Big Brawny, James Deegan and his son were in Deegan's den. Jimmy was on the phone with his mother, who had called from New York. They had been talking for almost five minutes.

". . . beside the neat cowboy with the lasso . . . what else happened?"

"Well, we met a very nice-looking lady doctor who cured a calf from a snakebite. She gave it a shot."

"Jimmy, have you been getting your shots like our doctor said?"

"Sure thing, Mom . . . now, here's Dad back, I'm gonna go watch Pepper fix supper."

He handed the phone to his father.

"Hello again, Liz."

"Jimmy seemed in a hurry . . ."

"Well, I'm not . . . the boy's got a lot to see and do around here."

"Like his father. Tell me about the very nice-looking lady doctor who cured a calf from a snakebite."

"She's a very nice-looking lady doctor who cured a calf from a snakebite."

"Not very funny . . ."

"Then don't laugh."

"Who's laughing? Blonde or brunette?"

"Just not my type."

"What *is* your type?"

"Look in the mirror."

"That *is* funny, particularly since we're separated . . . Say, whose idea was it?"

"I forget. Are you going out with any of your old . . . admirers?"

"They're not so old . . . and the answer is *no* . . . too busy. I'm still at the office now

— working."

"Yeah, I haven't forgotten how it is with you and work."

"You weren't exactly a homebody, your-self, mister, with all your *enterprises.*"

"Ouch! Let's change the subject."

"Of marriage?"

"Of . . . blame, Liz."

"Done."

"Hey, lady, the good times outdistanced the not so good . . . maybe they still can."

"From a distance?"

"Maybe if we both gave a little . . ."

"My man, sometimes a *little* is too much."

"My lady, are we playing 'Can you top this'?"

"No. But next time, if there is a next time, we've got to play for keeps. Think it over; now, truth, how is Jimmy doing?"

"Okay, for a boy with a disease . . . and separated parents."

"The medicine helping?"

"We'll know in a few years."

"In a few years we'll know a lot of things."

"I hope so, lady."

"So long, Jimbo."

"So long, Stranger."

Elizabeth Deegan, cofounder and partner of Liz-E-Design, went back to work at her office in New York.

James Deegan went to the dining room for supper at the Big Brawny.

"Ty-Roan!"

"Yes, sir, Mr. Skinny."

"Why have you stopped the presses?"

"First off, Mr. Skinny, we've only got one press, and ol' Bonnie's makin' protest noises. She needs a rest."

"She's got all week to rest. And, by the way, did you notify our distribution department, while I was writin' the front page, to be here early?"

"All done, Mr. Skinny. A dozen of our young 'uns'll be here at first light to spread the *Beacon* Extra. I told you that when I brought you back that turkey sandwich, don't you remember?"

"Yeah, I remember now, and I'll get around to that sandwich. Well done, Ty-Roan, you're a first-class Assistant Everything . . . think I'll keep you on for another hundred years."

"Thanks, but no thanks," Ty-Roan said as he started the press.

"What was that you said, Ty-Roan?"

"I said 'thanks' — twice, Mr. Skinny."

The Big Brawny dining room would be described in a magazine as "Western Ele-

56

gant" — beams — leather — carved heavy wood tables and matching chairs.

Toward the end of dinner, James Deegan, next to him Jimmy, also present Joe Higgins, and pilot Al Norkey, an imposing square-built figure with a square-built face and penetrating eyes.

A large dog of indeterminate breed was curled near the kitchen door.

Martha, a middle-aged helper, had entered to start clearing. She started near James Deegan's shoulder.

"Finished, Mr. Deegan?"

"Thank you, Martha," Deegan nodded, then smiled at his son. "Jimmy, you did all right by that steak."

"I was hungry, Dad."

"Boys grow eating and sleeping," Al Norkey's voice was about as warm and charming as it could get.

James Deegan pointed.

"Jimmy, what about the rest of that asparagus?"

"Do I have to?"

"I guess you can save some room for dessert."

Martha smiled and took Jimmy's plate.

Joe Higgins patted his ample midsection and beamed.

"Sure was a relief about that calf."

"Yeah," Deegan nodded, "in spades."

"Veterinarians," Al Norkey's voice took on some implication, "didn't look like that in my time."

"She knows her business, too," James Deegan gave Norkey an unsociable look.

"That calf's already improving," Higgins interceded. "That shot did the trick, all right."

"Speaking of animals, Mr. Deegan," Al Norkey changed the subject to his own business, "the roundup's going to be duck soup, and plenty worthwhile. Saw swarms of 'em."

"Couldn't hardly miss 'em," Higgins added. "Gettin' so there's more mustangs than beeves around here."

"Not when I'm finished. You settle for five dollars a head, Mr. Deegan?"

"Fine, but I don't care about that. Just get 'em off my range."

"Don't worry, they'll be off."

Norkey pointed toward the dog resting by the kitchen door and smiled.

"Course, some of 'em might come back in a can for Fido there."

Deegan shot a warning look at Norkey as Jimmy started to say something.

"Dad, what does he mean?"

"Jimmy, why don't you go to the kitchen and have your dessert with Pepper? He's

58

made something special for your diet."

"Okay."

Jimmy rose and started for the kitchen door, paused, and pointed to the dog.

"Can Rover come with me?"

"Sure thing, Jimmy," Deegan assumed a light, jovial attitude, "but don't give him any of your dessert . . . it's not on his diet."

"Come on, Rover."

Rover didn't hesitate to follow Jimmy into the kitchen.

The men at the table were silent as he left.

Deegan's attitude, and voice, were no longer light and jovial as he looked square at Norkey.

"Be careful what you say around the boy."

"Yes, sir, I'm sorry, Mr. Deegan." Norkey knew how and when to apologize, even if he never meant it.

"It's not easy for a boy his age to understand the situation."

"Right . . . sorry," Norkey repeated.

"Well, gentlemen," Joe Higgins did his best to temper the tone on a trivial note, "it's time to spread the bedroll and sink into slumberland."

It rang and rang and rang and rang.

Ben thought it would give up, and resisted, but the ringing persisted. He finally got out of the bunk, skin-naked.

For the past few days, he had been sleeping in the cab of the pickup with his clothes on, except for his hat and boots — excluding a couple of times when he came across a handy motel.

He made it across the cabin floor and reached for the phone in the dark of night.

"Hello."

"Ben, m'boy, it's Skinny, Skinny Dugan, remember me?"

"You're the only Skinny Dugan I know."

"You ought to know. I baptized you, remember that?"

"Sure, I do, I was almost one year old."

"How you doin', son?"

"Leaning forward all the way."

"Good, and good morning."

"What time is it, Skinny?"

"Just past three."

"Do you always get up this early?"

"Haven't been to bed yet. Been puttin' out an Extra for tomorrow's *Beacon* . . . make that today."

"Big news, Skinny?"

"Bet your boots, all about you comin' back here to roost. You comin' into town this mornin'?"

"Got to get some groceries."

"Good, otherwise I was gonna have Ty-

60

Roan deliver you a few copies."

"Well, thanks, Skinny, but I'll pick up a copy along with the groceries."

"Fine, just fine."

"How is Ty?"

"Slowin' up some, but then again, he never was lightnin'. If I miss you in the mornin', I'll see you sooner than later. By the Lord Harry, I'm sleepin' on my feet."

"So am I, Skinny, and thanks for calling. Good to hear your voice."

"And vice versa . . . By the way, you must know your neighbor the Baron of Big Brawny?"

"James Deegan? I do."

"What do you think?"

"I think we'll be neighborly enough. He's got a nice young son. You know the boy?"

"Never met him. But sometimes his father and I get each other's mail, Deegan — Dugan. Tried to interview him oncet. But the Baron's a mite shy when it comes to publicity."

"That's no sin."

"It is in the newspaper business. Good night, Ben, what's left of it."

"Good night, Skinny."

Ben's hand went to hang up but missed the cradle the first time in the dark.

He thought about lighting up a Lucky but

had a better idea.

He headed back to the bunk.

Chapter Six

A dozen young citizens of Sheridan, who constituted the Distribution Department of the *Sheridan Beacon,* had appeared at first light, and thus promptly, proceeded to deliver the Extra weekly edition of tidings throughout the community.

By midmorning, just about every adult who could read, or knew someone who could read the reportage to him, became aware of the return of Sheridan's famous native son.

There were no cannons booming, flags waving, bonfires burning, or brass bands playing, but there appeared to be more than a modicum of excitement about the weekly dispatch, which usually carried flashes concerning births, deaths, fistfights, an occasional divorce, an unusual rainfall, the fact that someone's dog or cat had been run over, or the latest depth of the Depression, plus a scattering of local advertisements . . .

and, of course, another account describing Sergeant Skinny Dugan and his charge with Colonel Teddy Roosevelt's Rough Riders up San Juan Hill as they Remembered the *Maine.*

But today's Ben Smith story, bylined Skinny Dugan, did stir up more conversation, even caterwauling, than any edition this year.

EXTRA — EXTRA — EXTRA

The front page of the *Sheridan Beacon* blared. The masthead included the usual credits.

Publisher Editor Scribbler
SKINNY DUGAN
Associate Everything
Ty Roan
Roving Reporters
A. Nonymous

The banner headline exclaimed.

BEN SMITH'S BACK AND WE GOT HIM!

Ben Smith, three-time All-'Round Champion Cowboy, has won every sort of event ever performed on the rodeo circuit, including bronc riding, bulldogging, barrel racing, and shooting.

I mention this just in case some of you local Rip van Winkles, who have been sleeping the last twenty years, and who are unaware that the Great War is over, Prohibition has come and gone, and something called the Great Depression has hit this country in its vitals, have not heard of him.

But today's good news here in Sheridan is that our own homegrown buckaroo, Ben Smith, has come home to roost where he was born and growed up — the Little Brawny.

But something else you won't hear from Ben Smith is that he won three medals for valor, including the Purple Heart for being wounded at the Argonne Forest, in bloody battles with the Krauts that might've even matched us Rough Riders who showed them Spaniards up San Juan Hill who ate the cabbage.

But right about here, let me go back to the Little Brawny long before Ben Smith was born.

A short spell after the Civil War, a tall Texan rode up north and into town with a saddlebag bulging with greenbacks. Enough to pay cash money for a spread known as the Little Brawny. When asked his name, he told them "Smith" . . . later, he added Benson, Benson Smith. Some rumors floated that he might have robbed a bank, but nothing was ever proved so the rumors ceased.

During that time, Jesse Chisholm, a half-breed Cherokee, blazed a trail north from Texas to the cattle market in Missouri and Kansas.

Not long after, Ben Smith's grandfather Benson Smith gathered all the beeves in the territory and blazed a trail south from the Little Brawny to these same markets — and prospered — and the Smith family flowered.

Ben's grandmother and his mother both had some Indian blood in them. The blood flowed but seldom showed.

Ben's father, Jefferson Smith, took over when old man Benson died of a broken neck from a fall off a stallion in 1890. The Little Brawny continued to prosper.

Jeff married a lovely schoolteacher, Louella O'Donnell, and our Ben Jefferson Smith was born in 1896 — the Little Brawny continued to prosper.

Ben mostly grew up there, but he did go to the University of Oklahoma and gradu-ated with a degree in animal husbandry, then along came war and he joined the U.S. cavalry in 1917 and fought under Blackjack Pershing in the War to End All Wars. Ben saw plenty of action and danger — I wrote about it up above — however, he survived. But both his mother and father died in the disastrous epidemic of 1918, and the Little Brawny survived but no longer prospered, much of it burned to the ground.

Former captain Ben Smith managed to hold on to the Little Brawny, but with a considerable mortgage. He went to rodeo-ing in the years that followed and became famous, met all sorts of eminent highbrows including a couple of U.S. presidents, and made enough coin of the realm to pay off that mortgage. He was the first three-time All-'Round Champion on the circuit.

All that time, there was no bronc-stomper to compare to the living legend named Ben Smith.

But just recently, the high-hickalorum of hell on horseback decided it was time to hang 'em up and head for the ol' home-stead — the Little Brawny.

We're all happy to say rodeo's loss is Sheridan's gain.

WELL DONE AND WELCOME HOME, BEN SMITH.

■ ■ ■ ■

Sheridan was, more or less, like any other small western town — maybe a little more, maybe a little less.

But not much different.

On Main Street a three-story building, probably the oldest and most impressive, which currently served as Sheriff Tom Granger's headquarters and jail, courthouse for the circuit judge, and mayor's office — vacant at the present time, since at the last election no citizen consented to run for the office due to the payday — $80 a month and heavy paperwork. Most of that paperwork was handled by the chamber of commerce under the eagle eye of David Bergin, also president of the Citizens Bank.

Also on Main Street, small businesses, including Walt's Hardware and Lumber, Louie Martini's Barber Shop, Star Grocery, The General Store, Mary's Cafe, Kit Carson's Saloon, Sheridan Post Office and Telegraph, the Higley Hotel, and the *Beacon* building.

On one edge of the street, a livery stable, on the other edge, Jake's Steaks and a small park.

In the middle of Main Street, the Majestic

movie house with a prominent marquee.

NOW SHOWING
TOM MIX — The Miracle Rider
HOOT GIBSON — Hell's Trail
JOHN WAYNE — Blue Steel

Main Street had its share of vehicles, some mobile, some parked curbside, mostly of yesteryear vintage, and mostly Fords and Chevys, coupes, four-doors, pickups, trucks, and station wagons.

The citizens, perambulating and stationary, as usual, were mostly dressed in western attire, others in more gentrified apparel.

But in Sheridan, that day, there was one distinct commonality. Just about everybody was reading, or had read, the front-page story on the Extra edition of the *Sheridan Beacon.*

The sign on the window in stylish lettering:

Louie Martini
BARBER

"Read everything about you, Mr. Smith."

"Ben."

"Ben . . . you fight for your country? Or against the kaiser?"

69

"Both."

Another customer walked in and sat on one of the two empty Douglas chairs.

"Morning, Louie."

"Morning, Rafe. Ben Smith, this is Rafe Birch."

Both men nodded.

"Rafe, you're my second customer. Ben here come to town early to get a haircut, didn't you, Ben?"

"Nope."

"Then why?"

"Groceries."

"Star don't open till eight. I open at seven."

"Right."

"You didn't know that?"

"Nope."

"Want me to take more off?"

"Nope."

"Then look in the mirror. How do you like it?"

"Fine."

"Ben, you been here twenty minutes . . . haven't said twenty words."

"Not much sleep."

"Oh . . ."

"How much?"

"How much, what?"

"Haircut."

Martini pointed to the sign.

SHAVE AND HAIRCUT
Two Bits

Ben rose, pulled a quarter out of his pocket, and put it on the cash register.

"First haircut is free, Ben."

"Nothin's free."

"You didn't get a shave."

"Shave myself."

"Okay, if that's the way you want it."

"Yep."

"See you soon, then."

"Three months."

"Three months?"

"Winter haircut."

Ben was at the door, looking through the glass pane.

"Good."

"What's good?"

"Grocery's opening."

"Uh-huh. Well, so long, Ben."

"So long, gentlemen."

Ben went out the door and walked toward his parked pickup.

Martini motioned to his second customer.

"Didn't get any news from him. What's new with you, Rafe?"

■ ■ ■ ■

She moseyed out of the entrance of Kit Carson's Saloon, a lit cigarette in one hand and the *Sheridan Beacon* in the other. She was on the shady side of forty, but still fetching, with a valentine face framed by orange hair — dressed in immodest saloon attire and had nothing to be immodest about.

She spotted Ben Smith stepping out of his pickup and heading for the Star Grocery store.

She promptly headed toward Ben, waved the newspaper, and smiled that fetching smile.

"Morning, Ben. I'm part of the welcoming committee." Her voice was just as fetching.

Ben paused, nodded.

"Morning, ma'am. You work at Kit Carson's, I see."

"Just came out for a breath of fresh air and a smoke. I *am* Kit Carson, but I wasn't always. By the way, we've met before, but you wouldn't remember."

"Where?"

"Colorado."

"Colorado's a big span."

"Dur-ang-go."

"I remember."

"You were the king of the rodeo, and I was a lady-in-waiting. I've worked my way up."

"Congratulations."

"You haven't changed much, Ben . . ."

"Neither have you." Ben couldn't resist looking her up and down.

"You like my costume?"

"Some . . . costume," he smiled.

"I let 'em see just enough to want more, but they never get more . . . well, almost never. You still take an occasional drink these days?"

"Been known to."

She flipped her cigarette into the street.

"Well, if the occasion arises, the first drink is free, that is, if you get thirsty, or lonely."

Kit Carson turned and moseyed back toward her saloon.

Dr. Amanda Reese, after an early breakfast, walked out of Mary's Cafe, carrying a folded newspaper. Ben Smith walked out of the Star Grocery next door, with a large, overloaded bag of groceries in each arm.

"Good morning, Mr. Smith," she smiled.

Ben Smith turned, and a couple cans fell out of the bag and onto the sidewalk.

"Here, let me give you a hand," she said,

and did, retrieving the cans and placing them gently into one of the sacks.

"Thank you . . . ma'am."

"Amanda Reese. I'm the local vet."

"Not like in the army?"

"No, like animal doctor."

"Ah, my pickup's right in front. Let me dump this stuff in there."

"Let me help you . . ."

"Thanks, you're pretty handy. Say, Doctor, have we met before?"

"Sort of."

"How do you 'sort of' meet?" Ben smiled.

She unfolded the *Beacon* and pointed to his picture.

"I'm surprised you recognized me. That isn't exactly yesterday's photo."

"Besides, I've seen you rodeo, you were great."

"When you were a little girl?"

"No. Just a few years ago. Just before I came to Sheridan."

By now, the bags were on the front seat of the pickup.

"Well, thank you, miss . . . Doctor."

"Amanda'll do just fine."

"Say, *Amanda,* you being a vet, I'm looking for a good riding horse, if you come across . . ."

"Matter of fact, if that's the case, I'll send

74

Gotch Tompkins over to see you . . ."

"Who's Gotch Tompkins?"

"He deals in horses. Got a beauty. I helped bring her into this world."

"With those little hands?"

She held up both hands.

"They're not so little."

They weren't. She extended one, Ben took it, and they shook hands.

"Well, ma'am, you've got a good strong handshake; I'll say that."

"Thank you. You're settling on the Little Brawny, Mr. Smith, according to the *Beacon.*"

"After, and while, I do a little repairing."

"Well . . . good luck, Mr. Smith."

"Ben."

"Ben," she repeated.

By then, a gathering of about a dozen uninvited spectators had nearly surrounded them.

Two of those spectators, the biggest, took a step closer. Each of the men held a copy of the *Sheridan Beacon.* They looked alike, and their faces never heard of agreeable, but did their best to appear respectful.

" 'Scuse us, please, Mr. Smith. We're what you might call a welcomin' bid. I'm Claud Krantz and this here is my brother, Clem."

"Howdy," Ben nodded.

A few in the crowd that had gathered were smiling, but there were those in the gathering who knew the two intruders, or their reputation. Their faces were grim.

"Well, sir, we're here to get your autograph on this here picture on the front page, but you see, me and Clem are twin brothers, even though I was born about a dozen minutes afore him . . ."

The look on Ben's face turned a trifle impatient as Claud Krantz continued.

"Now, me and Clem here, just had our first disagreement in almost a week . . . know what about?"

"No."

"Well, you bein' a war hero and a livin' legend, we were disputin' as to which one of us'ud be the first . . . to knock you on your ass." He grinned.

There was a chafed change in Ben's voice.

"Take it on the easy, Krantz. There's ladies nearby."

"You duckin' behind their skirts?" Claud's grin broadened.

"No. But I'll be pleased to settle your dispute."

"How? Are you . . ."

Claud never finished.

Ben's left fist caromed into Claud's face, broke his nose, and he fell bleeding onto the pavement. Clem took a step forward and was met by Ben's double-quick left to the stomach and rapid right straight to the jaw that landed Clem on top of his dazed twin.

The crowd whooped and yahooed but was topped by someone's authoritative voice.

"What the hell's going on here?"

Then someone grabbed Ben's arm. Ben turned to confront him but stopped short when he saw the badge.

"Oh, hello, Ben, I'm Sheriff Tom Granger, welcome home, what's . . ."

Sheriff Tom Granger looked toward the pavement.

"Oh . . . the Krantz bullyboys again. You all right, Ben?"

Ben nodded.

"*He's* all right, all right," a voice in the crowd responded.

Sheriff Granger motioned to the Krantz brothers.

"Okay, tough guys. Looks like you met more'n your match this time. You know your way to the pokey. Sooner you get there, the sooner you'll get out, unless he wants to press charges."

He glanced at Ben.

Ben shook his head.

The Krantz twins wobbled to their feet, avoided looking at the mocking spectators, and staggered toward they knew where.

"All in a day's day," both brothers said.

"Be seeing you around, Ben," Sheriff Granger smiled, then followed his detainees.

Dr. Andrew Baynes Carter appeared from another direction. He was easily distinguishable from the other men his age. "Doc ABC" was a head shorter and carried a medical bag.

"Anybody hurt?"

"Mostly some egos," somebody said. "But one of the Krantzes got a busted beak," he laughed. "They went thataway."

Doc ABC proceeded toward the sheriff's office, but he had barely left the crowd behind when he was joined in lockstep by Clay Sykes, a venerable citizen, who was easily distinguishable by his perpetual green eyeshades, walrus mustache, red shirt, and yellow suspenders, and at this time, almost out of breath.

For the past three decades, Sykes had been, and still was, Sheridan's postmaster and telegraph operator for Western Union.

"Dammit all, Doc, this was about the only time I wasn't the first to know, but that damn telegraph key hasn't stopped triggerin' all mornin' . . . What the hell's goin' on?"

"I got there a little late, myself . . ."

"Anybody got kilt?"

"No, but some blood's been shed."

"Whose?"

"Follow me to the sheriff's office and we'll both find out all about it."

"That's what I'm doin' — followin' you."

Most of the crowd had started to disperse, but Kit Carson stood next to Ben Smith, a smile of approbation on her embellished lips.

"Ben, ol' boy, you haven't lost your steam. Neither have I."

As she moseyed away, Dr. Amanda Reese took a step toward him.

"You okay?"

Ben nodded.

"Mr. Smith, you put on quite a show *outside* the arena."

"The boys were just funnin'."

"Some bloody fun."

Ben feigned surprise.

"And you, Doctor, didn't tend to 'em."

"I tend to horses, not horses' asses."

"Take it on the easy, Doctor," more feigning. "There might be some ladies nearby."

"I'm not afraid of female competition, if that's what you mean."

"Not what I mean, and I'd say you're not afraid of anything."

"Well," she smiled, "a mouse makes me

kind of queasy."

The banter was interrupted by a hearty greeting by Skinny Dugan, who was followed close behind by Ty Roan.

"Mornin', Ben." Skinny Dugan extended his hand and Ben took hold. "Slept in and missed the ruckus, but heard all about it, everybody has."

"Skinny," Ben wanted to change the conversation, "do you know Dr. Amanda Reese?"

"Hell, yes," Skinny smiled, "prettiest filly in the county, and Ben, you know this here is Ty-Roan, he ain't so pretty. Ty-Roan, our next front-page story'll be how Ben Smith acquainted those insolent Krantz skunks to some fists and gravel."

"Skinny, please don't write anything about what happened out here this morning. I'd duly appreciate it."

"So would those Krantz skunks," Amanda added. "Most gallant, Ben."

"If you say so, Ben. See you later. Me and Ty-Roan haven't et breakfast yet."

They both proceeded toward Mary's Cafe.

But Amanda Reese was still looking at Ben Smith.

"Well, sir, so ends our morning and begins our day. I've got to make my rounds, and you . . . ?"

"Back to the Little Brawny."

"I'll see Gotch Tompkins and tell him you might be interested in that good filly."

"Yes, ma'am, I'm interested."

She began to walk toward her parked station wagon.

Dr. Amanda Reese didn't look back but said it loud enough.

"Be seeing you, Gallant Man."

CHAPTER SEVEN

James Deegan was on the phone in his den when Pepper and Jimmy hurried in.

"I'll be there, Mr. Bergin," Deegan said, and hung up.

"Dad," Jimmy smiled, "Pepper got the newspaper this morning, and look what it says all about that cowboy we met at the gas station — with his picture and everything."

Deegan took the paper and scanned the front page, put the paper on his desk.

"Yeah, quite a spread."

"He's famous!" Jimmy picked up the newspaper.

"Yeah, heard about him, but didn't recognize him at Randy's. Speaking of spreads, I've got to go into Sheridan and talk to Dave Bergin over at Citizens Bank. Seems there's a piece of property for sale next to ours and I want to know more about it. Might make a deal."

"You talkin' about the Little Brawny, Mr. D?" Pepper asked.

"No, on the east side, but contiguous."

"Dad, can Pepper and me . . ."

"Pepper and I, son."

"Pepper and I, go by and welcome the cowboy since he's our neighbor . . . ?"

"Well . . ."

"You'll be gone for a while anyhow, Mr. D, and I sure would like to meet Ben Smith along with Jimmy if it's okay, while you're away."

"I suppose that'll be all right, but I'll be back in a couple of hours."

"So'll we," Pepper nodded.

"Neat!" Jimmy had already started toward the door.

Gotch Tompkins, a spry sixty or so, with a patch over his left eye — question marks for legs in Justin boots, just finished reading the front page of the newspaper that Dr. Amanda Reese had handed him.

"Hell, every cowboy in the world wished he was Ben Smith. You say he's fixin' to buy a horse?"

"That's what he said he was fixin' to do," she smiled.

"Well, he couldn't do better'n Betsey over there."

"I think he and Betsey would get along fine . . . told him so."

"Iffen I make the deal you'll get ten . . . uh, five percent commission."

"Don't want any percent, Gotch. She's your horse, not mine."

"But you're Betsey's godmother. You ought to get somethin'."

"Satisfaction'll be more than enough. You'd better get her loaded and get her over there."

"Soon as I go to the toilet. And thank you, kindly, Doctor."

"Ty-Roan! I say, Ty-Roan!" Skinny Dugan was looking through the *Beacon* window at the brand-new blue Packard convertible parked across the street in front of Citizens Bank.

"Yes, Mr. Skinny, what is it?"

"I'll tell you what is it. Did you spot that Packard across the street?"

"No. I didn't."

"Well, I did. That's why I'm the boss. Never seen anything like it around Sheridan. Think I'll mosey on over there."

"You think whoever owns it might be news, Mr. Skinny?"

"I think whoever owns it might be news, and I'm wonderin' how it got this far without one of my spies spottin' it and let-

84

tin' us know. Those fellas are slippin'."

"Mrs. Layton, this is Mr. James Deegan. As I said over the phone, he owns the Big Brawny and a few other enterprises."

"That sort of reputation," Deegan shrugged, "is usually exaggerated."

"But not always," she smiled again.

Mrs. Layton was the most ravishing woman Deegan had ever seen in or out of Tiffany in New York City, and she glowed from head to heels. She was not dressed in western attire, more like the latest big-city fashion by Coco Chanel or Gucci.

And she favored the blue to match her azure blue eyes.

Mrs. Layton crossed her long, lovely legs and swung them slightly toward James Deegan.

Dave Bergin also noticed but was all business.

"You see, Mr. Deegan, Mrs. Layton was recently divorced and . . ."

"Jason and I used to spend some of our summers at the ranch. I got the Layton Ranch in the settlement and told Mr. Bergin I was thinking of selling it."

"Thinking," Deegan reacted, "Bergin, I thought you told me the Layton Ranch *was* for sale."

"I thought so, too." Bergin looked toward Mrs. Layton. "I believe that that's what you said."

"I might have. But since getting back and thinking about it . . ."

"Mrs. Layton . . ."

"*Laura* . . . please, James," she turned on that smile again, "as of now, we're still neighbors . . . and it's so beautiful. You really ought to come and let me show you around . . ."

"Maybe I will . . . when you're closer to making up your mind. How long do you think that will be . . . Laura?"

"Not long. Maybe a week or two."

"Yes, well, in the meanwhile . . ."

"Yes?"

"Maybe I'll think it over, too."

He rose.

"Good day, Mr. Bergin . . . Laura."

Skinny Dugan, hands on hips, stood in squinting regard by the blue Packard Victoria convertible.

Other passersby paused, gave it the once- or twice-over, as if viewing a mirage in a desert, then moved on.

James Deegan walked out of the Citizens Bank door, and Skinny Dugan took a couple steps toward him, then pointed back to the Packard.

"Mornin'."

"Morning, Skinny, what's left of it."

"First, I thought maybe you bought a new machine, then spotted your buggy parked over there. This 'un's something to behold, ain't she?"

"I'll say."

"Think there's a story goes with her?"

"Stories . . . well, while I'm in town, might as well stop over at Louie's and get a haircut."

"Yeah, I'll get one, too, one of these days. Well, don't take any wooden Indians."

"So long, Skinny."

As James Deegan's Chrysler pulled onto the street, she came out of the door and started toward the Packard.

Skinny Dugan stood with as much surprise and awe as he did upon viewing her convertible.

"Pardon me, miss, I'm Skinny Dugan, and I publish the Sheridan newspaper."

"Congratulations."

"And you're Miss . . ."

"*Mrs.* Laura Layton, and in a hurry . . ."

She moved toward the convertible and proceeded to get in.

"You passin' through, Mrs. Layton?"

"Not exactly. I own the Layton Ranch."

"Congratulations. Get here often?"

"Not exactly . . ."

"Can't understand how nobody sees you and this conveyance come and go."

"We had a private road built off the highway."

Mrs. Layton started the Packard.

"You know, ma'am, you ought to keep the top up when you park. On a day like this, the sun's awful rough on your leather upholstery."

"Appreciate your concern, but I don't care. I get a new Packard every year."

"Congratulations, but I'd like to get an interview."

"I read your paper this morning, it's quite . . . quaint. But I'm in a hurry."

"Like to get that interview for next week's edition . . ."

"That would be . . . quaint. Sorry, but I'm in a hurry."

The Packard started to steer onto the street.

"I'm sorry, too . . . or, am I?"

The Packard was already roaring up Main Street.

James Deegan, a striped apron around his neck and shoulders, sat in the barber chair, while Louie Martini trimmed his hair, even though it hardly needed to be trimmed.

"Mr. Deegan, I didn't expect to see you until at least next week."

"Well, Louie, I had an appointment in town and thought I might as well kill two birds . . ."

"What do you mean, Mr. Deegan . . . 'kill two birds'?"

"Uh, you see, Louie, that's just an old hunter's saying, and . . ."

A blaring horn honk from the street blanked out Deegan's voice. He turned in his chair.

The Packard convertible had slowed at the sight of Deegan's Chrysler in front of the barbershop long enough for Laura Layton to wave, smile, then accelerate.

"She wasn't smiling at me, Mr. Deegan. She must be a new girl in town."

"She's not exactly a *girl*."

"I'll say."

"And that tomato doesn't miss a trick."

"Is that an old hunter's saying, too?"

"No. Just my observation."

"You know her pretty well, huh, Mr. Deegan?"

"No comment, Louie. I don't want to read about it in Skinny Dugan's newspaper."

Ben Smith knelt on the small front porch in front of his cabin, a can of sixpenny nails at his side, a hammer in his hand, pounding one of the nails into a loose board and accompanying the task by singing the words to a song between whacks.

"A man'll come home . . ."

Whack.

"To the place of his youth . . ."

Whack.

"In search of the things left behind . . ."

Whack.

"He looks for a place . . ."

Whack.

"For a smile on a . . ."

His singing and whacking were interrupted by a faint reverberating sound of a light plane above.

He stood and looked up toward the west as Norkey's aircraft swung toward the ridgeline, and then there was another different sound as the pickup came closer.

Pepper drove, Jimmy next to him in the front seat, as the pickup pulled up and Ben approached.

Jimmy waved his copy of the *Beacon*.

Ben waved back.

"Howdy, neighbors. Come out and say hello. I don't get many visitors, except from . . ." Ben glanced up at the sky and quickly decided to change course . . . "Well, step on out, have a look-see at what's left of the ol' homestead."

They did, and closed in near Ben.

"Haven't met your saddle pal, here, Jimmy."

"This is Pepper. He works for Dad."

"Oh, sorry your dad couldn't come along."

"He had to go into town on some business."

Ben extended his hand to Pepper.

"Ben Smith."

Pepper accepted eagerly.

"I sure know who you are, Mr. Smith."

"Ben."

Jimmy held up the newspaper.

"Everybody around here who read the paper knows all about him today!"

"Say . . . uh, Ben. The fella brought out the paper said those belligerent Krantz brothers came at you aggressive, and you settled their hash right quick. Sorry I missed that, and Jimmy, this fella can ride anything with hair on it . . ."

"He can lasso, too — gonna teach me, aren't you, Ben?"

Ben smiled.

"We'll get around to it, but I've got a little fixin' up to do around here . . ."

"Looks like you already started." Pepper pointed to the hammer still in Ben's left hand.

"Just nailing down some loose boards on the porch till I get some lumber and tools. How'd you fellas happen to come by?" Ben pointed the hammer at Pepper's pickup. "Did you get lost?"

"No . . . Jimmy asked his dad if we could come by, and truth is, I did want to meet you. Why, I saw you when you won . . ."

"Well, I'm glad you got here. Why don't you come inside? I got some cold tea for Jimmy and a nice cold bottle of beer for the two of us, Pepper, if you're so inclined."

"I am."

The trio started toward the cabin but stopped short.

Another vehicle pulled off the dirt road. Another pickup, this one towing a horse trailer, approached.

"Looks like this is my day for company." Ben dropped the hammer on the porch.

"Why . . . that's ol' Gotch Tompkins," Pepper said. "He's a good ol' boy."

It didn't take long for the good ol' boy to debark, move up, and stick his hand out to Ben.

"Ben, you remember me? Been a spell. Gotch Tompkins."

They shook.

"Sure do, Gotch. Quite a spell. You do know Pepper here and . . ."

Gotch nodded.

"Pepper. Hi, boy. Say, Ben, Dr. Amanda stopped by and tells me you're fixin' to buy a good horse."

"I am."

"Well, I got one to sell."

"That so?"

Gotch pointed to the trailer.

"Brought her along for you to look over."

"Well, let's look her over."

"That's a start."

A few minutes later, the animal, a sorrel, was out of the trailer . . . Ben looking her over, patting her flanks, rubbing her muzzle.

Pepper and Jimmy watched, but Gotch was enthusiastically making his pitch.

"She's a young 'un, deep chested, spirited, with a lot of bottom."

"Looks good," Ben nodded.

"Rides better. She ain't no kidney killer. Smoother ride you'll never get. I call her Betsey. You buy her, you call her anything you want."

"Betsey, huh?"

It was obvious that Ben had taken to the animal.

"If you got a saddle, throw it on her, if not, I got one in the pickup . . . just in case."

"I got a saddle and a bridle."

"Well, throw 'em on and give her a whirl."

"I will, and might be we'll make a deal."

"That's up to you," Gotch smiled. He felt he was getting closer.

"No, that's up to *us*. There's a little matter of price."

"Oh, yeah . . . price."

Ben Smith swung into the saddle strapped on the filly — a classic portrait of the magnificent animal and Ben astride, tall and straight.

He already looked years younger and happier.

Ben glanced at his audience, which in the past had been in hundreds of places, composed of thousands of spectators. Now there were three who watched. Gotch. Pepper. Jimmy.

Without words, Ben was communicating with the horse.

The animal reacted. Forward. A few steps. Backward. To the left, then right, as Ben gently laid the reins to the left and right.

Ben nodded at Gotch.

"Give 'er a go, cowboy," Gotch waved.

Ben didn't need encouragement. Neither did Betsey.

So it began.

Ben rode the spirited young mare. Firmly but gently. First a trot — a gallop — then a glorious ride — with all hooves flying off the ground — as the West was a hundred years ago, when survival of rider and horse depended on speed and skill.

On the open landscape toward the horizon — burning the breeze — then a swift, graceful turn — gaining ground with every stride — over a broken fence — through a muddy pond — toward the two men and boy, who had never seen anything like it before.

Damn few had.

Ben Smith had been on many horses, in many places: the open range, in open-air rodeos of the West, enclosed coliseums of the East — and even in England and the Continent. He had ridden and contested before every sort of spectator — men, women, and children, cowboys and crowned heads; presidents — McKinley, Coolidge, Hoover, and FDR; generals — Pershing and MacArthur; and had seen all sort of sights — the Hollywood Bowl, the Statue of Liberty, the White House, the Tower of London, in war and peace, and the Eiffel Tower in war.

He had ridden in most of the forty-eight states — in rodeos, the high plains, and deep valleys, in everyplace but a place called home. He had:

. . . known the high country
where lone eagles fly,
the desolate, no-path terrain . . .
. . . the hollow cry
of the lonesome man.
. . . You can't ever go home again.

But here on the ridgeline, as he rode Betsey back toward the cabin on the remnants of the Little Brawny, he was closer to home than any time he could remember.

Jimmy and even Pepper just stood speechless and looked at Ben as he finished in a smooth dismount and patted Betsey.

Gotch moved in, smiling.

"There's an old saying, 'there's nothin' better for the inside of a man than the outside of a horse.' Well, I'll say you two took to each other."

"You're not so far from right," Ben nodded.

"Want to do a little business?" Gotch inquired.

"Don't mind. What price?"

"Cash money?"

"Coin of the realm."

Gotch looked at Ben, then the horse, rubbed the patch over his eye.

"Three hundred."

"Done."

"Damn — shoulda said three-fifty, but I'm glad o' one thing . . ."

"What?" Ben squinted.

"Offered Dr. Amanda a commission if we made a deal . . ."

"And?"

"She refused."

Jimmy found his voice.

"Ben . . ."

"What is it, m'boy?"

"I told you Dad gave me a pony."

"Right."

"Well, would you come over and teach me all about horses?"

"Son, nobody knows all about horses," Ben smiled, "but I'll teach you some of what I know . . . now, wanna go inside, have something cool to drink?" He looked at Gotch. "And that's where the money is."

Gotch was already on his way.

"Let's go."

CHAPTER EIGHT

There was much work waiting to be done on the Little Brawny, but it could wait.

Something else couldn't.

Betsey.

Ben wanted to get more acquainted and take care of her first.

A couple more rides, then grooming his new companion.

He took to talking to her while he was doing just that, as well as at other times.

"Well, young lady, you're looking very spiffy, but there's one thing that's not just right . . ."

The horse seemed to react, at least it seemed so to Ben.

"Oh, don't worry, I'm not talking about you. It's that bridle and bit. It's too worn, and that bit don't fit. But I can do something about that over at the livery before we take another spin. Then . . ."

There was that familiar but unwelcome

sound and sight from above.

Norkey's light plane dipped invasively close, then pulled up to a higher level, moving away.

Ben looked at the fading aircraft, then back to Betsey.

"I'd like to do something about that, too."

". . . and, Mom, you should see that cowboy, his name is Ben, Ben Smith, you should see him ride . . . he's going to teach me, and to lasso, too . . ."

"That's fine, Jimmy, but don't overdo it. Save a little energy for school this fall, there are a lot of other things to learn."

"You sound like Dad."

"Do I? Well, he's a wise old party. We both are."

"I know . . ."

"Do you? I love you, Jimmy — we both do."

"I know that, too . . . Here's Dad."

Jimmy handed the phone to his father, then hurried out of the den.

"Hello again, Liz. This is that other 'wise old party.' "

"You're not so old. I exaggerated a little bit about that part."

"What about the 'wise' part?"

"That, too, and it goes for the two of us,

or we wouldn't be . . ."

"Be what?"

"This far apart."

"Are you talking about geography?"

"Among other things . . ."

"That again?"

"That *again.*"

There was a pause in the conversation.

"Liz, maybe we can do something about that. At least for a while."

"What do you mean?"

"I mean, uh, well, there's a piece of property that might be for sale next to the Big Brawny . . ."

"Are you talking about the Little Brawny?"

"No, no. This is the Layton Ranch on the other side. It'ud be a good addition to our spread."

"And?"

"And, well . . . this lady who owns it. She just got a divorce. I met with her, and she's thinking of selling . . ."

"What's that got to do with *us*?"

"Well, if she decides to sell, I'd like you to fly out and take a look at it with me."

"Why?"

"Because . . . because if we do get a divorce . . ."

"Yes?"

"That might have some effect on the settlement."

"Wouldn't have any effect on me."

"It might on your lawyer. Besides . . ."

"Besides, *what*?"

"The three of us, you and me and Jimmy, could be together again for a while."

"My friend, I'm a trifle busy. There's the new season to . . ."

"Oh, that again. Well, first things first."

"Hey, that cart's before the horse. Let's see if the 'gay divorcée' wants to sell."

"Sure, Liz, but don't you think that sounds a little like . . ."

"Like what?"

"The old stall-aroo?"

"You're rushing to judgment."

"I hope so. So long, Stranger."

"So long, Jimbo."

During his drive from the Little Brawny, Ben thought about his homecoming of just a few days and how most of it summed up much more agreeable and positive than disagreeable and negative.

He was disappointed that old Zander Brown had left the Little Brawny, but the truth was that the fine old gentleman no longer was in shape to work and was going to be near his sister and in a place where he would be taken care of.

Some of the old-timers that he remembered were no longer around. New characters, even before he actually got to the Little Brawny — Randy at the gas station; young Jimmy Deegan, friendly and eager; and his father, who was just so-so friendly.

Some of the rest:

Skinny Dugan, not as skinny, but still the son of an old bull moose, and his trusty sidekick, Ty-Roan. There were Pepper and Gotch Tompkins, both faint echoes of the bygone West.

Yes, things change and so do people, and mostly for the better, but there's always some unpleasantness, such as the encounter with the Krantz duo, but Sheriff Tom Granger seemed to hold his own and then some.

The most unpleasant situation was the plight of the diminishing mustangs, which he considered the shame, no, the disgrace of the new-old West.

But there was one horse those damn mustangers would never defile — beautiful, darling Betsey.

And that led Ben to the pleasant thought of how that came about, thanks to a beautiful, independent lady named Dr. Amanda Reese.

By that time, Ben was within the city limits of Sheridan, if you could consider

Sheridan a city.

Nobody was in a hurry. Not the citizens in automobiles, pickups, trucks, bicycles, or on the sidewalks. Ben couldn't help smiling at the difference between these small-town folks and the citizens of most of the big cities of New York, Chicago, Detroit, and San Francisco, and other overpopulated municipalities.

But the pace in even those big cities had slowed since the Roaring Twenties, when everybody was in a hurry to make more money, go to movie palaces, and drink more bootleg booze. During these threadbare thirties, those same citizens had lost some of their frenzied pace and purpose.

But since Ben could remember, the pace in Sheridan had remained the same — not too fast — not too slow. Everything and everybody quite ordinary.

But not exactly.

As his pickup neared the sheriff's office, it slowed down.

Three men were standing on the sidewalk in front. Sheriff Tom Granger and Claud and Clem Krantz.

A final word from Granger, and the Krantz brothers turned and walked across the street toward a parked truck with a prominent sign.

Krantz Bros.

CARPENTRY

HAULING

The two pedestrians obviously looked at, and recognized, the driver. One of them rubbed the taped bandage across his nose, then marched in lockstep with his brother toward their truck.

Sheriff Granger also had recognized Ben and motioned him to pull over.

Ben did.

Sheriff Granger leaned in and rested his elbow on the open window ledge.

"Morning, Ben."

"Morning, Sheriff."

"Glad I saw you just now."

"Why?"

"That's why." Granger pointed to the Krantz truck as it swerved onto Main Street and pulled away. "Wanted to give you a friendly heads-up."

"My head's usually up."

"Good. Because nobody knows what those Krantz brothers are liable to do."

"Like what?"

"Well, they jumped you once, didn't they?"

"They tried."

"Well, maybe they'll try again . . . this

104

time, in the dark. I warned 'em against it. But . . ."

"But what?"

"The two of 'em just stood there with that aggrieved look on their ugly faces."

"They can't help it if they're ugly . . ."

"No, but they didn't take kindly to how you done 'em in front of half the town. I reminded them how you didn't press charges."

"Thanks."

"Yeah, but with them . . . well, be on the lookout and let me know if . . ."

"If what?" Ben smiled.

"Let's say if they make any false moves."

"Okay, Sheriff, and thanks again."

"Say, where you heading this morning?"

"Going to pick up something for my new companion."

"Companion?"

"Betsey."

"Betsey? Who's Betsey?"

"Bought her from Gotch Tompkins."

"A horse?"

Ben nodded.

"*The* horse."

With an ample supply of hay, oats, and sundries, Ben's pickup was parked in front of a barnlike structure on a side street of

Sheridan.

Above the entrance, a large faded sign.

AL'S EMPORIUM
Feed — Saddles — Sundries
LIVERY — STABLE

Ben came out of the entrance, tucking a receipt into a pocket and a brand-new bridle looped around a shoulder where his lariat sometimes rested.

He stopped short as a station wagon pulled up, parked near his pickup, and Dr. Amanda Reese stepped out with a broad smile.

"Howdy, Mr. Ben."

"Howdy, Dr. Amanda."

"It's a small world, isn't it?"

"It is in Sheridan."

She pointed to the pickup.

"I see you've been doing some shopping."

"Yes, ma'am . . . and more to come."

"Such as?"

"Hardware, lumber, et cetera, et cetera, et cetera."

"Business certainly is booming since you came to town. But," she smiled again, "we've got to stop meeting like this."

"Why?"

"I can't think of a single reason."

"Neither can I."

"I heard you bought Gotch Tompkins's horse."

"Thanks to you, Betsey's all mine."

"She's a fine animal. I helped bring Betsey into this world. Congratulations."

"Uh . . ."

"Uh, what, Mr. Smith?"

"Speaking of horses, you own one?"

"Sure do. Domino's right in there."

"Maybe . . . the four of us, you, me, Domino, and Betsey, can go riding sometime."

"More than 'maybe.' "

"What about swimming?"

"What about it?"

"Well, there used to be a small lake we used to call our swimming hole, Devil's Lake, nearby. Is it still wet?"

"Rode by it last week, still wet."

"You have a bathing suit?"

"Wouldn't go swimming without it."

"Maybe we can ride over, take a dip."

"Why not a picnic? I'll provide the sandwiches, you bring the beverages."

"Sounds logical. Meanwhile, Betsey and I've got a little fixin' up to do at the Little Brawny."

"I get out to the Big Brawny from time to time."

"You do?"

"I do."

"Well, if you ever get thirsty along the way, stop by, have a sody pop, and visit your . . . godchild."

"I'll do that."

She started to walk toward the entrance.

"And take care of Betsey."

"I'll do that. And you take care of . . ."

"Of what?"

"Of all those four-legged critters around Sheridan."

Ben drove the pickup at a slow pace, slower than the other cars, trucks, and pickups along the way. He was in no hurry and besides, he wanted to think about her.

Dr. Amanda Reese. The "doctor" part could mask a lot of things.

Was it Mrs.? If she was, she probably wouldn't go riding, picnicking, and swimming with him — or anybody else.

Divorced? Could be, although anybody would be a fool to let go of someone like her.

Still single? Unlikely, unless all the men she ever met were low on vitamins.

There was something about her that lingered. Perfume?

She probably didn't use any, and if she

did, it would have gotten mixed with all the animals she was around and handled.

Something about her that lingered, the slightly crooked smile. The sparkling blue eyes. The slight tilt of her face when she was making a point. Her sense of humor.

Maybe it was the way all that came together.

But she was not quite like any other woman that Ben Smith had met along the way — and there were many, the most outlandish, for some reason, came to mind now — maybe in contrast to Amanda Reese.

His thought flashed back, not very far, to the latest "blond bombshell" of the screen.

Belinda Blake (née Novak).

It was in the early thirties, in, where else? Hollywood.

It had all been arranged by Ike Epstein, the most flamboyant press agent in, where else?

Hollywood. His motto was "I'll tell the world."

A limousine was to pick up Ben Smith and deliver him to Chasen's, where Belinda Blake would be waiting to have dinner with him and talk about a movie she was about to star in — and produce.

The Actress and the Cowboy.

Epstein added that there was "Quite a bit

of money to be grabbed."

Ben was far from broke, but it was the nadir of the Great Depression, and months before the next rodeo circuit.

He was not averse to grabbing quite a bit of money.

He stepped out of the limousine and into Chasen's, not overly dressed as a cowboy, and warmly greeted by name by Mrs. Dave Chasen, who, among other things, was famous for never forgetting a face or a name.

Mrs. Chasen greeted him by name, even though she had never met him, and led Ben Smith to an intimate private dining room.

Belinda Blake, in modest wardrobe that nevertheless revealed most of her physical assets, greeted him with a movie-screen smile, rose, and proceeded to kiss him as an anonymous photographer flashed his camera, then disappeared, followed by Mrs. Chasen.

"Please, sit down, Ben. Before drinks and dinner, which has been ordered, and Epstein joins us, I want to ask you something . . . personal."

Her voice was very "personal" and provocative. "Is that agreeable?"

"Yes, ma'am."

"Do call me Belinda?"

"Yes . . . Belinda. Ask."

"Will you marry me?"

"Say again?"

"Perhaps I shouldn't have been so . . . abrupt, but here's the whole scam. It was Epstein's idea and a damn good one — for both of us. Allow me to proceed."

Ben managed to nod.

"I'm about to star in a picture which will be released in about six months. I'm known as a 'bombshell' — my only competition is the young tart Harlow — the so-called It Girl, Clara Bow, has faded, so has Ann Harding — but I've got to keep that bombshell bullshit alive. My costar in *The Actress and the Cowboy* is Frank Cooper, but he's happily married, Catholic, and won't cooperate. So we give you a small part but a good run in the picture and you're famous, being a real three-time All-'Round Champion Cowboy — you are, aren't you?"

Ben shrugged and nodded.

"I know damn well you are. So, while we're shooting, we put on a hot little romance — get engaged — Epstein goes to work on one of his 'tell the world' publicity bonfires — we fly to Arizona, get married before the picture comes out, and the whole world goes to see *The Actress and the Cowboy,* all this time you're getting five hundred

111

smackers a week and enjoying the bedtime benefits of married life."

"For how long . . . Belinda?"

"Oh, don't worry about that, I've been married twice before and will be again after the picture runs its course and we divorce."

Before Ben could fully comprehend that proposal, the door flung open and who else but Ike Epstein, pranced in.

"Hello, kids — how're you two lovebirds getting along?"

"Uh, pardon me . . . Belinda, Mr. Epstein, but I gotta go to the men's room."

Ben opened the door to the men's room. There was a sign on the lower level.

WATCH YOUR STEP

Another on the even level.

WATCH YOUR STEP

Ben did what he had to do, then turned back.

A sign by an upper level.

WATCH YOUR STEP

Then an even higher level.

WATCH YOUR STEP

And near the door.

and Your <u>Fly</u>!

Ben flew.

That was the last time Ben Smith ever saw Chasen's, Belinda Blake, and Ike Epstein.

His thoughts harkened back to Dr. Amanda Reese.

But not for long. In the rearview mirror he saw something he didn't like. Something he'd been warned about.

Chapter Nine

Unless there were two trucks exactly alike, the Krantz brothers' truck following him belonged to the Krantz brothers.

The truck trailed at varying speeds. Sometimes at a distance, sometimes close enough to recognize their stolid faces.

Never too far. Sometimes too close. More often, too close.

Ben raced through his options. He could stop in the open here in the street, or keep driving to someplace where he might have a better advantage.

He chose the "might have" and kept driving, changing directions — so did the truck.

He kept driving until he spotted a familiar sign. It wasn't sanctuary, but it was company.

RANDY'S INDEPENDENT GAS

He pulled in. The truck slowed down, then

kept going.

Even before the pickup stopped near one of the two pumps, young Randy was out the door, having already recognized the pickup and its driver.

"How do, Ben?" Randy grinned.

Ben was out of the pickup and reconnoitering for any sign of the truck.

None.

"Leaning forward, Randy. Might as well fill 'er up."

"You bet."

Randy went at it.

"That was some story in Skinny's paper, smack on the front page like he said, big enough for a blind man to read — he sure was excited about that scoop I gave him . . . Say, you haven't been doin' much drivin' . . . only took five gallons."

"That right?"

"Yeah, just about everybody that's come in has already seen it."

Ben continued reconnoitering.

"That so?"

"You bet. Say, I got a few copies left inside if you need a couple for your scrapbook."

"I haven't got a scrapbook."

"You don't? Well, I do, and I'll paste a couple in there, seein' as I gave him the scoop."

"How much?"

"How much, what?"

"How much for the gas?"

"Oh, yeah, the gas . . . five gallons, fifteen cents a gallon . . . seventy-five cents, the toll."

"Here's a George Wash, put two bits in your safe deposit box."

"My what?"

"Your pocket."

"You bet, and if you got any more scoops, 'preciate if you give 'em to me. Skinny trades me a free ad for every one."

"I'll remember that, Randy."

"Want me to check the oil and water, Ben?"

"Nope. Haven't been doing that much driving."

Driving the partially loaded pickup back toward Sheridan, Ben occasionally glanced at the rearview mirror for any reflection of the truck.

There was none — so far.

He had dealt with bullies and braggarts, drunk or sober, who wanted to show off in front of buddies or blondes, then brag about decking the famous rodeo cowboy.

In most cases, it ended with Ben telling his potential opponent that he had a wooden right arm but would give it a go in an arm wrestling contest after he bought the challenger a couple of drinks. Sometimes it ended with the challenger asking for Ben's autograph, other times, with the challenger on the deck.

With the Krantz brothers it might end different.

In their previous encounter, Ben hit first and fast, but the next time, as the sheriff warned, they might jump him in the dark, or around a corner.

It so happened that the pickup was approaching Sheriff Tom Granger's office and Ben thought of stopping and telling him what happened with the Krantz clan. But what could the sheriff do about what they had done?

Charge them with making some "false move?"

Ben had ridden wild-eyed bucking broncos and wrestled sharp-horned bulls. In war, he had faced armed enemies who intended to kill. He had survived and prevailed.

He didn't come home to worry about a couple of big bozos — or did he?

Ben dismissed the thought and decided to proceed toward Walt's Hardware and Lumber.

He was on Main Street, approaching the only stoplight in town. The light was in his favor, so he proceeded at the proper pace until he saw a woman just off the curb with a boy about ten. The woman was pointing to Ben's passing pickup and the boy was running into the street toward it, waving a newspaper in the air.

Ben hit the brakes, and the boy jumped onto the running board, shoved the newspaper halfway through the open widow.

"Hey, mister, will you sign your picture on the paper? Please!"

"Sure, son."

The light had turned red. Ben took the newspaper.

"Have you got a pencil?"

The boy shook his head.

"Well, I have." Ben took a pencil out of his shirt pocket. "What's your name?"

"It's for my mom."

"What's her name?"

"Uh, Mildred Ross — but everybody calls her Millie."

"Then Millie it is." He wrote *For Millie* and signed it. Handed it back through the window.

"Got to go, son, the light's turning green."

The boy jumped off and started toward the curb.

"Careful, son, of the traffic."

Ben took off as Millie was smiling and

waving good-bye.

An hour later, in front of Walt's Hardware and Lumber, Walt Swicegood, husky, middle-aged, and Tommy, his fourteen-year-old, tall, towheaded son, were just about finished helping Ben load the pickup with paint, hardware, and lumber for the Little Brawny.

"Ben, Tommy'll go with you and help unload. I'll pick him up later."

"Thanks, but I can manage, Walt."

"Won't hear of it. Part of our service; besides, I got to swing by that way and see Mrs. Layton. She called and wants me to come out and talk about some work on her ranch."

"Well, if you say so. I appreciate the help and the company." Ben looked at Tommy and nodded.

Just then, the venerable Clay Sykes, who was always in a hurry, approached in a hurry.

"Howdy, Walt." Sykes nodded at Tommy, then turned to Ben. "You are Ben Smith, aren't you?"

"Have been since I can remember. Have we met?"

"A long time ago, but you wouldn't recall. You were about his age, or maybe younger."

He pointed to Tommy. "I'm Clay Sykes, run the post office and Western Union station. Your picture's been in Skinny's paper more'n anybody's 'cept Pete Germano, ex-governor, and he's dead now."

Clay Sykes extended his hand and they shook, but that didn't slow down Sykes.

"Sorry I missed that ruckus with those Krantz grizzlies, but you showed 'em how to kiss the ground. I went over to Granger's office with Doc and reviewed the payoff."

"Yes, well, pleased to see you again, Clay."

"Maybe and maybe not. Got a telegraph for you . . . to be held till your arrival."

"Well," Ben pointed to the loaded pickup, "I've arrived."

Clay reached into a pocket and handed the unopened telegraph to Ben.

"Do you really know those fellas who sent it?"

Ben put the telegraph into his shirt pocket. "Don't know till I read it."

"Well, aren't you going to open it?"

"After I get home."

"Suppose it's urgent?"

"You ought to know, Mr. Sykes, you read it, didn't you?"

"I . . . uh, have to read it when I take the message, don't I . . . Mr. Smith?"

"Then I'll be back."

"You know who it's from?"

"I have a notion."

"Do you really know those fellas . . . or is this a gag?"

"You'll find out if I do answer it, Mr. Sykes, unless I write them a letter."

"He'll find out anyhow, Ben," Walt smiled. "Ol' Clay Sykes knows everything that goes on in Sheridan . . . sometimes before it happens."

"And sometimes," Ben also smiled, "I wish I had me one of those crystal balls. Pleasure meeting up with you again, Mr. Sykes."

"Yeah." Sykes glanced at the loaded pickup. "Looks like you're fixin' to stay."

"First, I've got a lot of fixin' up to do."

"Yeah . . . I've seen the Little Brawny."

While they were at Walt's loading the pickup and listening to Clay Sykes, young Tommy had not participated very much. In fact, his vocal contribution could not have been more than two or three sentences, and none of them memorable.

As they started the drive to the Little Brawny, Ben assumed it would be more, or less, of the same, dead air.

He considered breaking the silence by turning on the radio or by kicking off some conversation by introducing a topic that would jump-start a reply or reaction.

But Ben needn't have worried. Tommy was the one who commenced conversation, in a measured pace at first, but it didn't take him long to gain momentum.

"You know, Mr. Smith . . ."

"Ben."

"I been thinking . . ."

"About what?"

"Mrs. Shuler over at the high school. She's been teaching us a class about American contemporary literature, and she started off with Hemingway's short stories, you know, 'The Killers,' 'Fifty Grand,' the adventures of Nick Adams . . . maybe you read some . . ."

"Some."

"Well, that got me to reading a couple of Hemingway's novels over at the library — *A Farewell to Arms* and *The Sun Also Rises.*"

"That's some pretty deep stuff. Go ahead, Tommy . . ."

"Well, I'd like to be like him."

"Hemingway?"

Tommy nodded.

"You want to be a writer?"

"I don't think I could ever be that, but I'd like to live the kind of life he does and you do."

"Now, hold on, if you're comparing me to

Ernest Hemingway, you're a mile apart."

"Oh, no. You both left home when you were young. You both went to war. Been to places overseas like England and France, had all sort of adventures, and saw the world, and here I am in a flyspeck called Sheridan."

"You're young yet."

"Sure, but I got to start thinking about when I grow some . . ."

"And do what, for openers?"

"I'm not sure about openers, but after that . . ."

There was a pause.

"What?"

"I want to bust the world open and see what's inside."

"Some didn't like what they saw . . . there's also rumbling about another war. A couple of fellas named Hitler and Mussolini are making noises and talking tough."

"You know, I almost hope another war starts. I'd be just about the right age and be among the first to go."

"A lot about war is storybook stuff. A lot of people die."

"The two of you came back."

"But we were among the lucky ones."

"And you both are better off for the chances you took."

"Like I said, we were among the lucky ones."

"Well, I could get lucky, too, but I'm not sticking around here."

"Tommy, you've got to do what you've got to do. I wouldn't be one to try to discourage you . . . you go ahead, bust the world wide open, and see what you can find in there."

"Thank you, sir. Means a lot to me, besides, another famous American writer, Jack London, said something like, 'I'd rather wear out than rust out.' "

"Yep. And he died before he was forty."

Ben's pickup swung into the Little Brawny.

Just less than three hours later, Ben and Tommy had unloaded the pickup; Ben had taken Betsey for a short stretch of her legs; both Tommy and he had laid out her daily meal, then groomed her while Ben told her what a nice day it had been and how tomorrow would be even better.

Betsey seemed to agree with a nod of her curved neck and flowing mane.

On his way back from Laura Layton's ranch, Walt had stopped by to pick up Tommy but made abundant references, not about her ranch and what needed to be done, but about her face and frame and how nothing need be done to any part of either.

Walt made sure that the portion of his conversation about the Layton lady and her attributes was spoken only to Ben, and out of Tommy's earshot.

On their drive back to Sheridan, Tommy Swicegood retreated to his usual laconic self, but not in his churning thoughts — all about his conversation with Ben Smith.

Neither he, nor Ben, could predict the future, but some of what they said would come true.

The whole world was on the brink of chaos and might crack apart at any time. The coming decade would be among the most devastating and historic since the time of dwellers in caves.

Japan had decimated China and raped Nanking. Those couple of fellas that Ben mentioned invaded first Ethiopia and later Poland. Planes out of the rising sun bombed Pearl Harbor, and it all flared into World War II.

Young Tommy Swicegood was one of the first to leave his high school sweetheart, Mary June, behind and enlist in the marines . . . one of the first marine privates to land on the beaches of Guadalcanal . . . one of the first marine corporals to wade onto the sand of Saipan . . . and one of the first marine sergeants to fall at Tarawa.

Sergeant Tommy Swicegood would not be among the luckiest, nor among the unluckiest.

He lived — but lost his left leg just above the knee.

He was among the first veterans to return to Sheridan. Mary June and he became husband and wife.

Tommy Swicegood did not bust the world wide open.

But he left his mark on it.

Near sundown, Walt and young Tommy Swicegood arrived in Sheridan, back from the Little Brawny, and drove past Kit Carson's Saloon.

Inside Kit Carson's, the two Krantz brothers sat at a corner table, draining beer and chuckling about what they were going to do to Ben Smith.

As Kit Carson strolled by, Claud grinned, "Hey, Kit, how about more beer?" Then turned back to brother Clem, both still grinning.

Kit hailed the waiter.

"Attention, Baldy, Laughing Boys need more beer."

■ ■ ■ ■

On the porch of the cabin, Ben Smith watched the sun go down.

Sunrise and sunset were his two cherished parts of the day, no matter what happened in between — he had lived to see it, and there was always the prospect of a better tomorrow.

A man named Will Rogers once said, "Life begins at forty."

That might not be true.

Ben Smith's life was just past forty, and had been crammed with struggle and success, with near death and high living, with pain and prosperity, with disappointment and laughter — and what happened in between.

All in all, it was easy — easy the hard way.

But here, back at the Little Brawny, one life had ended, and a new life was about to begin.

Then, out of the descending sun, he saw, then heard, Al Norkey's aircraft.

The mustangers were heading back to the landing strip of the Big Brawny.

It was time for Ben Smith to go back inside.

The unopened telegram was still in his pocket.

CHAPTER TEN

Ben had fixed and eaten supper. A can of Campbell's chicken soup, fried bologna sandwich on rye, washed down with a bottle of Lone Star beer.

He had taken the dirty dishes — a soup bowl, a resting plate for the sandwich — and all the rest — and placed them in the sink for tomorrow morning's wash.

He had wiped off the dining table, which also served as desk, and sometimes workbench.

There were four Douglas chairs around the table. He adjusted the one he used so it would conform with the other three.

There were three choices for his evening's smoke. Strike up a Lucky, a pipe, or light up a Marsh Wheeling cigar.

He chose the cigar.

Ben walked toward the lone easy chair in the cabin, next to a floor lamp — a small side table on each side of the chair — tin ashtray on one table, a small Philco radio on the other.

The radio was turned off.

Ben left it off.

He lit the cigar, pulled the unopened telegram envelope from his shirt pocket, smiled, took a puff of the Marsh Wheeling, opened the envelope, and started to read.

DEAR OL BEN
IFN YOU EVER DECIDE TO GIVE UP THE LIFE OF EASE IN SHERIDAN — THERES ALWAYS AN EMPTY SADDLE AND A SWAY-BACK SORREL WAITIN FOR YOU TO RIDE AGAIN — ON SCREEN AND OFF WITH THE GOWER GULCH GANG.
    SIGNED (IN ALPHABETICAL ORDER)
                        BUCK JONES
                          TOM MIX
                      WILL ROGERS.

Ben thought about his three pals — what he and practically everybody else knew — their backgrounds and fame.

But there were the rollicking times he shared with the Gower Gulch Gang that Ben thought about most.

There's an old saying.

"You get old when you start tripping over your memories."

But some memories are worth tripping over. And besides, Ben wasn't that old.

In the mid to late 1920s, among the highest-paid western stars at William Fox's studio and probably in Hollywood, only one of them was actually born in the West, William Penn Adair "Will" Rogers, in Indian Territory, which later became Oklahoma. His family's line consisted of one quarter Cherokee blood and, as Will often said, "They didn't come over on the *Mayflower,* but they met the boat."

Even in his youth, Will excelled in riding and roping, which led to ranch, and then circus work, a stint in Australia, then the St. Louis World's Fair, vaudeville, and New York, perfecting his act, by this time highlighted by western-style commentary of uncommon common sense peppered with dollops of personal and political discourse such as, "I only know what I read in the papers" and "I am not a member of any organized political party. I am a Democrat."

For more than a decade he starred on the stages of the Ziegfeld Follies, captivating thousands of audiences, including the common throng, high society, presidents, and royalty.

Along came silent movies, first at Fort Lee, New Jersey, and finally a fateful move to Hollywood and Hal Roach, Samuel Goldwyn, and ultimately at Fox, where he remained, famously and financially — along with newspaper articles and radio appearances, for the rest of his life.

To everyone, Will Rogers was "everyman," but there was no other man ever like him.

During the Roaring Twenties, there were two other western stars at Fox, Tom Mix and Buck Jones.

Thomas Hezikiah Mix, who was born in Mix Run, Pennsylvania, and grew up on farms and in stables, riding ponies, shooting pistols, and throwing knives.

A stint in the army and several short stints in a series of marriages led to a hitch as town marshal in Oklahoma, then to the world-famous 101 Ranch with its Wild West touring company, then rodeo championships in Arizona and Colorado, shooting, riding, and roping.

After *The Great Train Robbery* and *The Squaw Man,* Hollywood became the cowboy mecca, and it didn't take Tom Mix long to ride in the parade. He started by doing stunts, then galloped to top-salaried stardom via scores of action-packed horse operas at Selig then at Fox, earning $7,500 per week and dethroning William S. Hart as King of Cowboys. While Hart with his horse, Fritz, were heroic, Tom and his horse, Tony, blazed a more flamboyant and fashionable image of what the West might, and should have, been — more circus and cavalier than Hart's raw realism, with Tom obviously doing his own stunts and paying the physical price.

Audiences of all ages loved the Douglas Fairbanks of the West.

Of the Fox western troika, Buck Jones, born Charles Frederick Gebhart, in Vincennes, Indiana, led the most dangerous and heroic real life, which included combat in the Philippines in Troop G, 6th Cavalry Regiment, after enlisting underage, and he was wounded in action during the Moro Rebellion — discharged and later, after recovering, reenlisted and served another hitch before he was twenty-one.

The expert young ex-cavalryman also went into cowboying at the famed 101 Ranch in Oklahoma, where he met and married his lifelong companion, Odille "Dell" Osborne. During her pregnancy, they moved to the promised land of the West, which for a time proved not at all promising, as he eked out a Spartan existence between stunt work, bit parts, and professional boxing events. While heavyweight world champion Jack Dempsey didn't have anything to worry about, the motion picture western moviemakers began to take notice of the rugged rider of the Painted Desert.

From Poverty Row at Gower and Sunset, he galloped to Universal, then to Fox in 1925, with over 150 films, adding another star to the western sky with salary to match — not far behind Tom Mix and the more homespun and versatile Will Rogers — where the three formed an offscreen camaraderie as well.

It was not unusual for the trio to visit the not-as-fortunate veteran cowboys whom they knew from the early days, greet them with a friendly handshake, and press a hundred-dollar bill into their callused palms. Some of those cowboys had charged up San Juan Hill with Teddy Roosevelt and others had fought with Black Jack Pershing in the War to End All Wars.

That's when Will Rogers, Tom Mix, and Buck Jones labeled themselves the Gower Gulch Gang.

During the winter of 1926, after appearing in a Los Angeles rodeo event, three-time All-'Round Champion Cowboy Ben Smith was featured in a two-reel short subject by Fox entitled *Rodeo Rough Riders*. The money was good and welcomed — but there

134

was something better. Ben was welcomed by three Fox cowboy stars who wanted *his* autograph.

Three famous fans named Will Rogers, Tom Mix, and Buck Jones.

They forged a resolute friendship that lasted longer, much longer, than silent movies. The Gower Gulch Gang knew a cowboy's cowboy when they watched Ben Smith work at it with a rugged grace and seemingly effortless command.

After that, whenever Ben came to Los Angeles the three buckaroos showed him the town and were pleased to be seen with him and even tried to convince him to "get into the movie racket." But Ben would have none of it.

"I'm not an actor. I have to be myself."

"Well, who the hell do you think I am?" Tom Mix grunted, "John Barrymore?"

"Not with that punctured profile," Buck Jones smiled.

"Me," Will Rogers noted, "I just play myself . . . only more so."

"Thanks, but no thanks, fellas." Ben shook his head. "When the time comes, I'll just head back to the ol' homestead and the real West."

"With the real scent of horse manure instead of orange blossom," Mix observed.

Ben nodded.

"In the meanwhile, I sure do favor your company . . . and seeing the sights."

The sights that Ben favored seeing with his pals included the Pacific Ocean, the Santa Monica Pier Hippodrome, the La Brea Tar Pits, and the Hollywood Bowl.

But his new amigos also introduced Ben to some of their favorite fun fairs: the Cocoanut Grove, where Joan Crawford won another dance trophy; the Blossom Room at the Hollywood Roosevelt Hotel, site of the first Academy Award presentation; the Hollywood Hotel, where the Talmadge sisters tangled with the Marx Brothers; Roscoe "Fatty" Arbuckle's Plantation Cafe, where John Gilbert squired Greta Garbo on and off the dance floor; and there were other social sanctums where Mix, Rogers, Jones, and their guest mingled with celebrities Ben had seen only on the screen and who looked much smaller in person.

Ben enjoyed all of it, but none of it rubbed off. He changed not a whit. Through half a dozen years when he came and left, he was still the same laconic, but stalwart son of the West, who felt most at home on horseback, while Mix and Jones found favor in fast cars, and Will Rogers, who, between performances and polo games, took to flying in airplanes with his close pilot friend, Wiley Post.

Tom breezed through a couple more marriages, but Buck and Will were steadfast to the end of their married lives.

Ben did get a hoot out of their visit to Sid Grauman's Chinese Theatre on Hollywood Boulevard.

The Sunday sun was still trying to shine through the coral sky after a Saturday night and early Sunday of making the rounds of the usual hot spots to see and be seen with all four revelers wardrobed in tuxedos — Ben's borrowed from Buck.

Tom parked his Phaeton, partly in the street and partly on the curb, and he and the passengers made their way to the dawning palatial entrance.

A police car pulled up. Two uniformed officers exited and made a serious approach.

"You fellas lose something?" the shorter lawman barked.

"Maybe a little sobriety," Will Rogers remarked as the taller lawman shone a flashlight in Will's face, then blurted:

"Well, I'll be damned. Jim," he addressed his partner, "if it ain't Will Rogers, himself."

"Plus, his pardners," Will added. "Jim, meet my fellow knights of the trail. Mr. Mix, Mr. Jones, and our friend, Ben Smith, the illegitimate son of Buffalo Bill. He's new in town."

"Well, I'll be damned," Jim also chimed in. "It's a pleasure, fellas."

"Vice versa," Tom nodded.

"Mind if we show Buffalo Bill's son some of the signatures?"

"Go right ahead, fellas, but take it on the easy."

The officers turned and walked to their car.

"I'll be damned," one of them said again.

At their visit to Sid Grauman's Chinese Theatre, Ben's companions pointed out the hand- and footprints of the movie immortals, including Gloria Swanson, Harold Lloyd, Norma Talmadge, Douglas Fairbanks, and Mary Pickford.

Will and Buck did not fail to bring Ben's attention to a block of cement that framed the imprint of Tom Mix's hand and boot prints, his .44, and his horse Tony's two front hoofs.

The always gracious Tom Mix guided them to another inlay in cement . . . that of his predecessor in Cowboy Kingdom . . . William S. Hart.

Ben thought about his last visit with the Gower Gulch Gang.

By 1933 things were different in Hollywood and the USA. There was a new president, hailed as FDR. Prohibition had ended. So had silent motion pictures. The Great Depression was in session.

Prosperity was just around the corner — so was World War II.

William Fox was gone. Young Darryl F. Zanuck had taken over and dubbed the studio Twentieth Century Fox.

Will Rogers was still riding high over there, still with the fattest deal on the lot and thriving now in talking pictures.

Both Tom's and Buck's days at the studio were over, but their careers were far from over. Tom succeeded with his own circus, in radio and at Mascot Pictures in a serial called *The Miracle Rider* — money was still flowing and fleeing — so were Tom's marriages.

Buck was as popular as ever, with a good deal and a passel of good features at Columbia, including westerns and even contemporary movies.

Ben had won first-place money and a trophy at a Los Angeles rodeo — where Will, Tom, and Buck were in attendance, and the Gower Gulch Gang was ready to celebrate — although they didn't know it — for the last time together.

They had made reservations for a private

dining room at a new favorite outpost in town. The Hollywood Gardens, owned by a newcomer from the East, Frank Sennes, a young, personable character who had already made friends with hundreds of celebrities, including stars, studio chiefs, sycophants, sightseers, and Sheriff Eugene Biscailuz.

From the start, the Gower Gulch Gang was instrumental in promoting and publicizing the Hollywood Gardens. Will Rogers wrote a column that included a homespun homily.

> . . . the layout looks part Art Deco, part Southern comfort, and the rest, Monaco casino. The eats are deluxe — delicious . . . the drinks smooth, but oh, my . . . and the music, part Paul Whiteman, part Gershwin, and what's left is St. Louis blues . . . The private dining rooms are as colorful and cheeky as they come — Crumb Castle — Belly Cheater — Sundown Room — Sunrise Room — Winner's Luck — Loser's Lament — Retake Room — Stranger's Delight . . . the delight will be all yours . . . and the tab is tolerable.

After that, Frank Sennes's Hollywood Gardens was the magnetic merry-go-round of the town's hoity-toity and hoi polloi.

As usual, the Gower Gulch Gang was greeted at the entrance by Frank Sennes himself.

"Good evening, compadres. The Winner's Luck Room is ready whenever you are. You know the way," Sennes smiled.

As usual, the entrance of the Gower Gulch Gang garnered a vocal and visual reaction among the throng of citizenry, from celebrities to career seekers, to the flotsam of the Hollywood scene.

Even more so on this occasion, as the gang came dressed in western apparel. Tom's included a decorative gun belt and his .44 residing on his hip. Will had a lariat slung around his left shoulder. Buck's Stetson towered toward the ceiling, and Ben toted his winner's trophy in a bushman bag.

As they made their way toward the private room, Buck paused, then stopped.

"Just a minute, fellas. I want to say hello to somebody."

Mix and company followed Jones to the bar, where a tall, lean, handsome young man sat next to a burly, craggy-faced, bleary-eyed, somewhat older character — with a near-empty whiskey bottle between two empty shot glasses in front of them.

"Hello, Duke."

John Wayne turned and reacted as if he were gazing at living monuments.

"I think," Buck said, "you remember a couple of these fellas from your time at Fox."

"Remember? I was propping when I met the three high-and-mightys on the lot."

The three high-and-mightys smiled. The bleary-eyed man filled his glass and swallowed the contents.

"Tom helped me get that part in *The Big Trail.* Mr. Rogers taught me a few tricks with his lariat. And you, Buck, kept me going later over at Columbia when the going got rough with that bastard Harry Cohn."

"Duke," Buck motioned, "I'd like you to know Ben Smith . . ."

"Oh, I know Mr. Smith, all right. Never met him, but I sure as hell know *of* the best All-'Round Cowboy in God's country."

Ben Smith extended the hand that wasn't holding the trophy bag. As they shook, Duke nodded toward the bleary-eyed man.

"This is a friend of mine, Ward Bond."

Bond also nodded and filled his glass again.

"Hear you're doing all right, Duke," Jones said, "over at Monogram."

"Well, I don't know about that," Duke shook his head. "They got me playing a

singing cowboy, of all things, named Singin'
Sandy . . . with somebody else's voice."

"Well, keep at it, son," Will Rogers smiled.
"Singin' cowboys might come into fashion
someday."

"We're having a little celebration in a back
room," Tom said. "You and your friend care
to join us?"

"Thank you, Mr. Mix, but Ward and I've
got early calls, so we're going over to the
Athletic Club and steam off some of this
red-eye. Honor meeting you, Mr. Smith."

"Thank you, Mr. Wayne."

"Duke. Just plain Duke . . . and adios,
gentlemen."

Duke helped disembark Bond from the
stool and guided him toward the door.

Throughout the conversation, all the
tables in the room were occupied, including
the two nearest tables to the bar. Around
one table sat five of the biggest mortals in
sight. At the other table, a solitary smallish
man playing chess against himself. Both
tables were within earshot of the conversation between the Gower Gulch Gang and
Duke Wayne.

The solitary smallish man paid no mind
to what was being said. The five behemoths
did their best to overhear.

The Gower Gulch Gang paused momentarily at the chess player's table.

"Evening, Bogie," Tom Mix greeted. "Who's winning?"

"I always win," Humphrey Bogart snarled sibilantly.

And that was true in the early New York days. Between stage plays, Bogart would challenge six contestants at a time for money and invariably collect from all six.

Bogart inhaled a Lucky Strike and stubbed it out on an ashtray containing a half-dozen used-up Luckys.

"Well, good luck," Tom said.

"I don't need luck. I've got brains, yes, I have," Bogart said, and he lit another Lucky as the Gower Gulch Gang walked away.

Bogart finished the drink on his table, took a final look at the chessboard, nodded approval, then briefly assayed the five pilgrims at the next table.

All five jumbos were costumed in nearly identical wardrobe from head to heel: gray Stetsons extra-wide brimmed, gray buckskin jackets fringed shoulder to sleeve, heavy leather belts with egg-shaped silver buckles embossed with longhorn imprints, buggerred britches stuffed into gray midlength Justin boots with three-inch heels. They had consumed, and were continuing to consume, bourbon from one bottle in front of each consumer.

Bogart rose, shrugged up his trousers with both wrists, then sauntered over to the next table and leaned toward the biggest pilgrim.

"Say, stranger, you know what those four counterfeit cowboys remarked to me about you when they passed by?"

Bogart didn't wait for an answer.

"They remarked that they didn't want to drink in the same room with you five homos on the range."

Bogie let it soak in for a beat, then went on his way toward the entrance, where Frank Sennes was greeting Alan Mowbray.

"Too bad, Francis," Bogart interrupted, "I can't stick around for the ruckus. Got a date with an impatient virgin."

Bogie glanced back at the five pilgrims who were finished conferring and started to rise unsteadily. They began to totter toward the dining room wing of the Hollywood Gardens.

Bogart smiled and headed for the door. Frank Sennes shook his head and headed for his office. Alan Mowbray shrugged and headed for the bar.

Inside the Winner's Luck Room, the Gower Gulch Gang, with Ben Smith, were examining the repast on the long table laced with an elaborate buffet and assorted bottles of liquid libation.

Two tuxedoed attendants were standing by to accommodate them when the door slammed open.

The five bourbonites crammed into the room.

One of the attendants rushed toward them.

"Sorry, gentlemen, this is a private party."

"Not anymore!" came the gruff response from the biggest intruder.

One of the other Longhorns slammed the door shut.

"What can we do for you fellas," Buck Jones said, "before you turn around and leave?"

"We ain't leavin'," Big Longhorn blared. "Not before we get somethin' settled."

"Well, get to gettin'," Rogers drawled.

"That little fella told us . . ."

"Told you what?" Mix questioned.

"That remark you counterfeit cowboys passed . . . that you wouldn't drink in the same room with us hobos on the range."

"We made no such remark," Will Rogers smiled.

"Prove it!"

"Prove it, how?" Buck Jones shrugged.

"I'll show you how." Big Longhorn walked to the buffet table and lifted a bottle of bourbon by the neck with each hand.

"We're gonna have a few drinks together . . . all of us!"

"I'm getting just a little annoyed at all of you," Tom said. "And your bad manners."

"What are you gonna do about it?"

"Just this."

Tom Mix fast-drew his .44 and fired twice. Each bourbon bottle shattered, and Big Longhorn stood frozen, still holding the bottle necks.

The other four Longhorns — "Gee-Haw!" — and sprang toward the Gower Gulch group — but not far.

Will Rogers's lariat looped tight around a Longhorn's neck, the rope jerked, and the Longhorn met the floor hard.

Buck's right fist smashed into another Longhorn's jawbone, his left exploded into the fourth invader's right eye, and both toppled at the same time.

Ben swung the bushman bag that held the trophy into the fifth Longhorn's Stetson and down he went.

Just then, the door slammed open again and four men made entrance. Three imposing men and Frank Sennes.

"I'm Sheriff Biscailuz, and these two are deputies. What the hell is going on here?"

"Oh, just a slight misunderstanding," Will

shrugged.

"Doesn't look so slight." The sheriff looked around at the disabled Longhorns.

"Not anymore," Buck said.

"I called the sheriff and told him what I thought was going to happen."

"It happened," Will loosened the lariat.

"It was all that Bogart's doing," Sennes said. "He's what we Italians call a *istigatore.* A needler. Loves to start trouble, then walk away."

Sheriff Eugene Biscailuz was not the biggest man in the room, but something about him spelled "authority" — his eyes, his voice, his manner — and he was well acquainted with the Gower Gulch Gang.

"You fellas want to prefer charges against these unlawful cinch-binders?"

"Naw, they were just a little off their range." Will looped the lariat around his left shoulder.

Biscailuz pointed to the door and nodded toward the Longhorns.

"This way out, cowboys."

On his way out, the biggest Longhorn paused in front of Tom Mix.

"Thank you, sir . . . and I sure do enjoy all your movies. Mr. Mix, you're a real straight shooter."

When the others had left, Frank Sennes

stood at the open doorway and looked around, then at the Gower Gulch Gang.

"Sorry about the interruption, fellas."

"We'll pay extra for the damage," Buck said.

"On the house, friends," Sennes smiled. "It's all on the house."

Buck Jones ambled over to Tom Mix.

"I didn't know your .44 was loaded, Tom."

"What good is an unloaded .44? Let's get on with the celebration."

They did.

During that celebration, Ben Smith was officially inducted as one of the Gower Gulch Gang.

And that was the last time Ben Smith was with the Gower Gulch Gang.

The Marsh Wheeling was mostly ashes in the ashtray.

He slept tranquilly in his bunk that night, rose before dawn, fixed and consumed a Spartan breakfast of coffee and toast, washed last night's and this morning's dishes, walked to the cabin door, opened it, took a step onto the porch, and stuck fast — staring at a sight he didn't want to see.

Claud and Clem Krantz standing — smiling — triumphant and defiant.

CHAPTER ELEVEN

Ben Smith was not cowed.

He stood rock still.

Not triumphant.

But defiant.

"All right, fellas, maybe you've got a beef coming. I went at both of you without warning. But if you want some of me now, I'll take you one at a time in a fair fight, whoever comes first."

Claud took a step ahead.

"All right, mister," Ben nodded, "you first."

"Not so fast. First off, you done me a favor."

Ben waited.

Claud grinned.

"For years I had trouble breathin'. Doc ABC kept tellin' me I had a 'dee-vee-ated septum,' whatever that means. And with one punch you un-dee-vee-ated it, and I can breathe clear now."

"And me and brother Claud been thinkin'" over the whole kettle o' fish."

Brother Claud nodded in agreement.

"Not for the first time, we was outta line tryin' to disfavor you in front of all those people — but you showed your spine, good and plenty — and we're here to do somethin' about it."

"Do what? And how'd you get this close without my hearing your truck?"

"We shut off the motor and glided in — pretty smart, huh?"

"Yeah, pretty smart. What's next?"

"Just this," Claud turned toward their parked truck and hollered, "All right, folks, pull back the tarp on that truck and come on out!"

The tarp was pulled back, revealing about a dozen people, mostly men and three women, now standing and smiling.

"Just a few friends," Clem said to Ben, "who want to welcome you home and help put this place a-right in jig time."

Ben shook hands with both of the Krantz brothers.

"All in a day's day," they both said together.

Then all went to work on the cabin, corral, barn, smokehouse, and bunkhouse.

The first few minutes seemed like mass

pandemonium.

Within twenty minutes, more like organized pandemonium.

Among the volunteers were a half-dozen workers on the Krantz brothers' construction crew.

The Krantz brothers had their faults, such as a "look out, cowboy" sense of humor, but when it came to the construction business, they were all business.

"Hey, Jake," Claud nudged Jake, "get a wider brush. You ain't paintin' a portrait — that's a barn."

"Pete," Clem leaned in, "that nail's already sunk in. What're ya tryin' to do, kill it?"

"Ladies, you call them windows clean?" Claud remarked, "I couldn't see through 'em with a magnifyin' glass."

"Hey," someone yelled, "the bunkhouse is in pretty good shape inside and out. No leaks from the roof, windows all boarded — just needs a little dustin'."

"Well, get a broom and start dustin'," Claud yelled back.

So it went.

Dr. Amanda drove up in her station wagon.

Ben wasted no time greeting her, while she was still in the driver's seat.

"Surprised?" she said.

"Yeah."

"So was I when they told me about it. I'll bring by some curtains later. Just stopped by to say hello. Making my rounds."

"Well, hello," Ben said.

"Still on for that picnic?"

"You bet."

Dr. Reese drove off.

"Skinny Dugan?"

"No, I'm Ty Roan."

"I want to speak to Skinny Dugan."

"I'll give him a holler."

Ty Roan hollered.

"Hey, Mr. Skinny! Telephone!"

"Who is it?"

"I don't know."

"You didn't ask?"

"Why? Are you gettin' particular?"

"Gimme that phone . . . Hello."

"Mr. Skinny Dugan? Editor, publisher, and scribbler of the *Beacon*?"

"Correct in every detail. This is Skinny Dugan."

"I'm Laura Layton, owner of the Layton Ranch; we met in town, remember?"

"Yeah, I remember; you were in a hurry."

"You wanted to do an interview about me for your next edition."

"That's right . . ."

"Still want to do it?"

"I do. When?"

"Now."

"Okay, I'm ready to ask you some questions."

"Over the phone?"

"Sure."

"I don't do interviews over the phone. It's so distant, but I've sent a driver to pick you up and bring you to the ranch . . . much more intimate and personal. You'll get a feel of the place. He'll be there shortly . . ."

"In the Packard?"

"Heavens, no. We have a station wagon for such occasions."

"Well . . . I'm pretty busy."

"It's now or never . . . and bring your notebook."

"Never use one."

"You don't take notes?"

"Don't need to. Never have."

"We'll have lunch."

"Never eat lunch."

"Then, we'll have a drink."

"Now you're steamboatin'."

"See you for midday cocktails and the interview."

Laura Layton hung up.

The noon meal at the Little Brawny was

154

mostly mobile, consisting mostly of hot dogs and soft drinks provided by the ladies. Some of the workers had a hot dog in one hand and a hammer or paintbrush in the other.

Ben was doing his share of repair and still trying to figure out the Krantz brothers.

Betsey was out of the barn, probably wondering what all the noise and activity were about.

"Well, Mrs. Layton, you've showed me your . . . spread and it's in grand shape. I've had a couple of tall bourbons, and it's the smoothest bourbon money can buy. Now, shall we get to the interview?"

"Of course. Just providing some atmosphere."

"I've got all the atmosphere and bourbon I can take. Let us proceed with the libretto."

"That was quite an article you wrote about Ben Smith. I imagine you know him better than anybody else in this town."

"I imagine. I baptized him. I'm his godfather."

"He's not married, is he?"

"Nope."

"Ever been married?"

"Nope."

"You think he's here to stay?"

"Yep."

"You think he'd consider selling the Little Brawny?"

Skinny shrugged.

"You know his spread and mine border the Big Brawny."

"That's a geographical fact."

"But both our spreads rise higher than his. So, water flows from our high streams into his lower territory."

"Sounds logical."

"So, without us, Deegan would be hard up for water to feed his land and cattle."

"You want me to include that in your interview?"

"I'll sue your ass if you do," she smiled.

"Look, Mrs. Layton, is this supposed to be an interview about you, or about Ben Smith? Why don't you ask him those questions?"

"You don't ask a man like Ben Smith those questions unless you already know the answers."

"Well, you ain't gonna get 'em from me. Now, you want to answer a few questions?"

"Oh, I've already thought about that."

She handed Skinny a dozen pages of typed paper.

"This is my official bio. Use as much or as little as you please, and good day, Mr. Dugan."

■ ■ ■ ■

The workers in the bed of the Krantz brothers' truck were standing and waving "so long" to Ben, who stood nearby, shaking hands and talking with both brothers.

"Sorry, we got to take an early quit, Ben," Claud said, "but we said we'd get these folks outta here before sundown."

"Early quit? You people've been here for twelve hours."

"Time slips by when you're havin' fun," Clem smiled.

"Fun? It would've taken me a couple of weeks to do anything near it . . . and not as well."

"We'll be back to put on some finishin' touches when the paint dries," Claud said, "and when we're sober."

"Since you wouldn't take any money, this time . . ."

"This was a shivaree," Clem pointed to the people in the truck.

"Yeah, well, when the time comes, I'm officially hiring the Krantz Construction Company at the going rate."

"Maybe . . ." Claud said, "or maybe we'll see you when my septum gets dee-vee-ated again."

Both brothers walked away saying, "All in a day's day."

Dr. Amanda Reese had finished her rounds in a bit of a hurry and was driving back toward town, but she intended to make a stop along the way. She was nearing the Little Brawny to deliver and hang those curtains — or so she would say. But just then, she heard the melodic honk of an automobile horn.

It could probably be heard a block away.

She turned and saw the convertible Packard, top down, driven by the most striking woman she had ever seen in Sheridan — or near, or far.

The Packard passed her, then made a sharp turn on the dirt road toward Ben Smith's cabin.

Dr. Reese hesitated, but decided to follow — at least for a while.

Until the Packard's melodic horn sounded again, this time even louder.

Dr. Reese pulled the station wagon under a tree but within sight of the cabin.

Ben Smith was either expecting his visitor or had heard the horn.

He was standing on the porch.

Her station wagon made a U-turn away from the Little Brawny.

"Howdy. You lost, ma'am?" Ben stood at the door of the Packard.

"No. I found what I was looking for. You are Ben Smith, are you not?"

"I am."

"I'm Laura Layton, own the Layton Ranch. Do you know about it?"

"I've heard about it."

"I'd like to talk to you, but not out here."

"Then come on inside, Mrs. Layton."

She did.

Laura Layton looked around.

"Nice and cozy."

"I don't know about the 'nice' part."

She pointed to the bunk.

"Are those your sleeping quarters?"

"Temporarily. I intend to build a bed-room."

"Good idea. You have indoor plumbing?"

"Water closet is behind that door if you need to use it."

"Not at the moment. Mr. Smith, I'm a lady who doesn't waste time and comes right to the point, and as I said, I'd like to talk to you."

Ben pointed to the table and chairs.

"Well, then, sit down and talk."

She settled and smiled.

"Mr. Smith, would you be interested in selling the Little Brawny?"

"No, ma'am."

"You sure?"

"Damn sure."

"Not at any price?"

"Well . . . ten million dollars might move me a little."

"I'm serious."

"I'm not."

"Then I'll shift gears."

"Go ahead, shift."

"You know that your property and mine lie between the Big Brawny."

"So?"

"So, I was thinking of selling mine, but I may have a better idea that includes you, without your selling the Little Brawny but making quite a bit of money in the bargain."

"What bargain?"

"Together, we can put the squeeze on Mr. James Deegan to the point where he'll sell to me, and I'll cut you in for quite a penny for cooperating. You see, your land and mine, though much smaller than his, both extend . . ."

"You're talking about water supply . . . that's the squeeze, isn't it?"

"You're way ahead of me, Mr. Smith."

"I might be a country boy, ma'am, but I wasn't born lately. Besides, I don't think you could squeeze him enough to make him sell."

"I think I could . . . talked it over with my business manager. He got me a fat settlement on my divorce. He's a crafty old cougar. With him this sort of thing is a chess game and he knows how to play . . ."

"Dirty."

"Not exactly, but he knows how to tangle Deegan up in court until it's not profitable with dry land and thirsty cattle, while you and I . . ."

"That's far enough, Mrs. Layton. I don't care to hear any more, now, or ever."

"I'll settle for the 'now' part, but in the meanwhile . . ."

"In the meanwhile, 'back at the ranch, ranches,' what?"

"Give me your word as a gentleman that you will not reveal the topic of our little conversation to our neighbor James Deegan."

"As a gentleman like me, to a lady like you, I will be . . . discreet . . . if at all possible."

"That's good enough for now . . . and if I do change my mind and sell to him, I'll cut you in for a nice piece of change."

"No, ma'am, you can keep your nice piece of change. I'll keep my peace of mind and show you to the door."

Even as he said it, Ben thought that the gentlemanly thing to do was walk her to her automobile. It was getting darker, and even though it was unlikely that a pack of wolves might attack her — and even though Ben would give the wolves benefit of the first charge — he'd still bet on Laura Layton to win.

As Ben opened the Packard's door, she turned and kissed him full on the lips and then some.

It was not a familial kiss.

"Good night, Mr. Smith . . . nice meeting you."

"Good . . . night, Mrs. Layton," he managed to say — as the Packard roared off.

No sooner had Ben shut the cabin door than the phone began to ring.

"Hello."

"Ben, m'boy, it's Skinny."

"Evening, Skinny."

"Thought you might still be outside with them Krantz boys and their work gang, so I waited for after dark to call . . ."

"You know they were coming to help?"

"I did . . . *that'll* be in the next edition about the shivaree . . . how'd they do?"

"They did plenty . . . good and plenty. Seems like everybody knew they were coming but me."

"Don't know about 'everybody,' but I'm a newspaperman . . ."

"What's on the newspaperman's mind, Skinny?"

"Did an interview with that Layton woman earlier today. She gave me her official bio . . . full of lies that might as well have been capitalized, so I thought I'd call you and give you fair warning that . . ."

"Skinny, my good-fairy godfather, you can save your breath to cool your soup . . . she came over and gave me an earful, and an eyeful, of her charms. I didn't fall for either, so don't worry about it . . ."

"That's my godson!"

"Good night, Skinny."

"Good night, you ol' curly wolf."

Ben lay in his bunk with a wry smile on his face, thinking — she's a slick piece of lace, that Layton woman is.

She had more than one ace up her sleeve and knew how and when to deal them.

She said she was a lady who doesn't waste time and meant it.

First card — Mr. Smith, would you be
      interested in selling the
      Little Brawny?
      Blanko.

Second card — A little conspiratorial alliance to squeeze James Deegan dry — and force him to sell — with Ben reaping a piece of the profits.
Ditto.

Third card — A gentlemanly vow of nonrevelation as far as Deegan was concerned for a considerable commission.
Questionable.

Fourth card — A promissory kiss with a not-so-tenuous taste of further inducement.
To be continued?

Four aces — Pretty hard to beat.

But not a pat hand as far as Ben Smith was concerned.

Still, Laura Layton was a slick piece of lace and probably had more up her sleeve.

Chapter Twelve

"Norkey, I'm not going to mince words. This isn't paying off. The pickings are lean. Hardly worth my while, and there's not much in it for you so far. Probably not enough to cover the cost of your plane, truck, and squad."

Pepper and Joe Higgins were standing nearby.

"Well, things have been kinda slow, Mr. Deegan, but . . ."

"But if they don't speed up pretty damn soon . . ."

"They will."

"They better. I'm not playing games here with those damn mustangs. They're consuming more grass and water than the Big Brawny can afford to lose. I'm in the cattle business, and there's no profit in those damn mustangs. They're draining me dry. I want results from you and fast. By roundup there'll be nearly a thousand cows, steers, and bulls . . . We want them fat and content for market, don't we, Joe?"

"That's right, boss," Higgins nodded.

"Well, they won't be if those mustangs keep feeding on my grass and bellying up to my streams."

"I'll get the job done. I've done it before down in Arizona."

"I don't give a hoot about Arizona. The Big Brawny's not in Arizona. It's right here where we're standing . . . Pepper!"

"Yes, sir, I'm right here."

Pepper took a step closer.

"Right here," he repeated.

"Take care of Jimmy. See he gets his shot if I'm not back in time. Keep him busy. I've got that damn early meeting with the chamber of commerce and some other business in town."

"I know, and I'll do it all."

"You do it all, too, Norkey, or else. Get going. You're burning daylight."

James Deegan made a fast turn toward the parked Chrysler.

Pepper waited until the appropriate distance.

"Ain't seen him so steamed up since the last Oklahoma rain."

"What the hell is Oklahoma rain?" Norkey asked.

"Dust storm, and you'd best storm the hell outta here."

The Chrysler was on its way and so was Norkey.

"Oh, by the way, Joe," Pepper said, "Good mornin'."

"Yeah!"

Higgins turned and walked toward a corral.

Ben, with an easy swing, settled into the saddle.

He had been talking to Betsey most of the morning.

"Betsey, m'lady, you been standing around too much. What you need is a good stretch of the legs, and you're gonna get it this morning."

A few minutes later, driving his Chrysler toward Sheridan, James Deegan spotted Ben some distance away, riding toward the Big Brawny. Deegan was not hardly in favor of his son cavorting with the cowboy.

At the same time, Dr. Amanda Reese drove from Sheridan past Deegan on the way to her rounds.

The Sheridan Citizens Bank also served as headquarters for the Sheridan chamber of commerce, and the chamber's meetings were held in the bank's boardroom. Dave

Bergin, who was president of Citizens Bank, also served as president of the chamber of commerce.

James Deegan was surprised when he saw Laura Layton's Packard parked in front of the bank. He was even more surprised when he saw Laura Layton parked in the boardroom of the bank among Bergin and the other six male officials of the chamber.

"Good morning, Mr. Deegan. Glad you could make the meeting," Bergin said. "By the way, Mrs. Layton asked if she could sit in. Get acquainted since she owns the Layton Ranch. If that's agreeable to you?"

"Sure, it's agreeable."

"Then, please take a seat."

James Deegan took a seat next to Laura Layton.

It was the only empty seat in the room.

They were just outside of one of the corrals at the Big Brawny.

Ben and Betsey, Jimmy and his pony, a paint, and Pepper.

"I call him Pinto," Jimmy said.

"That's logical," Ben smiled. "He's a nice little animal, but you're still not quite tall enough to throw a saddle and fit a bridle on your pony."

"Maybe by next year."

"You bet. By then you'll be a foot taller, but meanwhile keep watching how Pepper does it."

"I will."

"But the main thing about learning how to ride a horse is getting on and riding it."

"Oh, I've ridden some before."

"I know, but are you ready to go for a little turn around some of your dad's real estate?"

"I am."

"Then, come on, son. I'll give you a little boost up. Stick your boot in that."

It was soon obvious that this was not the first time Jimmy had ridden his pony. Ben and Jimmy on their mounts and Pepper trailing in a pickup, past the outbuildings and onto the open range.

Jimmy never looked happier or healthier as they rode into a more remote area, swarms of cattle grazing in the distance.

"Ben, look!"

"Yep. They're fattening up." Ben didn't add "for the kill."

"Jimmy, m'boy, you're holding the reins a little too tight . . . no need to . . . loosen up."

"Like this?"

"Just like that."

Jimmy smiled and waved back to Pepper in the pickup.

Pepper responded.

Jimmy looked around, then to Ben.

"Are we on your land now, Ben, or on Dad's?"

"Not quite sure, the boundaries are . . ."

Ben was looking up, then pointed to the sky.

"See those birds?"

"I see 'em."

"Those are quail. You ever get lost or thirsty, you follow them. Quails are never far from water. Remember that."

"I'll remember."

Suddenly, there was sound from the sky — and then another kind of bird — the light plane flown by Norkey — and in the distance, a truck trying to keep up with the plane.

The plane approached — banked closer — then changed direction and whipped away.

James Deegan found himself walking toward their parked cars with Laura Layton.

"That meeting wasn't exactly thrilling, was it?"

"They never are, but you can't tell when some of those yahoos are liable to pull something sneaky."

"Is that why you attend?"

"That's why."

"You don't trust human nature?"

"Not till I get to know the human."

"Might be *we* ought to get to know each other better."

"*Might* be."

"How about dinner some night? We can go Dutch so one won't think the other is trying to bribe . . ."

"No need to go Dutch. We can flip a coin for who pays. By the way, have you been thinking about selling?"

"Still thinking. Got a few other things on my mind."

"Well, first things first."

"Yeah, there's that dinner. Don't call me. I'll call you."

"We'd better be getting back. Your dad'll . . ."

"Ben . . ."

"What, Jimmy?"

"I don't see Pepper. Do you?"

There was a pause as Ben looked back and reconnoitered.

"Yeah . . . he's a ways back there, parked under a tree. Probably rolling up a Bull Durham. He'll catch up to . . ."

Ben stopped in midsentence.

Something in the distance had caught his

attention.

First, a moving dust cloud invaded the stillness. Then, the source of the cloud became evident.

Gathering speed along the canyon escarpment, a herd of mustangs, led by the black — the same herd Ben saw from the cabin at the Little Brawny — now sweeping along the mountain slope, tails and manes streaming in the wind.

Twenty or more following the lead of the great eagle of the turf — survivors of Andalusian ancestors — fleeting across sagebrush toward the narrow-channel threshold to a deep, high-walled canyon.

The dust settled and disappeared with the herd into safe haven — for the time being.

Norkey's plane turned in another direction in search of another quarry. The truck followed.

Jimmy was awed.

"Never seen a mustang like that leader — mag-ni-fes-ent!"

"Ben, whose horses are they?"

"They don't belong to anybody, Jimmy. They're mustangs."

"Mustangs?"

"Been roaming wild and free for hundreds of years. But there aren't too many of 'em left. Not enough."

"What happened to them?"

"Civilization."

"Civilization?"

"Right," Ben grinned, looking at the sky. "Seems like that black outfoxed Norkey . . . for a while," Ben said. "Come on, son, your dad'll be waiting."

Jimmy's dad was waiting, and he had company. Beside Higgins, Dr. Amanda Reese also was there — sitting on the shady side of the porch, cocktails in hand.

There was a silent impatience in James Deegan's demeanor — until he caught sight of Norkey's plane coming in for a landing.

Deegan set his glass on a table and rose.

"Excuse me. I want to talk to him."

Higgins waited until his boss was barely out of earshot.

"The Great White Hunter is back."

"You sound disappointed."

"I was hoping he'd run out of gas at five thousand feet."

"Now, Mr. Higgins . . ."

"That's not all . . . and crash into his truck."

Ben and Jimmy, on horseback, and Pepper in his pickup appeared along the trail leading into Big Brawny as Norkey's plane had landed and he and Deegan walked back.

"All right, Norkey, how did it go this time?"

"That big black bastard got away, but we'll get him. The good news is . . ."

"There better be some."

". . . is I spotted another herd, prime stock, led by a roan. We'll have a bunch of 'em tomorrow. It'll be like shootin' fish in a barrel."

"I don't want to get rid of fish. I want to get rid of mustangs."

"Mr. Deegan . . . ?"

"Yes?"

"Is that invitation to dinner still on?"

"I guess so."

Amanda and Higgins walked up toward Ben, Jimmy, and Pepper — then Jimmy's father and Norkey.

Ben helped Jimmy down from the saddle, and Pepper was now beside them.

Deegan's face was not smiling, but not exactly solemn.

"Hi, Jimmy," he said, then with a slight edge, "We were beginning to get a little worried."

"Sorry we're late, Mr. Deegan," Ben said. "My fault."

Jimmy was still excited.

"Dad, we saw mustangs! You shoulda seen them!"

Norkey tried not to react. Higgins and Amanda approached. Deegan nodded toward her, then Ben.

"This is Dr. Reese."

"I've met Mr. Smith." Dr. Reese did not smile. Then to Ben, "I came by to check on a calf."

Deegan continued with the introductions.

"You know my foreman, Joe Higgins, and that's Al Norkey. I've asked them to stay for dinner."

"Dinner?" Pepper said. "Well, ma'am, it won't be Parisian dee-light, but I'll hustle somethin' up to cheat the belly, laced with my secret ingredient. Big medicine. Garlic."

"Oh, sure," she smiled, "that *is* big medicine."

"How would you know, ma'am?"

"My mother was Greek."

"She was?"

"Gloria Moulopoulos."

"That's all Greek to me." Pepper was pleased. He figured he'd made a joke. He then walked off toward headquarters.

Deegan glanced to Ben without great enthusiasm.

"Would you care to join us, Mr. Smith?"

" 'Preciate the offer, Mr. Deegan, but I'd best be getting back home." Then to Jimmy, "Adios, cowboy."

"See you soon, Ben . . . Dad, you should've seen . . ."

"Jimmy . . . it's time for your medicine."

Deegan guided his son toward the house. Higgins and Norkey followed.

Ben started to saddle up, but turned back to Amanda Reese, who was still standing.

There was a moment of awkward silence.

"I . . . uh, didn't know you were part Greek . . ."

"There's a lot of things we don't know about each other. Did you know I intended to stop by last night with those curtains I promised? Drove by but saw you had company . . ."

"Ma'am?"

"The Packard. Thought it was a 'Do Not Disturb' sign."

"No, ma'am. Just a little business on Mrs. Layton's part. No sale. She offered to buy Little Brawny."

"You refused the offer?"

"Yes, ma'am."

"Will you quit calling me 'ma'am,' it's Amanda, and since you're staying, I *will* bring those curtains by."

"Anytime." Ben swung into the saddle. "So long, Amanda."

Pepper popped his head in from the kitchen

door and smiled toward the diners — Deegan, Jimmy, Norkey, Higgins, Amanda . . . and Rover.

"How was it?!"

"Pepper, it was . . . de-lish-eus. Thank you."

"Thank you, ma'am. My half-hour specialty. Hurry-up stew . . . and that secret Greek ingredient."

"Reminds me of my mother's home cooking," Amanda smiled.

Pepper nodded and disappeared.

"Dad, can I have my dessert with Pepper?"

"Sure enough."

"Come on, Rover."

Jimmy scampered toward the kitchen but looked back.

"Dad, you should've seen those mustangs!" And he was gone.

There was a moment of silence.

"He won't be able to see them much longer, will he, Mr. Norkey?"

"I know you're an animal doctor, ma'am. But what I do is legal and necessary."

"And the way you do it?"

"This isn't some sport, ma'am, it's . . ."

"I know it's 'necessary' to drive them crazy and shoot them from an airplane — no — not a sport . . . or sporting."

"Amanda, I don't like it any more than

you do, but . . ."

". . . but you hire Mr. Norkey."

"They deplete the range and . . ."

". . . and there's so little range and so many mustangs."

Amanda looked at her watch, then as pleasantly as she could muster.

"Well, it's getting late. I'm going to have to skip dessert."

She rose, and so did the men.

"Please thank Pepper, and say good night to Jimmy."

Deegan took a step.

"I'll see you to your car."

Amanda's voice was firm.

"I'll be fine. Stay and finish your dinner . . . and business."

Ben finished currying Betsey in the barn. He set the brush down on the bench. Rubbed his palm over the horse's head and muzzle.

Betsey nickered. Ben nodded.

"Yeah, good night, horse."

He walked toward the barn door.

Amanda, driving her station wagon, looked at her watch through the fading light of sundown.

Ben ate his dinner at the table under a solitary light. Meat, beans, coffee. He looked toward the small Philco radio but decided not to turn it on.

He heard a sound, a faint motor, he rose, set the cup of coffee on the table, and walked to the door as the motor sound grew louder, then ceased.

As the cabin door opened so did the door from her station wagon, and Amanda stepped out, carrying a sizable package.

"Well, good evening, ma' . . . Amanda."

She moved closer.

"Are you receiving? Or am I too late?"

"Never too late. Just finished dinner but there's coffee and I thought you were having dinner with . . ."

"I was, but my stomach began to revolt when the subject turned to mustangs . . . so I thought I'd stop by and drop off those curtains." She held up the package.

"Well, come in and drop 'em. We'll avoid the subject of mustangs."

"With you that wouldn't be necessary. I think we'd agree on that subject."

"Well," he smiled, "we'll see what else we agree on." He motioned toward the door. "This way, Dr. Amanda."

Inside, she looked around the cabin.

"Very nice."

"It'll do for playing solitaire."

"Not like last night?"

"Told you that was a bum beef . . . Put the package down. I'll clear the dishes."

"*We'll* clear the dishes. Mighty nice for a bachelor. Have you always been a bachelor?"

Ben picked up some items from the table.

"We'll just stack 'em for tonight — that's morning duty — old bachelor tradition."

"You haven't answered the question."

"Oh, I thought I did. Always."

"Must've left a lot of disappointed ladies on your trail."

"Not so disappointed. And you?"

"Let's say that's another story for another time."

"Anything you say . . . or don't say."

"Well, I'm not the silent type."

"Good, because you've got a nice voice."

"Thanks."

"Say, there's a pretty good bottle of rye around here someplace. Would you care for a nightcap?"

"No thanks, I've got to drive home, but some other time."

"And some other place?"

"Not necessarily. The Little Brawny's a nice place, nicer than the Big Brawny."

"Thanks," he pointed to the package, "what do I owe you for the curtains?"

"No charge. They're a housewarming present, but I'll help you hang them sometime, unless that's against another bachelor tradition . . . and what about that ride and swim and picnic we talked about . . . sometime?"

"Would tomorrow be too soon?"

"You speak pretty fancy for a cowboy when you want to. Where did you learn?"

"I've seen a few Cary Grant movies; he'll never play a cowboy."

"Who's Cary Grant?"

"Are you kidding?"

She nodded. "Yeah, he's the one with a dimple on his chin. I just saw him in a movie with Jean Harlow. He played an aviator during the Great War."

"Some call it 'Great.' "

"Were you in it?"

"Didn't think they played Cary Grant movies in Sheridan."

"This was at a big-city convention . . . about that ride and swim and picnic, I'll be here before nine a.m. with Domino in tow."

"Good. I'll have the dishes done by then and the beverages ready."

"Save the rye. I'll bring the sandwiches and swimsuit."

"I'll walk you to your car. The end of a very nice day."

"Veltio avrio."

181

"What's that mean?"

"Greek . . . for 'tomorrow will be better.' "

CHAPTER THIRTEEN

With more than a dozen drovers, more than a couple hundred head of cattle were being driven in a comparatively organized pace and fashion from a fertile valley toward a less-favorable grazing area but still a part of the Big Brawny empire.

James Deegan and foreman Joe Higgins stood alongside of a pickup with the Big Brawny logo painted on both doors.

Deegan made no effort to mask his annoyance at being at this place at this time.

"All right, Joe, now what the hell is this between you and Norkey, and what the hell is going on before first light in the morning and what you wanted me to see?"

"The sonofabitch said I had to get these beeves outta here to a practically barren ground, or else . . ."

"Or else, what?"

"We're liable to have a stampede on our hands in a couple hours, like he's the one givin' me orders, instead of you — what we don't need is them runnin' crazy and losin' valuable weight they been puttin' on right here where the grazin' is good. I just wanted you to know and see for yourself . . ."

"Norkey might be a sonofabitch, but he's not an idiot . . . he must have a reason, and a good one, accordin' to him . . . Go ahead."

"Said yesterday he spotted a herd of mustangs led by a roan near them beeves, and he's flyin' in after them this morning and doesn't want the cattle to scatter and run off 'cause of the low-flyin' plane."

"Yeah, he told me about the mustangs but not about the rest."

"Well, damn it, he should've. You're the boss, aren't you?"

"Damn right."

"Well, I thought you ought to know and see what's goin' on for yourself."

"All right, Joe, I'll talk to him about the chain of command around here. Let's see what happens and take it from there."

"Well, I can only take so much from him and . . ."

"All right, Joe! I said I'll talk to him and straighten things out."

"You might catch him before he takes off this morning."

"I'll catch him, Joe. You stay here and see

to things. I'll catch him."

"Good morning, lady. You're early."
" 'Drather be a half hour early than a minute late."
Dr. Amanda Reese had arrived with the horse trailer in tow, delivering Domino.
"Good habit. I finished the dishes an hour ago. Let's make ready."

At the Big Brawny airstrip, near the light plane, James Deegan was talking, Norkey was listening. Out of hearing distance, Norkey's truck and crew were waiting.
Weegin, shotgun in hand, waited to board the plane next to Norkey. Anson, the truck driver, wiped at his chin with obvious impatience. Next to him, Baker. There were three other mustangers on the truck bed. Crane, Dorn, and Estes.
The truck was loaded with heavy tires, ropes, and other necessary equipment of the mustangers' trade.
"I'm sorry, boss, but I thought Higgins was the foreman . . . and I . . ."
"He is. But I'm the boss. If I'm on the property, and for something like moving a whole herd of cattle from a fertile valley, I want to know and okay it. So, come to me, or both of us. If I'm not here, that's a dif-

ferent story."

"I'm sorry, Mr. Deegan. I was anxious to get some results. I'll do what you said. Now, can we get going?"

"Get going . . . and get mustangs."

"We'll do both."

"Are we still on the Little Brawny?"

"Yep."

"The Little Brawny's not as little as I thought. Maybe you ought to call it the Not-So-Little Brawny."

They had been riding for well near an hour, with Ben on Betsey and Amanda on Domino.

And they moved on until they came to a tree-lined glen centered by a good-sized body of clear blue water that could have accommodated an Olympic swimming team.

Ben pointed ahead.

"We have arrived, m'lady."

"Is this what you called a swimming hole?"

"That's what we called it."

"This is phenomenal . . ."

"What's so phenomenal about it?"

"I feel like I've been here before. It's . . ."

"It's what?"

"Almost a replica of MGM's back lot where I watched them shoot a Tarzan picture . . ."

"How come you were there?"

"In Tarzan pictures they use animals. They also use animal doctors."

"Doctor, you've been places and done things."

"Look who's talking. Shall we dismount?"

"Yes, ma'am . . . unless you want the horses to go in, too."

They dismounted.

"Say, Amanda, where's your swimsuit?"

"I'm wearing it."

"Me, too."

"Shall we disrobe . . . discreetly?"

"Pick a tree . . . there's plenty."

They did.

A few minutes later, they were both in bathing suits.

They both liked what they saw.

"Well," she said, "are you hungry? What comes first, the picnic or the pool?"

"Can't swim after we eat, the pool comes first."

"I can't swim."

"What?"

"I said, 'I can't swim.' "

"I'll teach you how. You got a good start — looks like you could float."

She smiled.

"That won't be necessary . . . I was only kidding."

"About not being able to swim?"

"That's right."

"Well . . . I'm sort of disappointed, but, let's get wet."

"Let's."

Norkey's light plane was over a familiar landscape from which the herd had been moved — and below, Anson at the wheel of the traveling truck with Baker beside him with the rest of the crew, Crane, Dorn, and Estes, on the bed of the truck, loaded with oversized tires, ropes, and equipment.

Norkey's and Weegin's eyes followed the truck, then looked ahead and to the left and right, trying to catch sight of their elusive prey.

And after a time, they dipped.

The herd of mustangs, led by the roan, trailed by more than a dozen followers.

At first, the herd moved slowly, seeking whatever was edible.

Having spotted the herd, Norkey swooped his machine toward the ground.

The roan and then the rest of his herd reacted to the ominous sound of the engine. A sound they had heard before, a sound from which some of them survived and some were left behind and died.

Now, the roan, heeled by the mares,

instead of something edible, sought safety. At the moment their own safety was speed.

The truck accelerated, following the plane and the stampeding horses.

The roan galloped, head low, eyes glaring, hooves flying.

Norkey smiled, in complete command, knowing his machine would outlast the flesh and muscle of the animals.

Weegin lifted his shotgun closer to the open window.

Anson, driving the truck, pressed harder on the accelerator, gaining on the tiring herd, nodded toward Baker as dust from the herd swept past the bouncing truck.

The roan and herd had passed their maximum speed and were running on their instinct to survive.

The propeller whirled in its invisible circle as the tireless roar of the motor drove the plane steadily forward.

The tires of the truck spun over the unhinged earth.

Ben and Amanda swam with smooth, steady strokes, from the center of the clear blue pond, glancing and smiling at each other, as they neared the shoreline, where they anticipated picnicking and spending a pleasant afternoon.

The mustang herd, still led by the roan, still running, but perceptibly slower — muscles aching — frothing at the mouth and sweating — weakened by the relentless pursuit.

The plane banked and dipped close to the ground almost alongside the flagging herd and zeroed in on the roan.

The truck barreled ahead and closer.

From the plane, Weegin aimed the shotgun at the leading roan — and fired.

The roan, hit by the blast, fell with a sickening finality.

The mustangs, no longer a herd, scattered, leaderless, defeated — still chased by the truck.

Norkey's plane circled and came back for a look at . . .

The roan.

Lifeless.

"Never had a chicken sandwich that tasted good as this," Ben smiled.

"Baked with that special Greek sauce," she winked, "garlic."

They hadn't said much during their time together that morning and afternoon.

They didn't have to.

She had said the setting was much like the man-made location of an MGM back lot — with artificial pond, trees planted by a greens crew, with shiny boards to reflect both sun and the key light of electricians.

But this was no artificial setting constructed by a motion picture team.

This was the real thing.

They had known each other only a short time — according to the calendar.

But the calendar measures only days and weeks and months — not feelings, or depth.

They were both reluctant to talk about feelings or depth — as yet.

"You're a good cook, ma'am. A woman, even a woman doctor, should be a good cook."

"So should a cowboy, especially a bachelor cowboy."

"I am a good cook. Sometimes the best commissary around, have to be."

"What about the bachelor part?"

"What about it?"

"Have you always been a bachelor?"

"Always."

"With all those ladies you must have known at home and on the road . . . there must've been someone you thought about . . ."

"Marrying?"

"That's what we're talking about."

"There was . . . you remind me of her."

"I look like her?"

"No."

"Then, what?"

"Oh . . . certain things . . . the way you tilt your face . . . your crooked smile, your eyes, the way you arch one eyebrow, the lilt in your voice . . ."

"All right, Ben . . . a very vivid description. But then, why are you still a bachelor?"

"She's gone."

There was a long pause.

Too long.

"Ben, I don't know how else to say this but to just say it."

"Go ahead."

"You just said the wrong reason."

"What do you mean?"

"I mean I was falling, really falling, I was hoping you were, too."

"What makes you think I'm not?"

"*Maybe* you are . . . but for the wrong reason. Ben, I'm myself, not somebody else, I want to be myself . . . not somebody else. A substitute. A stand-in."

"That's not what I said . . ."

"Of course not. But maybe that's what you meant. I've got to find out . . . and so do you."

"Amanda . . ."

"All I'm saying now is that we've got to give it some time. I made a mistake once when it came to men. Today was perfect. Let's not do, or say, anything to spoil it. When I was watching them making that movie, I used to hear them saying, 'This is a wrap.'"

"Is that what you're saying, Amanda?"

"Not a wrap. But . . . a break."

There was still some sunlight, but this would be the final phase of the day's roundup. The mustang crew was using heavy chains and ropes — men with winches dragging fallen animals still hog-tied, mustangs loosened from heavy tires, up a ramp onto the hauling kill truck.

Rivulets of blood streamed from the overloaded bed of the truck.

No part of the mustang roundup would be wasted — shipped to the processing plant — slaughtered, salted for pet food — and shipped again — meat in heavy barrels — hooves, ears, and tails for glue — and bones and scraps for chicken feed — hides for baseballs and shoes — blood for fertilizer.

The light plane and pursuit truck were parked nearby as the sky wranglers contemplated the day's roundup.

Norkey, Weegin, and Anson faced the kill truck while Weegin reloaded his shotgun.

Norkey looked at his watch.

"Damn."

"What's wrong, Al?" Weegin asked.

"The haul wagon's loaded, and it's early yet."

"You're complaining about a loaded wagon?" Anson shrugged.

"Naw, but too bad the wagon's not bigger. We could've nailed another half dozen."

"Yeah," Weegin nodded, "but Deegan's got to be more than satisfied with this haul."

"Sure, but I'm not. Not by a damn sight."

If this were a chapter in a book that either one of them would write, it might be entitled "The Long Ride Home," or maybe, "The Long Silent Ride Home," silent, except for hoofbeats, the rustle above from leaves of trees, or the far-off occasional call of the lonesome coyote.

What had been the sunlit, cheerful morning ride to the pond and picnic had turned to the dimming gloom of sundown.

Somber and silent.

Except for the inner echo of their voices that afternoon.

. . . you remind me of her . . . the way you

194

tilt your face . . . your crooked smile . . . the lilt in your voice . . .

. . . then, why are you still a bachelor?

. . . she's gone.

. . . you just said the wrong reason . . . I was falling, really falling . . . hoping you were, too . . .

. . . what makes you think I'm not? . . .

. . . I want to be myself . . . not somebody else. A substitute. A stand-in.

There was more, not much more, but enough.

They were back at the Little Brawny.

And this was not the end of a perfect day.

"Jimmy, why don't you give Pepper a hand in the kitchen with supper? I've got to talk to Mr. Norkey about some business. Then you and I can make plans about tomorrow."

"Sure, Dad. Pepper's gonna show me how he makes cherry pie al'amody."

"Good. And did you say good night to your mom for me?"

Jimmy nodded.

"She said she'd rather hear you say good morning. What does that mean?"

"It means I have to talk to Mr. Norkey about some business . . . now, scat."

Jimmy scatted out of his father's den.

"Like I was saying, Mr. Deegan, just take

195

a hinge at today's work record. And tomorrow'll be even better."

"Don't fly tomorrow."

"What? There's the remnants of that roan's herd, and that black and all his beauties still around out there . . ."

"They'll still be around out there after tomorrow."

"What's up?"

"Not the plane, not tomorrow . . ."

"You tell me you want mustangs one day, and the next day . . ."

"The next day I'm taking Jimmy riding around the ranch . . ."

"So?"

"So, I don't want him to see you buzzing around and how you and your crew chase down and deliver those mustangs."

"But . . ."

"There's no 'buts' about it, Norkey. Those are my instructions. Take tomorrow off, okay? I'll tell you when to go hunting again. It'll be soon enough."

"Okay, boss. But it can't be too soon. Good night. Think I'll go into town and have a couple drinks."

"You do that."

It was a werewolf moon, full and bright, a hunter's moon, a blossoming sight, a theatrical moon of artificial light.

But it was a melancholy moon that shone down on the Little Brawny and two uncertain people that night.

The horses unsaddled. Betsey in the barn. Domino in the trailer. And it seemed that even the horses sensed that something was not quite right. Their heads bent a bit lower, their eyelids a little laggard.

Something amiss.

These were not the same two people who rode out in the morning. Their faces seemed somehow different, even their voices when they spoke and that was seldom.

It was almost as if they hesitated to do, or say, anything, because it might be the wrong thing to do or say — here and now.

"Ben . . ."

"Amanda . . ."

Both spoke at the same time.

But neither said anything more.

She turned, walked to her station wagon, started it, and drove away.

He stood and watched until her car and trailer disappeared then turned and walked toward the empty cabin as the moon looked down in the still of the night.

A saloon is a saloon, is a saloon, is like saying the West is the West, is the West — in a saloon there's the bar, the bartender, and the tables, and Douglas chairs, and drifting smoke. In the West there's the plains, the valleys, the mountains, and drifting clouds.

The same, but different.

Each saloon takes on the personality of the owner. Each span in the West takes on the earmark of the geography.

Rough and tough, aggressive and troublesome — like the Bella Union Saloon in Deadwood, where a man named Hickock would meet his destiny holding aces and eights in his hand and a bullet in his back.

But this was Kit Carson's Saloon in Sheridan, where a group of friends would meet and indulge in a pleasant game of two-bit-limit poker . . . and bad jokes.

And that's what was going on that night at a couple of tables while Kit, herself, sat at a corner table cheating at solitaire with a bottle of Courvoisier within easy reach.

At another corner was an upright piano fronted by a fat man known as Gaylord, who was fingering the keys somewhat to the tune of "Shenandoah."

At the bar, Baldy and a couple locals were matching pennies.

At the largest table, there sat Skinny Dugan with Ty Roan and some of his staff, also known as spies — Randy Rawlins, Doc

ABC, postmaster Clay Sykes, and Louie Martini.

At a nearby table, Al Norkey's crew — Weegin, Anson, Baker, Crane, Dorn, and Estes.

At the far end of the bar, the two Krantz brothers drank beer from the bottles.

The strains of "Shenandoah" stopped abruptly at the outburst of Skinny Dugan's voice.

"*Damn!* Your pot, Randy Ragamuffin!"

"You shouldn't try to fill an inside straight, Skinny," Randy grinned.

"I'll bust a cinch tryin' . . . I did it in Cuba."

"Did what?" Clay Sykes asked. "Bust a cinch?"

"This isn't Cuba," Randy added.

"A little more respect to your elders, ragamuffin," Skinny Dugan countered.

"Are we playing poker here?" Doc ABC wondered.

"Whose deal?" Martini inquired.

"Pay attention, Louie," Skinny gathered the cards. "My deal."

Most of the occupants turned in surprise as Dr. Amanda Reese entered the saloon.

"Well, good evening, Doctor," Kit Carson smiled after turning up a one-eyed jack.

"Evening, Miss Kit. Came in for a pack of

cigarettes. The drugstore's closed."

"So, it is . . . Baldy."

"Yes, ma'am?"

"Bring over a deck of . . . Luckys, is it, Doctor?"

"Doesn't matter."

"Comin' on the run," Baldy affirmed.

Baldy came on the run, opening a fresh pack of Luckys on the way.

"Here you be, ma'am, and a book of lucifers to scratch. That'll be double dimes, please."

"On the house and bring another glass. Please sit down, Doctor, and you look like you could use a sip or two of brandy."

"Pretty good diagnosis, Miss Carson. Thanks, I will."

"Didn't know you smoked, Doctor."

"I don't." She lit a Lucky. The snifter arrived. Kit Carson poured a double.

"Confusion to the enemy," Carson toasted, and they both sipped.

"That brandy's been keeping good company," Amanda nodded. "Thanks."

"You're welcome. Now, sit back and tell Mama all about it."

"About what?"

"That's what Mama wants to know. A saloonkeeper's good company, too. Go ahead, spill. It'll do you good, get it off your . . .

mind." She poured more brandy.

"Gaylord, play something soothing."

Immediately, there came "Shenandoah" again.

"It was all beautiful. Perfect . . . then he started to compare me to . . ."

"To what? Who?"

"An old girlfriend . . . Ben. That's 'what' and 'who.' "

"The same old story . . ."

"Not quite. I didn't give him a chance to finish."

"That was a mistake. You should've let him finish, might've changed the story altogether."

"Well, he did finish, said she's gone."

"That's not an ending, could be a beginning . . . for you."

"I told him I didn't want to be a substitute . . . a stand-in."

"So, you're in a standoff, instead. Dumb play. Listen, lady, you stumbled over a little purple pride — and now you sit here in a saloon with . . ."

"With what?"

"A wise old party who did it easy the hard way. Let me tell you a story I've never told before. It's short but seemed long. You care to listen?"

"Go ahead." Amanda lit another Lucky.

"Before I was Kit Carson, I was, well, never mind, I was somebody else, an actress of sorts. Stage. He was an actor, bit of a ham, but okay. A good solid man. We fell for each other, but I stopped falling. I was too damn persnickety. I thought I would land Jack Barrymore. But I landed in a saloon instead. He owns an air-conditioned movie theatre in Toledo, with a beautiful wife and two kids in college. I threw a pearl away and kept the oyster. There ain't many around like Ben Smith — and I've been around — there never were and there never will be — strong, honest, and true. In fact, if I were a dozen, well maybe even ten years younger, sister, I'd give you a run for your money in that department. Don't know how I'll end up. If it ain't Kit Carson, it might be Calamity Jane, or Sadie Thompson in some other gin mill. I'm not comparing me to you, but take him and treasure him before one of you lets go. Hold on. Hold on tight, or you'll regret it, maybe not soon, but for the rest of your days and nights."

Kit Carson poured more brandy into both snifters.

Al Norkey walked in, clean-shaven and wearing a pressed plaid suit. He stopped and semibowed at their table.

"Good evening, ladies. Either of you two

care for some company?"

Kit Carson didn't even look up.

"Not from someone who smells like a perfume peddler."

"Just took a French bath," Norkey smiled.

"Next time try an American shower, but it won't do much good," Carson took a sip.

"Good night, kids, it's been nice visiting with you."

Norkey walked toward his crew's card table and pulled out a chair.

"I'll sit in for a few hands, boys."

"We were about to fold," Weegin said.

"Deacon Deegan's declared tomorrow a holiday."

"What?" Anson rubbed his chin.

"Just deal." Norkey sat down. "We've got all night."

Both Krantz brothers walked past the card table without saying a word — until they approached the two women.

"Good night, ladies," Claud Krantz said, and glanced back at Norkey's table, "unless you want us to stick around, just in case . . ."

"There won't be any 'just in case,' fellas, but thanks anyhow and good night."

Amanda rose.

"Well, Miss Carson, thanks for the hospitality and the story from that wise old party. I'll think things over."

"You do that, Doctor. You do just that."

"Boys," Skinny Dugan declared, "this is the damnedest, dullest poker game I ever sat in. Nothin' happens around here — no item for the next edition — didn't catch any of you brigands cheatin' — and I lost four and a half greenbacks, to boot. Good night and good riddance. I'm going to let nature take its curse."

"You mean 'course,' " Doc ABC said.

"No, I mean 'curse,' remember the Dust Bowl."

CHAPTER FOURTEEN

Ben lay in his bunk at the Little Brawny —
or was it some other place, some other time?

It was a late-autumn night or early-
autumn morning in no-man's-land with two
soldiers in a shell hole between persistent
unfriendly and friendly cross fire.

Captain Ben Smith and Lieutenant Frank
Flemming were fast friends. Both officer
material since they met at Fort Riley almost
a year and a half ago in the same cavalry
brigade. It's not hard to become fast friends
when surrounded by enemies trying to kill
you. And it didn't take long when they
traded saving each other's lives — more
than once.

Frank Flemming, a big genial Irishman
with a Gaelic sense of humor — good, very
good athlete, but not as good a marksman
or horseman as Ben Smith.

Each had his good-luck tokens, Flemming
had two of them, an Immaculate Concep-

tion medal and a small photograph of his younger sister, Dawn.

Ben's good-luck token was his Browning model 1911 pistol, issued by the U.S. cavalry.

When Ben first saw the picture of Frank's sister, his vocal reaction was, "Why, she's just a little wisp of a girl."

"Ben, that picture was taken three years ago when she was fourteen, and . . ."

". . . and what kind of name is Dawn?"

"She was born January first, 1900, at the dawn of the first day of the twentieth century. Dawn, pretty good, eh?"

"Yeah, Frank, but I don't know if something else is pretty good or bad."

"What?"

"This damn quiet. Too damn quiet. No rifle shots or bombs in almost ten minutes."

"Well, I thought about that, too. Ben, you're my superior officer. How did we get into this mess? First, it's too noisy, then too quiet. Tell me how. Tell me why?"

"We volunteered — because we're patriots."

"*We volunteered.* What's with the plural business? *I* was perfectly happy in the dear ol' cavalry. You, Captain Smith, volunteered *us* into the infantry, remember?"

"Well, I do, and I don't — it was all pretty

fuzzy, but as I recall I hadn't slept in two or three days, and I found myself walking up three flights of steep stairs in a spit-polish estate the AEF had confiscated somewhere near the western front with orders to report to some spit-and-polish general who turned out to be a gen-u-ine hero of the Spanish and Philippine Wars — and then there was that disturbance down in Mexico with a fella called Pancho Villa . . . Frank, what was his name again, that spit-and-polish general?"

"Very funny, Ben. But I'll wager you snapped to attention at the sight of General Black Jack Pershing."

"Damn near snapped my spine. Treated me damn near as an equal. Said the war couldn't be won without him and me working together to beat the Boche."

"Sure, he did."

" 'Ben,' he said, 'I purely admire your rifle and pistol record. Best in your division.'

" 'Thanks, Jack,' I said, 'you're a pretty fair shot, yourself.' "

"Sure, you did . . . treated him almost like an equal, didn't you? Now, do you want to get closer to the truth, and how you really got those captain bars?"

"I'll get as close as I can remember between walking in a first lieutenant and walking out a captain of my own company."

"Go ahead. I've already heard ten different versions. I'll add one more to the collection just to break the monotony of the Great War."

"Well, we chatted — that is — *he* chatted, mostly about the importance of the cavalry in warfare — in Cuba, for instance, where we had a lot of cowboy volunteers including that self-made cowboy, Teddy Roosevelt, but he ended up saying that this was a different century and a different war — and how he was going to make one last big push to breach the Hindenburg Line and force the Krauts to surrender — and for that push he needed infantry — not cavalry.

" 'Smith,' he said, 'you've already been awarded two medals. I'm going to see that you win another one, but it will probably be . . . posthumously — however, in the meanwhile, you'll be promoted to captain. Because whether you know it or not, you're volunteering the hell out of the cavalry and into the infantry. Not that it matters, but, how do you like them potatoes?'

" 'That's just dandy, sir,' I said, 'and speaking of potatoes, there's this Irish second lieutenant I'd like you to promote to first lieutenant. We've been a team since Fort Riley in Kansas, and . . .'

" '. . . And I wouldn't want to take a chance of losing the war by breaking up your team, so,' Pershing picked up a bulging envelope and shoved it at me, 'here are your orders in triplicate — and just remember this . . . *old soldiers never die* . . . do you know why?'

" 'No, sir. Why?'

" 'Because . . . they have to live to get old.'

"And that, Lieutenant Flemming, is just about how I remember it."

"You mean, this time."

"Yeah, this . . ."

"Hold it!"

Lieutenant Flemming raised his rifle, took aim . . . then lowered the rifle, turned, and leaned back against the side of the shell hole.

"What's a-matter, Frank? He duck?"

"No."

"What?"

"I don't think the kid ever shaved, yet."

"Well, pal, I . . ."

In that instant, there were three instead of two soldiers in the shell hole.

"Well, well, if it isn't Sergeant Muldowney," Flemming said. "What da ya hear from the mob, Sergeant?"

"Just one word . . . armistice!"

A strange thing about war and peace — at

209

the beginning of war you become part of a large, very large family — and as the war goes on the family shrinks smaller until two or three of you in your unit become close as brothers. Ben Smith and Frank Flemming were even closer than most brothers.

And you swear that after it's over, if you survive, regardless of geography, or anything else, you'll stay as close as brothers, even closer, because in that time of war, brief as it was, you faced death together almost every minute of every day and night.

But in most cases, geography or something else does make a difference and you are suddenly split or drift apart.

And that was the case with Ben and Frank.

While still feeling and healing the visible and invisible scars that war leaves, there were letters and even a few phone calls with promises of "Let's get together soon, sometime," but it never happened — not for a long time — for years while hard times hit Ben as both his mother and father fell victims to the deadly plague of 1918, fire destroyed the handsome headquarters of the Little Brawny, and Ben joined the hard life of rodeoing.

Frank made the varsity of Notre Dame's football team his freshman year under Knute Rockne's freshman year as coach, but almost mysteriously dropped out the following year.

It was just after Ben won his second All-'Round Champion Cowboy title that it happened at the Roaring Twenties Chicago indoor arena.

Ben still held the trophy in his hand, and the runner-up champion, Curly Kaine, was at his side as he spotted Frank and the lady, both bundled with coats, scarves, hats, and hoods they wore against the freezing winter streets they had crossed to see the contest. It was almost as cold inside the arena as it was outside in the streets.

The heating system in the arena had gone on the fritz, but as she stood there, her face, her eyes especially, had all the warmth and sparkle of a summer garden.

But it wasn't the cold he was feeling, or the knives in his knees, or the flush of another victory in the arena — it was something else — and she was standing beside his best friend. It had never happened to him before, and he didn't expect it could, or would, ever happen again.

"There never was a cowboy that couldn't be throwed."

And it had happened to Ben Smith, there and then.

It wasn't the first time that words failed Ben Smith, nor the first time that his friend had come to the rescue in that department.

"Well, Captain, my captain, what did you expect? A salute?"

"No. But now I know why you've been hiding all this time. You didn't want me to see your bride until you were married. Congratulations, Lieutenant, and as for you, Mrs. Flemming, I . . ."

"But I'm not Mrs. Flemming."

"You're not?!"

"No." She smiled. "Still *Miss* Flemming."

"For two reasons." Frank Flemming pulled open the lapels of his heavy coat. "Lieutenant Flemming is now Father Flemming and this is my new uniform. White collar and black regalia."

"Huh?"

"That's a brilliant reaction, bucko."

"And this is . . ."

"My sister, Dawn."

"But, but . . ."

"But, what?"

"What happened to that wisp of a girl in the picture?"

"She grew up to be an old maid of twenty-four years."

"Please, 'Father Flemming,' not until my birthday next month."

"Well, I'll be . . ."

"Be what, Captain?" Father Frank Flemming grinned.

"I'd be . . . pleased if you accepted this here trophy as a present on your approaching birthdate."

"Okay. My birthdate . . . fifty years from now."

"Wisp. We've got a date. Oh, by the way, this young fella is Curly Kaine, my . . . second-best pal next to former lieutenant Frank Flemming."

So it began . . . and got better . . . for almost a year.

The happiest, most prosperous, most beautiful year of Ben Smith's life.

He was in love.

She was in love.

It was the Roaring Twenties.

Running wild.

Lost control.

But not Ben and Wisp.

They were in control.

Of the present.

And the future.

They would be married on her twenty-fifth birthday. January 1, 1925.

By then the mortgage would be paid off on the Little Brawny and Ben could pick and choose his rodeoing. Wisp would have her master's degree — her topic was landscape architecture. And as the song declares, "Life is just a bowl of cherries" from then on. And they would be together forever. Well, not forever, but until death them did part.

In the meantime, during the rest of this year they would steal as much time together as possible — between Ben's rodeo schedule and Wisp's teaching at the University of Toledo and working on her master's — it wasn't nearly enough.

Letters. Telephone calls and infrequent rendezvous whenever and wherever possible, sometimes even just for a few precious hours. Toledo, Nashville, St. Louis, Des Moines, Kansas City.

To talk and touch each other like any two people in love — almost like any two — but they had vowed to wait until Father Flemming married them to consummate their union. Until then, they would meet and touch and talk — sometime silly and sometime serious.

"You mean you'd actually trade the beautiful Maumee River of Toledo for the muddy wide Missouri of the Wild West?"
"Only if you throw in a couple of crabs."

214

"Wisp, where've you been all of my life?"

"Waiting for you."

"Ben . . . my darling, when are you going to quit rodeoing? You were lucky in the war and the rodeo so far, but you're getting pretty . . ."

"Busted up? Yeah, you get some bruise or gash every time. But don't worry, Wisp, I'll quit before . . ."

"Before what?"

"Before you know it. Okay, pardner?"

"Okay, if you say so . . . pardner."

It was October, and like most Midwest Octobers, crisp and sere.

The place Abilene. The event, the Annual Halloween Rodeo with big, very big prize money, and Wisp had arranged to be there for just that night.

Ben was in the chute again and had been doing fairly well, but not quite up to his usual standard. Young Curly Kaine was a close second, and Wisp was surprised when he came up to her with a look on his face she had never seen the few times she had seen him before.

And his voice was different, more mature and confident.

"Excuse me, Miss Dawn . . ."

"Yes, Curly, you're doing very well tonight. Congratulations."

"Miss Dawn, I know you want Ben to quit rodeoing; oh, I could tell from that first time we met. Well, ma'am, I'm going to beat him tonight . . . and I think that'll be a step in the right direction."

He turned and started to walk away, but before he took another step.

"I hope so, Curly . . . and good luck to all three of us."

An hour later the announcer could barely contain the surprise and excitement in his voice.

"Ladies and gentlemen, this well could be Curly Kaine's night — one more ride — if he can stay aboard Blue Blaze for eight seconds he'll beat out his rodeo mentor and good friend, the veteran champion ol' Ben Smith, for first prize money — Oh, oh! — Here comes Curly out of the chute smooth and easy — three — four seconds — lookin' good, almighty good — a real travelin' man or my name ain't Herbie Joe Brown — five, six, oh, oh — one electrifying buck that's all it took — Curly flew off, pop goes the — hold on — just a second — this doesn't look good — that fall seems much worse than — Curly's not moving — the medical team and other cowboys, Ben Smith among the first to be there — and now Curly's

— I'm not going to speculate — we'll have a report for you as soon as possible — all of us hoping and praying for the best — we'll have some music from Smiley Huston and his gang before the next rodeo event."

But there never was a next rodeo event for Curly Kaine. Within seconds he was dead of a broken neck.

Wisp's hands covered her face and the tears in her eyes.

"Ben, it wasn't just Curly I was looking at out there. It was you. You said you get something every time. Well, Curly got his, a lot younger than you are now . . . and not just a bruise or broken bone . . . something more permanent. You're a champion. Retire a champion. You've got enough money. You've got the Little Brawny . . . and you've got me. But not if you don't quit. Because I won't, I can't, be around when it happens. I won't be with someone else. But I'll be somewhere else. Do I have to say anything else?"

"No, you don't, Wisp. Because I'm quits . . ."

"You mean it, Ben?"

"Just as sure as the turning of the earth. I've got a contract to do one more rodeo on Thanksgiving Day less than a month from now. I don't expect you, I don't want you to be there. But win or lose, I'll meet you the next day. Frank'll marry us, and we'll head for the Little Brawny in double harness. How does that sound . . . pardner?"

"It sounds like heaven."

Ben Smith won the big prize money on that Thanksgiving Day rodeo contest . . . but he lost.

He knew there was something wrong by the look of Father Flemming's face. He had never before, not even during the war, never before had he seen that look in the eyes of his friend, who stood at the door that night.

"What is it, Frank? What's happened? Is it Wisp?"

"She called just before she left Toledo. She was going to drive up and surprise you. There was an accident on Telegraph Road. Drunk driver. Head-on."

"I want to see her . . ."

"No, you don't, Ben. Fire. Explosion. It was quick, but horrible. You want to remember Dawn the way she was last time you saw her."

It made no sense to him that night ten years ago . . . and still made no sense at the Little Brawny that night.

Wisp lost her life because she couldn't

bear the sight of Ben in harm's way at the Thanksgiving Day rodeo.

But that was the first time he left the arena without a mark on him . . . except for the invisible mark he carried for the rest of his life.

CHAPTER FIFTEEN

FATHER FRANCIS ALOYSIUS
FLEMMING O.F.M.
FOREIGN SERVICE RECORD
Incomplete and Unconfirmed

June 1, 1933. Father Flemming became a missionary priest at Saint Ambrose Church in Nanking, China.

November 15, 1937. Japanese forces bombed, invaded, and ravished the city of Nanking. Over 200,000 soldiers and civilians, ministers and nuns, doctors and nurses, young and old — brutalized and killed. International newspapers and radio summed it up in four words — the Rape of Nanking.

Father Frank Flemming was never seen, nor heard of, since.

CHAPTER SIXTEEN

If he ever did sleep that night, Ben Smith awoke early — an old army habit — and before. As a boy at the Little Brawny from the sound of a rooster — during the war at the sounds of battle, bugles, and bombs — and sometimes the quiet, too quiet, before the onslaught — and even during the rodeo years, with aches and pangs from falls off broncs and bulls.

Ordinarily, Ben would make his own Spartan breakfast at the cabin, but this morning he decided to go to Mary's Cafe, where he first saw Dr. Amanda Reese coming out the door.

But if that were the reason, he didn't want to admit it, even to himself.

Mary's Cafe had quite a chronicle of past and present even for a small western feedery. In the old days, it used to be called the Rock and Rye Saloon. The locals called it the Drink and Die.

More gunshot deaths took place there per square foot than at any other whereabouts in Sheridan — until the two partners who owned it — Rance Martin and Jake Lewis — got into an altercation and killed each other.

Mary Bricky took over and hired Piggy Barnes, an old cattle drive gut robber, to do the cooking, and Stumpy Grace, a peg-legged ex–chorus girl with a wooden stump, as waitress. Both employees were efficient. The interior still looked more like a saloon than a cafe.

But the back bar was turned into an open stove and steam table, and the eats were ample, nourishing, and cheap.

There was never a check. Mary sat at a stool near the cash register at the front of the bar.

On his or her way out after breakfast or lunch, the customer would sum up, "Ham and eggs, mug o' coffee."

"Still twenty-five cents."

No tipping was allowed. Un-American.

The usual morning customers were there, including the Krantz brothers at their usual table, when Ben Smith walked in.

"Over here, Ben ol' buddy," Clem Krantz hailed.

Ben nodded and sat.

Stumpy Grace almost beat him to the table.

"Call it, Ben."

"Just coffee and just black."

"On its way."

Ben looked around at the other customers.

"She left a few minutes ago, pal," Claud said.

"Who?"

"Drank her coffee but didn't touch her scrambled eggs," Clem added.

"Didn't go to waste," Claud smiled. "Clem ate 'em."

Skinny Dugan came in and sat at the table's empty chair.

"Morning, you cabin robbers."

Stumpy was there with two mugs of coffee, placed in front of Ben, the other in front of Skinny Dugan.

"Saw you coming, Skinny."

"Yeah, Ty-Roan's coffee tastes like tar."

"Then why don't you make a pot yourself?" Clem suggested.

"Mine's worse," Skinny said. "But I might, if I ever get around to it. How's by you, Ben?"

Ben nodded and did his best to smile.

"Say, Ben," Clem did smile, "we're sort of idle today. Suppose brother Claud and me come over and give you a hand with some more fixin' up at the Little Brawny?"

"Not today, fellas, thanks, I've got some stuff I got to do on my own and take Betsey out for a stretch of the legs."

"Hey, Ben," Claud took a fast gulp from his coffee mug, "when are you gonna start running some cattle of your own? You're supposed to be in the cattle business, aren't you?"

"Yeah, well, first I've got to get me a couple of bulls and a few cows."

"Well, then, I'm glad I dropped by," Skinny exclaimed.

"Why?"

"Troy Johnson's gonna sell or auction off some of his prize stock, needs the cash, gonna put an ad in the *Beacon*."

"When?"

"Said he'd let me know in advance. I'll tell him you're interested."

"Yes, I am."

"When you go," Claud said, "we'll come along."

"To pick the stock?"

"Hell no," Clem shrugged. "We wouldn't know a mule from a matagorda. But we can haul a load or two back to the Little Brawny after you pick 'em."

"Sounds good."

"All in a day's day," they both said.

"What are friends for," Claud added.

"Most special, good friends," Clem winked.

"Well, good friends," Ben rose, "in that case, I'll pop for the morning meal all around."

Her nearly naked body gleamed in the morning sunlight with an abrupt turn as she heard the sounds. Footsteps? Human? Male? Animal?

Amanda stood less than a full second, then reached for the clothes she had spread on the rocks near the picnic pool where she and Ben had been less than twenty-four hours ago.

She had been up before dawn, wanting to get out of her cottage-office, had had nothing to eat or drink since the picnic, except brandy and smokes with Kit Carson, skipped her morning shower, and headed for Mary's Cafe.

That didn't work, either.

In a haphazard moment she thought of, and drove to, the picnic area.

The pool looked inviting, refreshing, cleansing, and there was no one in sight.

Then the sound.

She veered and caught a glimpse of bushy

tails, two squirrels, disappearing through a rock formation.

Even so, there was no more thought of swimming.

Other thoughts raced through her mind.

Of yesterday . . . yesterdays . . . and yester years. When she was young and married and thought she was in love, but that didn't work out, either.

It's strange how the mind works. Now she was near her midthirties, and, of all things, a current popular radio soap opera flashed. She seldom had the time or the inclination to listen to soap operas, but now one echoed through the airwaves of her mind.

An announcer's voice:

"And now, 'The Romance of Helen Trent.' The real-life drama of Helen Trent, who fights back bravely to prove that because a woman is thirty-five or more, romance need not be over, that romance can happen at thirty-five."

Amanda Reese was not yet thirty-five. Beautiful, youthful, and healthy — with a further physical description any female, any age, would covet: Height five foot six. Weight 127 pounds — and to quote one of the radio commercials — "round and firm, and fully packed."

How close she had come to romance — and more — as close as yesterday.

It is strange how the mind works.

And sometimes —

How strange the change from major to minor.

By midmorning, the day was like any other midsummer morning at the Big Brawny — high, wide, handsome, and picture-perfect.

Deegan on his favorite horse, Jimmy on Pinto, and Pepper, even with his crooked leg, astride his gentle mare.

But Jimmy had never been as close to the land and his father.

Miles of level land rimmed by purple ridges. The outskirts peppered sparsely with line shacks, some dating back dozens of decades. A winding shallow stream flanked by too few trees and a summer scraggy blanket of grass that the cowboys called cow-feed.

Branded beeves scattered in patternless battalions as far as the surrounding horizon. And now and then a glimpse of foreman, Joe Higgins, on his palomino, conferring with a curly wolf cowhand.

James Deegan reined up and waved at the distance as Jimmy and Pepper pulled up beside him.

"Well, what do you think, son? Bigger than some counties and we've only covered half of it. But we could do with some more water to go with it."

"So could I," Pepper said, and unstrapped his canteen.

Jimmy shook his head.

"Does all this belong to you and Mom?"

Deegan glanced at Pepper, who looked away.

"Well," Deegan said, "right now it does, but it's been in our family since before, long before, I was born, and . . . you both stay here. I'll be back in a few minutes."

James Deegan nudged his horse toward the light plane; Norkey and his crew were working around it fifty yards away.

"Norkey, I told you, no mustanging today."

"Take it easy, boss. We're not takin' her up. Just running some tests on the engine . . . seems to be sputtering some. That's okay, isn't it?"

"Yeah, that's okay . . ."

But there was another sound, not from the engine.

A sound too familiar on the Big Brawny.

They all turned and looked toward the oncoming drone.

Hoofbeats.

And then the bustling herd of mustangs, led by the black, swerved away from the grounded plane and people they had sensed, smelled, and seen on the cow-feed of the Big Brawny.

It had been a magnificent picture out of the historic western past, but too often by the current cattle rancher — and for Norkey, a lost round.

"You're the boss, Mr. Deegan, and I'm paid to follow orders, but we still got a chance to get those mustangs today if you say so."

"I don't say so. Not with my son in sight."

Norkey shrugged and reached for a pack of cigarettes in his shirt pocket.

Jimmy was still aghast and Pepper not far from it when Deegan rode back.

The boy pointed in the direction that the black's mustangs had fled.

"Dad, did you see them?!"

"Yes, son. I saw them."

The shadows lengthened.

Ben had been astride Betsey — riding lonesome and aimless — how long and where, he didn't know or care — until he heard and saw the mustang herd led by the black — then watched as they diminished the distance to the narrow-channel threshold — to a safe haven he had seen them enter before. A high-peaked canyon. Safe haven for wild horses, but too hazardous for any low-flying plane to give chase.

Ben Smith smiled, patted the nape of his horse, and spoke for the first time in hours.

"Sanctuary," he said, "for your cousins the mustangs. Sanctuary, for the time being."

CHAPTER SEVENTEEN

Pepper sat at the dinner table that night, along with James Deegan, Jimmy, and Joe Higgins, plus Rover.

"These days I don't know whether I'm more uncomfortable in the saddle or at the dinner table — besides this food tastes different when I don't cook it."

"Pepper, your old bones've absorbed enough punishment today. I thought you deserved some time off and let the kitchen help do the cooking and serving tonight."

"Tastes different, like I said, Mr. D, I don't cook it . . . and that saddle feels different to this ol' stove-up bronc twister than it used to. Next thing I know, you'll have me reclinin' on an ol' rockin' chair."

"Pepper," Deegan smiled, "why don't you just quit you bellyaching and . . ."

"It's not just my belly that's achin'."

"Well, quit anyhow. Jimmy, how do you like ranch life on the Big Brawny?"

"It's neat, Dad, and I'm getting to know all about horses, even those wild ones we saw out there."

"M'boy, there's a lot more to ranching these days than horses."

"There sure is," Higgins agreed. "Things have changed since I was your age."

"I guess so, but I like horses the best. Ben says that he . . ."

"Well, that's a start," James Deegan interrupted. "The Big Brawny'll be yours someday, son, and so will a lot of other things. I'm just a few . . ."

The phone on the small side table rang.

Higgins rose.

"I'll get it, Mr. Deegan."

"Thanks . . . Jimmy, you've got to decide whether this is part of the life you want . . ."

Higgins had picked up the receiver.

"Hello . . . yes, yes, he is . . . Just a minute. Long distance for you, Mr. Deegan."

"Okay." Deegan rose and took up the receiver. "Hello."

"Hi, Jim, this is Tom Drury. I'm at the Osage County Cattlemen's Association up at Grandview . . ."

"Yes, I know about it."

"Well, there's something about it you ain't heard, and you've got to come up here, pronto."

"Hell, Tom, I can't. My son just got here, and it's important that . . ."

"This is important, too, damn important!"

"What do you mean?"

"I mean your old pal Sam Birthistle, that giant independent, that road company Theodore Roosevelt, is up to one of his old tricks. Amongst other things, he says he's going to introduce a resolution to dissolve our cattlemen's association, says it's a waste of time and money during this Depression, and he's gathering a passel of votes . . ."

"Tom, you've got my proxy. You know how I'd vote."

"Not good enough. These ranchers have got to hear you say it the way you only can, and help me do some strategizing. Jim, I'm desperate. A lot of us are. This could blow up everything we've fought for . . ."

"You're the chairman and . . ."

"And you're the vice chairman, and you've got the voice and the smoosh. I can stall till you get here or else . . . no cattlemen's association. Get it?"

"Yeah, I got it."

"I already got a room for you."

"I'll drive up in the morning. It'll take a couple of hours."

"Don't spare the horses."

Tom Drury hung up.

James Deegan paused a beat, hung up, and paused again, thinking of Samuel Ogdon Birthistle. Drury had called him "a road company Theodore Roosevelt." T.R. had been dead since 1919, but Birthistle, all three hundred pounds of him, was alive, very much alive, and not a comic opera character — still, he did nothing to conceal his admiration of the twenty-sixth president of the USA — in fact, quite the opposite, from emulating T.R.'s eyeglasses, to an occasional "BULLY! — BULLY!" which escaped from his grinning mouth.

But it was all part of his outward persona. Birthistle was far from a comic opera character. James Deegan knew that Samuel Ogdon Birthistle could be devoutly serious — and dangerous.

Deegan walked back toward the dining table.

"Damn," he uttered.

"What's the matter, Dad?"

Deegan looked at Higgins, then at Pepper and Jimmy.

"I'm sorry, Jimmy. But I have to leave for a few days. Special meeting of the cattlemen's association."

"Uh-oh, one of those," Pepper groaned.

"That's right, 'one of those,' " Deegan nodded.

"Can I come with you, Dad?"

"No, lad. I'll be tied up day and night with those muleheads."

"Want me to do the usual packin' for you, Mr. D?"

"I guess, Pepper. Sorry, Jimmy. I'll get back as soon as I can and call you every day. Pepper'll keep an eye on you."

"So'll Ben. We got a lot to do."

Jimmy's reaction was not nearly what Deegan expected.

"So have I . . . first thing in the morning, I've got to call your mom."

As the sun was still topping out, James Deegan was on the phone with his wife, at the moment listening.

". . . at the Grandview Hotel? Why, Jimbo, that's where we spent part of our honeymoon, remember?"

"Like it was yesterday, only it wasn't . . . anyway, I wanted you to know I'll be away for maybe a couple of days."

"Dear one, what would the cattlemen's association do if you weren't there?"

"But I am here — and you're not; so I wanted you to know in case you called and I wasn't here — and to know Jimmy'll be in good hands and taking the medicine he needs."

"That's not all he needs."

"Don't rub it in, kid, we've been down this path before."

"Not exactly primrose . . ."

"Can we please postpone that part?"

"Sure, and I was working on a deal to surprise you, but not . . ."

"Now's not the time to talk about it. I'm working on a deal, too, his name is Jimmy, remember him? So long, Stranger."

Deegan hung up.

As soon as he did, he was sorry and thought of calling back, but the phone rang.

"Hello, Liz, I'm sorry . . ."

"Don't be sorry, and I'm not Liz."

"Who . . ."

"Don't get excited, but this is your neighbor Laura, Laura Layton. Good morning, neighbor."

"Good morning, Mrs. Layton."

"*Mrs. Layton?* My, my, we're so formal this morning."

"Okay, then, Laura, is this business or what?"

"It's not exactly 'or what,' but I've been thinking . . . remember I said, 'Don't call me, I'll call you'? Well, I'm calling about getting to know each other better, talking some business, and having dinner tonight."

"Well, well, that would be progress,

but . . ."

"But what? And it better be good."

"Not so sure it's good, but I'll be out of town tonight and a few other nights, cattlemen's meeting up at Grandview."

"I heard about that."

"How?"

"How what?"

"How did you hear?"

"I've got my eyes and ears . . . and spies."

"I'll bet you have."

"But I'll take a rain check when you get back. In the meantime, I'm still in bed, so I'll go back to sleep."

Laura Layton hung up.

Pepper loaded a suitcase into the rear compartment of the Chrysler station wagon and closed the tailgate. Deegan, Jimmy, and Higgins were near the open driver's door. Deegan tossed his briefcase onto the front seat.

"Jimmy, you be sure to take your medicine."

"I will, Dad."

"Joe, did you tell Norkey to keep out of range of headquarters?"

"I told him."

"Now, Jimmy, Pepper, Joe, and your mother know where I'll be staying if anything goes wrong."

Pepper was approaching and heard.

"Nothin'll go wrong, Mr. D."

Deegan put a hand on his son's shoulder.

"And you call your mom anytime you feel like it."

"Okay."

James Deegan kissed his son.

"So long, m'boy. I'll call you tonight." He slid into the front seat, but before he closed the door Pepper leaned in.

"You use your talkin' talent on them bush poppers, Mr. D," then closed the door.

Deegan nodded, started the engine, glanced at Jimmy, and the Chrysler pulled away.

Norkey's plane, with him at the controls and Weegin next to him, pulled up and away with the truck and crew on the ground following in an early start for the day's pursuit.

Ben Smith astride Betsey, the Chrysler making time on the road, were barely in sight of each other. Ben waved.

Deegan didn't, and the station wagon picked up speed.

Jimmy and Pepper had started to walk away from the pinto, toward headquarters, when Jimmy spotted something coming from another direction. A man on horseback and in no hurry.

"Pepper, look. It's Ben!"

It was. And he greeted them when he got close enough but didn't dismount.

"Morning to the Big Brawnys."

"Morning, Ben," Jimmy smiled, "glad you came by for a visit, we got . . ."

"Not today, cowboy. Got to get back, but I did see your dad, guess he's got business in Sheridan."

"Further than that," Pepper said. "Drivin' to Grandview for a few days on cattle business." Pepper winked. "So, Jimmy here's in charge."

"Well, then," Ben nodded, "I'd say then this outfit's in good hands . . ."

Jimmy pointed to Pinto in the corral.

"Ben, can't we go for a ride?"

"Sorry, Jimmy, like I said, just on my way back to the Little Brawny, got something I have to attend to."

"Maybe we can help you," Jimmy volunteered.

"Thanks, but maybe you noticed, darlin' Betsey needs a new shoe. Stepped on a sharp rock or something and got bent."

"Well, we got plenty shoes around here," Pepper said.

"Obliged, but no thanks. You fellas use 'good-enoughs.' Hers is a de-luxe, got a couple of spares at the Little Brawny just in case, but it'll only take a few minutes."

"Listen," Pepper grinned, "I'm still saddle sore. You two ride ahead. I'll fix up some eats, meet you there with my pickup, and we'll go somewhere, have a picnic, and take it from there. How's that for a plan?"

"Neat!" nodded Jimmy. "Okay, Ben?"

"Can't disagree. I'll help you saddle up, Jimmy." Besides, Ben thought to himself, maybe the change of company would help settle some of yesterday's dustup with Amanda.

Since the legal separation between his mother and father, Jimmy Deegan had not been much of a talker. He was more likely to wait until they said something, then save as many words as he could in his response — maybe in the hope that things between them would change, maybe in the concern that they wouldn't.

It seemed both his mother and father thought that his reticence was due, at least in part, to his medical condition — and that way there was less blame on each of them because of their split.

But around Ben Smith, he was a different boy, with more energy, enthusiasm, and questions, questions . . . And that was the case as the two of them rode from the Big to the Little Brawny.

"Ben, I heard some of the men on the ranch talk about another cowboy as a curly wolf. Is that a bad thing . . . what's the word I'm looking for, a . . . ?"

"An insult?"

"Yeah, in-sult."

"No, Jimmy, it just means an old-timer."

And so it went until they were along the Big and Little Brawny boundary.

Suddenly, Ben reined up and pointed.

"Look!"

"What is it?"

"Take a look!"

They were a faraway distance, but within sight of the narrow passage and just in time to see the magnificent black leading his herd of mustangs through, and into the open range, leaving a swirl of dust behind them.

"Gee whiz!"

"Gee whiz is right, Jimmy. But don't ever tell anybody what we just saw. Never."

"Why not?"

"Because that's the mustangs' safe harbor."

"A harbor, out here?"

"That's right. A place where they're protected."

"Why?"

"Because of high peaks and narrow passages where a plane can't fly close to the ground and a truck can't chase 'em — but not much grass, so they come out to eat."

"Gee."

"Right again. But if Norkey knew, he might figure some way to get in and go after them."

"Oh."

"It's the mustangs' secret, so promise you won't say anything to anybody. Promise."

"Sure, I promise."

"That's not good enough."

"Why not?"

"Because a promise isn't a promise unless you spit and promise."

Jimmy spit, some of it on his shirt.

"I promise."

"Good . . . and here comes ol' curly wolf Pepper and his pickup."

It's been said but never verified, that outside of the three states of New York, California, and Texas, this was the only place that measured up to its name and reputation — Grandview.

It was built along the soft slope that faced the sharp, towering peaks of a mountain range that changed colors as the sun and even the moon sailed through a sea of drifting cloud formations.

The Grandview Hotel, built less than a mile from the small western township of the same name, challenged the beauty and enchantment of the bleached structures along the Riviera.

It was a favorite getaway of the rich and infamous as well as ranchers from all western points of the compass, and for honeymooners who, before and after, had honeymooned with or without benefit of blessing of the church or civil marriage certificate.

A rumor, make that rumors, persisted that the Grandview Hotel was a front for a consortium of mobsters who didn't care if the enterprise made money so long as they could enjoy the pleasures of its pleasure dome, which included three gambling suites of high, higher, and highest stakes, for members only.

Of course, the customers had to produce a membership card at the door or buy one that cost one dollar to join.

All this and more, the reasons the cattlemen's association chose Grandview as the site of its special meetings.

Chairman Tom Drury and his vice chairman, James Deegan, sat at the sizable platformed table in front of the otherwise empty meeting room, with briefcases, papers, sandwiches, and drinks within easy reach during the strategy session.

"Jim, I've stalled the docket regarding the motion to dissolve the association until the last meeting to make sure you get here and have a chance to strategize as much as possible, and you could make your spiel — but now, I'm getting worried about doing that."

"Why?"

"Because it's given time for dear ol' Samuel Ogdon Birthistle, also known as S.O.B., to line up votes against us and for himself."

"Yeah, well, we can do some lining up ourselves."

The door opened. From a distance it could have been Theodore Roosevelt himself. But it wasn't. It was Samuel Ogdon Birthistle himself, all three hundred pounds of him. His mischievous smile and booming voice inquired:

"Is this a private conspiracy or can anyone join?"

"Come in," Deegan smiled back. "The door was unlocked, wasn't it?"

"A locked door seldom stopped me anyhow."

"And if it did," Drury said, "there's always the keyhole."

"That, too . . . say, who's paying for your lunch, the association?"

"No, Sam," Drury shot back, "we're goin'

Dutch."

"Oh, the odor of integrity. Well, in that case I think I'll go back and win a couple more hands of poker before the afternoon meeting and show you fellas how the cow ate the cabbage, and, nowadays, how the West is won without a Colt or Winchester. Good luck, compadres, you'll need it, and then some."

Birthistle belly-laughed, turned, and walked out, leaving the door open.

"Still the same old windbag," Deegan said.

"Yeah, but he usually gets it done."

"This doesn't happen to be 'usually.' Where's that list you were talking about?"

"Right here. I call 'em the leaners, one way or t'uther. X's are for the ones you know best, and O's are mine."

"Looks like we might need some luck and then some."

"After this afternoon's bullshit meeting, I'll pick you up for an early dinner. Then go after some of those agnostics together."

"Sounds like a fun date."

With a deluxe new shoe on Betsey, Ben and Jimmy on horseback, and Pepper in the pickup, they had started back toward the Big Brawny and a shady spot to make do for the picnic. Maybe they had crossed the unmarked boundary line and maybe not.

In the distance above, the light plane circled in a wide arc, Norkey and Weegin both on the lookout for any movement on the landscape below, while the truck followed, keeping the plane in sight.

Weegin reacted to something on his side, tapped Norkey, and pointed downward.

The black whinnied at the sound of the engine and bolted away from his alerted herd that followed, responding to every command and maneuver, faster and smarter than the mustangs that had been led by the roan.

The truck on the ground picked up speed in pursuit of the plane and mustangs.

Norkey's plane twisted then dove downward toward the long-legged black that raced fast and free.

Ben was the first, then Jimmy and Pepper reacted to the deadly pursuit.

They reacted by coming to a stop, knowing they were helpless to make any move to help the mustangs and hinder Norkey and his hunters.

In fact, it seemed the racing black, tracked by the frenzied mustangs, was charging toward Ben and his companions.

Closer and closer.

Until it was almost too late, but the black

twisted in an abrupt curve, changed directions, and the wild-eyed mustangs instinctively spun and heeled after their leader.

The pursuing truck made a fast turn, two wheels off the ground, almost turned over but recovered balance, and tore on.

Norkey's plane banked and dove within gun range of the tiring herd, then roared ahead toward the black.

Weegin took aim with the shotgun, fired.

Just after the blast sounded, the black turned and toppled from the impact.

The rest of the animals scattered, and the truck sped past the motionless horse on the ground in pursuit of the surviving prey, westward toward the mountain ridge.

Ben turned to the boy.

"Jimmy, you stay here!"

He waved Pepper on, then galloped toward the felled black. Pepper's pickup followed for close to a half mile.

Ben reined in and even before Betsey came to a complete stop Ben was off his saddle and moving toward the black.

Pepper braked the pickup and swung out the door.

In spite of Ben's admonition, both Jimmy and Pinto had been on the way.

Ben knelt close to the black. Pepper stood beside him as Jimmy rode up and dismounted.

Pepper was the first to say anything. "Damn!"

There were tears in Jimmy's eyes. "They killed him."

"Son, I told you to stay behind."

Jimmy covered his face with both hands. "They killed him," he said again.

Ben's face turned toward the boy. "Jimmy . . . he's not dead."

Jimmy lowered his hands, looked at Ben, then at the black to see if what Ben said was true.

The horse's rib cage showed slight movement, breathing, but the animal was too weak to move.

"Stunned," Ben said, "bleeding from the pellets."

"What do you think, Ben?" Pepper asked.

"I'll stay with him — get back to Brawny headquarters. Get help. Try to reach Amanda."

"I'm on my way. Jimmy, you come with me."

CHAPTER EIGHTEEN

Ben knelt close to the enfeebled horse still stretched on the ground. He had placed his kerchief on the black's worst wound after wetting the cloth from his canteen and spreading Betsey's saddle blanket on its body.

From the direction of the Big Brawny, Pepper's pickup raced closer, followed by Dr. Amanda's station wagon, then a truck from the ranch, outfitted with a lifting winch.

Ben, Jimmy, Pepper, and a group of cowboys from the Big Brawny watched while Amanda worked on the black, stopping the bleeding with salve after she had given the animal an injection.

With a long brush-tipped instrument in hand, she moved to the black's head and began working on its muzzle.

"What you doin' now, ma'am?" Pepper leaned in and asked.

"Aerating his nostrils . . . full of dirt . . . can't hardly breathe."

No word had passed between Amanda and Ben until he stooped and spoke so Jimmy couldn't hear.

"Will he make it?"

"Not out here."

Ben looked at the truck with the winch.

"We can lift him with that, but it won't be easy on him."

"No choice."

"We're closer to my place."

"Do it."

They did.

Within the hour, they were in the Little Brawny barn — Ben, Jimmy, and Pepper. Betsey in her stall and the black in another stall on the ground and partially covered by a blanket.

Jimmy sat on the floor, his back leaning against a wall, his face buried in his hands. Amanda looked from ministering to the animal toward Jimmy, then motioned to Ben.

Ben nodded.

"Jimmy . . ."

"Yes, sir . . ."

"Jimmy, it's best that Pepper takes you home."

"But, Ben . . ."

"You've got to get your rest . . . and your medicine."

"That's right, boy," Pepper said. "We don't want you getting sick, too." He helped the boy to his feet.

Jimmy looked at the black, then at Amanda.

"What do you think?" he whispered.

"I think you could say a little prayer."

The boy nodded again and tried to smile.

There was silence in the barn during the time Pepper and Jimmy left and even until the sound of Pepper's pickup started up then drove away.

The silence was broken by two different words spoken at the same time by two different people.

"Amanda."

"Ben."

A faint smile on both, then Amanda motioned.

"You first."

"How long are you going to stay . . . with him?"

"A horse'll stand up as soon as it can. I want to be here when he does, unless you want to get a different medic."

"No, ma'am. No way."

Jimmy was on the phone in the dining

room. Pepper stood close by.

". . . so, Mom, that's what happened."

"I'm sure the horse will be okay. Did you take your medicine?"

"I did. I'm going upstairs and say that prayer like the lady doctor said right after I call Dad."

"No . . . don't call him. Your dad's got business to take care of up there, and there's nothing he can do tonight. Talk to him tomorrow. Is Pepper still there?"

"Right here."

"Let me talk to him, and you go on upstairs."

"Okay, good night, Mom, I miss you . . ."

"That goes both ways, Jimmy. Put Pepper on."

"Here he is. Pepper . . ."

"Hello, again, Mrs. D . . . Uh, Mrs. Lizabeth . . ."

"Pepper, as I said to Jimmy, don't call . . . my . . . husband tonight. Let him go about his business and bring him up to date tomorrow."

"Sure thing, ma'am. Done and done. Good night."

Dr. Amanda Reese walked back toward Ben and sat across from him.

"Any change?" he asked.

"Not yet."

Ben rose.

"Where you going?"

"Inside. I'll scramble some eggs and bring 'em back so we can eat . . . and talk about old times while we wait."

"*Old* times?"

"Well, that's a start . . ."

"You sit back and stay. I'll scramble the eggs after I freshen up and maybe get rid of some of that fragrance of horses and barn-yards."

"I, uh . . . kinda like that . . . fragrance."

"If anything happens, come a-running."

"You bet."

James Deegan was at his desk in his room, going over a litter of scattered notes, when he heard the knock.

"Tom, come on in."

No response.

"Tom," louder.

Another knock.

Deegan rose and briskly walked to the door and opened it.

"I'm not Tom. Can I still come in?"

Laura Layton stood at the doorway, dressed as if she were on her way to an elegant San Francisco soiree.

Her smile was more invitational than elegant.

"Mrs. Layton, what are you doing in Grandview?"

"Do you want me to explain standing in a doorway, or invite me in?"

"Well, I was expecting Tom . . ."

"I presume you mean Chairman Tom Drury. Are you disappointed?"

"Come in."

She did and closed the door.

"You didn't want to have dinner in Sheridan and get acquainted, so I thought we might do it in Grandview. But that's only part of the reason."

"What's the other part?"

"I'm here to listen to the pros and cons and vote for or against dissolving the association."

"*You* have a vote?"

"I most certainly do. Check with your chairman, we did."

"Who's we?"

"My banker and adviser, Dave Bergin. We came up together — and maybe find a prospect to buy my ranch. Already ran into your friend Samuel Ogdon Birthistle downstairs."

"You touch all the bases, don't you?"

"Including home plate. That's why I

254

thought we could have dinner . . . and get to know each other."

"I've already got a date."

"Break it."

"Can't. Maybe tomorrow . . ."

A knock on the door.

"Maybe I'd better see who it is this time."

The phone rang.

"Go ahead, I'll grab the phone."

Deegan continued to the door. Laura Layton picked the receiver up from the desk.

"Hello."

"Oh, hello. Is this James Deegan's room?"

"Yes, it is."

"I'm Mrs. Deegan. Who are you?"

"My name is Laura Layton."

A pause.

"I've heard about you. Is my husband there?"

"Of course he is . . . answering the door . . . he'll be right here."

James Deegan was hurrying back, trailed by Tom Drury.

"Mr. Deegan," Mrs. Layton said, "Mrs. Deegan," and handed him the phone.

"Hello, Liz."

"You have a secretary now, or a companion?"

"Neither. All business."

"Monkey business?"

"Association business."

"Putting in long hours."

"What is it, Liz? Something wrong?"

"No. Talked to Jimmy and Pepper. They'll call you tomorrow."

"Okay, Liz, I . . ."

"Take it easy, Jimbo. I was just going to tell you about a deal I'm working on, but I've got to think it over anyhow. Go back to your business, I'll tend to mine . . . and have a good night."

She hung up.

"I'm sorry if that was rather awkward," Laura said, and smiled.

"Mrs. Layton," Deegan said as he hung up the phone, "this is Tom Drury."

"So I gathered." She started toward the door.

"Please stay, Mrs. Layton," Drury motioned. "We have time."

"I'm afraid I don't."

Laura Layton opened the door.

"I'm going to meet Mr. Bergin. What a waste of my expensive perfume."

There was no evidence of remnants of scrambled eggs, fried potatoes, toast, and coffee on the stacked crockery that Amanda Reese had brought in half an hour ago.

Ben and Dr. Reese sat on the barn floor,

leaning against a large bale of hay.

"Breakfast close to midnight. You sure do know how to scramble eggs, Dr. Reese."

"My specialty is soft-boiled eggs."

"I'd say that your specialty's whatever you want it to be . . . besides taking care of horses."

"There's one good thing about what happened to that horse."

"What?"

"It brought us this close together again."

"Don't you think that would have happened anyhow? Sometime? Somewhere?"

She shrugged, just a light shrug.

"Talk about somewhere, I went somewhere yesterday . . . back to our old swimming hole."

"You did?"

"I did."

"Want me to tell you something?"

She nodded.

"I thought about going there myself."

"Why didn't you?"

"I was afraid . . ."

"You! Afraid, of what?"

"That you'd be there — or that you wouldn't."

"Ben, you are a complex man."

"Does that mean," he smiled, "that I'm not as simple as I look?"

"It means . . . that I don't know, I don't care what happened before we met. No matter how, or why it happened. All I do know is that I'm better off with you than without you, and you're better off with me than without me. Here and now."

"Amanda . . ."

"No. Let me finish . . . countless snow-flakes fall on the earth every year. No two snowflakes are exactly alike, neither are people. Not she and I. Not you and anybody else I've ever known. Why it happened and how it happened don't matter. We don't need any more questions. At least I don't, not if I already know the answer. And for me the answer is you. Now, if you . . ."

"Stop right there. You just gave the answer for both of us. Come here."

He put his arms around her and kissed her for the first time.

They both knew it wasn't for the last.

It was well past midnight when James Deegan came back to his room. He and Tom Drury had exhausted their marathon campaign of buttonholing, bracing, and bullshitting every rancher, sober and drunk, they came across at the Grandview Hotel. They did their best to convince each of them the merits and advantages of sticking with the association.

The high and low point of the evening was at the hotel's ornate bar/dining room and a brief encounter with Samuel Ogdon Birthistle with two of his acolytes hosting the dazzling Laura Layton in all her glowing glamour and David Bergin with eyelids half-open and -shut, half-asleep.

Birthistle had converted to a more conservative evening wardrobe, but it still smacked of Theodore Roosevelt. So did his booming voice as he hailed Deegan and Drury.

"Well, well, if it isn't the two D's out angling for votes. How's the fishin', boys?"

"Just fine, Sam," Drury replied, "except for a few sharks in the water."

"I'll let you know," Birthistle grinned, "if I spot one."

"We already have," Deegan countered.

Laura Layton allowed a faint smile and not in Deegan's direction as he and Drury moved on.

Other than that, the odds on their night's effort appeared to have been about five-o, five-o.

Deegan was on the phone after having called the Big Brawny, and after what seemed like a hundred rings, Pepper answered and was explaining what happened during Norkey's mustang chase and how the result affected Jimmy.

". . . the boy's okay, Mr. D, but comin' on that mustang like that was quite a jolt."

"Did you give him his medicine?"

"Sure did."

"And he's sleeping now?"

"Sure is."

"I never should've let him go out there with that . . . cowboy."

"It wasn't Ben's fault."

"You tell Jimmy to stay away from that . . ."

"I don't think that *I* should tell him anything. You better do the tellin' when you come home."

"You're right. I'll talk to him."

"Best thing for that boy'ud be if that horse got well."

"You say that Dr. Reese is tending to it . . ."

"Day and night. Over at Ben's place."

"Pepper, when you see Norkey be sure he knows I said to keep the operation as far away from headquarters as he can."

"I can tell him that, Mr. D, but he's got to go where the mustangs are."

"You're right again, and I'm getting punchy. I'll take care of things when I get back."

"How's it goin'?"

"When a bunch of independent cattlemen get together they're still pretty damn independent."

"You ought to know."

"I'll be back as soon as I can."

"Good night, Mr. D."

"Good night, Pepper . . . thanks."

They were both asleep covered by a blanket on the barn floor.

Silence.

Until the sound — soft at first — then louder and stronger.

A nicker — a neigh — a whinny.

Ben and Amanda reacted.

The black, its eyes blinked — focused — started struggling to gather its strength — straining — every sinew and nerve — lifting his head barely off the ground.

Ben and Amanda rose and watched.

The animal, still enervated, exerted its pent-up strength — the will of the wild — slowly, lifting first its head and chest, higher, then the forelegs — wobbling. The blanket fell off.

Ben and Amanda took a step forward.

The black, inch by inch, body quivering, muscles rippling, by the first glint of dawn, the forelegs gaining elevation then with effort the hindquarters — higher, its flank off the ground, then its shiny black body — upward — higher, almost to its feet, unsteady, almost falling, but struggling and gaining the determination, the strength to stand.

Sunlight streaked through the barn window.

From her stall, Betsey whinnied.

Ben's arm was around Amanda.

"Go ahead and smile, Dr. Reese. It's going to be an agreeable day."

CHAPTER NINETEEN

The sun hadn't arched much higher when the barn was more populated. Near Ben and Amanda, Jimmy and Pepper watched the black standing in his stall. Jimmy was smiling. They were all smiling.

"Well, Jimmy," Ben said, "I know it's early, but we thought you'd want to see this."

Jimmy nodded.

"Never saw the beat of it," Pepper pointed. "Right up on all fours."

"He wasn't as badly off as it first looked. Still amazing. But as I said, a horse'll stand as soon as it can."

"Especially a wild horse," Ben said.

"But it'll be a while before he can run."

"Doctor, he'll run."

"Are you going to ride him, Ben?"

"Jimmy, some horses were meant never to be ridden. He's one of 'em."

"But we've got to give him a name, don't we, Ben?"

"I don't know. What do you want to call him?"

"Well, I call my pinto Pinto . . . and this one's black . . ."

"Then we'll call him Black."

Pepper put his hand on the boy's shoulder.

"Jimmy, we'd better get back, have some breakfast, and see about your medicine."

Then Ben and Amanda were alone again . . . with the horses.

"We had our breakfast around midnight, but can I fix you something this time?"

"Thanks. But I'll grab something at home, take a shower," she looked at her watch, "and get to work. But I'll be back."

Betsey whinnied.

Ben smiled, looked at Betsey, then at Black and to Amanda.

"Well, Dr. Reese, you brought one of them into the world and kept the other one from leaving it."

As Amanda's station wagon pulled away, Ben, before turning to go back to the barn, spotted the truck coming from the opposite direction.

Ben stood and waited until the truck stopped near the barn and the Krantz brothers stepped out, one from each side.

"That was Dr. Amanda," Claud pointed back toward the road, "wasn't it?"

"We heard about what happened with the mustang," Clem said. "How's that animal doin'?"

"Doing all right, thanks to her."

"We figured this to be a light day on account of we had a heavy night," Claud's voice was still on the hoarse side.

"So, we thought we'd come out here, sorta take it on the easy, give you a hand if there's anything we can do." Clem was still a bit on the bleary side from last night.

"But we did run into Troy Johnson and told him you wanted to do business," Claud said. "He's ready to do business when you are."

"Appreciate it, fellas, and I'm glad you're here to look after things, because I've got to see a certain party about a certain airplane."

"Glad to accommodate an old pal," Clem smiled.

"We'll be here till you get back," Claud nodded.

"I'll be back."

"I just stopped by for a minute, Jim."

"Take your time, Tom. Have a cup of coffee . . ."

"Already had mine, and we haven't got much time. No more stall-a-roo. I've got to schedule that vote for sometime tomorrow.

Some of the guys are grumbling — getting calls from their wives."

"I think we're getting closer . . ."

"But not close enough yet."

"Okay, so we'll split up today, cover more territory."

"Right, and Jim . . ."

"Yeah?"

"I'm counting on you and your speech — whatever that is — to swing more votes. You've been damn mysterious — even to me."

"I want it to be a surprise even to you — get a unified reaction."

"You'll get a reaction from me, pal — one way or the other."

The light plane, anchored by guy-wires, gleamed in the sunlight. Nearby sat the truck loaded with heavy tires. In the distance, cattle grazed.

Norkey and his crew were at work. Norkey and Weegin releasing guy-wires and steadying the aircraft. Anson, Baker, Crane, Dorn, and Estes around the truck.

Weegin was the first to spot the rider. He tapped Norkey on the shoulder and pointed toward Ben Smith mounted on Betsey as he approached.

The rest of the crew reacted and stopped

working.

As Ben stepped off his horse, Weegin picked up his shotgun. Norkey moved a little closer, followed by Weegin.

Norkey smiled, not really a smile.

"Morning, Mr. Smith. Something we can do for you?"

"There is . . . but you won't."

"If it's about those mustangs — we've got a job to do."

"Yeah, I saw some of your handiwork yesterday."

"Oh, you mean that black stallion? Been mustangin' for a long time. Never saw one like that."

"You're never gonna see him again if I can help it."

Norkey looked at his crew then back to Ben.

"Heard you picked him up. You and that animal lady."

Ben didn't answer.

"You know that herd is pretty slick. Didn't catch but a few of 'em."

"Too bad."

"*Yep.* But we'll get 'em. Won't we, boys?"

The crew laughed.

"Still haven't said why you came all the way out here."

"I just want you to know that I'm going

to be running some cattle . . ."

"Uh-huh."

". . . and some horses."

"So?"

"So, I'm telling you plain and simple, I don't want you, or your men — or any of your machines — on my land."

"I have no intention of crossing on your land . . ." Norkey smiled. "But . . ."

"But?"

"Were I you, I'd keep those horses from straying."

"Wherever they stray, my horses'll have brands on 'em."

Weegin, still carrying his shotgun, walked near to Ben. A little too near.

"Sometimes we don't get close enough to read brands."

"Mister, you're a little too close to me right now."

Weegin started to step even closer.

"Well then, bub, maybe you ought to back up."

Ben's left fist slammed into Weegin's jaw. Weegin and his gun dropped to the ground. Weegin reached out toward the shotgun, but Ben kicked it away. With the same motion, he pulled the Winchester from its boot.

Nobody moved. Nobody said anything.

Ben turned and swung into the saddle

with the Winchester across the saddle horn. He nudged Betsey and rode away. Not fast, not slow.

Laura Layton, in a change of costume, but still bright eyed and glamorous, sat at a small table with Dave Bergin, who was still a bit hazy, sipping coffee with half a grapefruit in front of him on the table.

Her bright eyes brightened even more at the sight of James Deegan.

"Good morning to both of you," said Deegan.

"You in a hurry?"

"Not necessarily."

"Then sit down, have a cup of coffee."

"Already had my coffee a couple hours ago."

"Then how about a little conversation?"

"Never too late for that."

He pulled out a chair.

"Converse," Deegan smiled.

"You know Mr. Bergin, of course."

"We've done a little business . . . in the past."

"Maybe you can do a little more. How's the voting coming?"

"It's coming."

"I always like to be on the winning side."

"Who doesn't?"

"But you've got to know how to pick it."

"I've done all right."

"So have I . . ." She smiled.

"So far. But you know the old saying about a gambler's lucky streak."

"I'm not a gambler."

"Have you made up your mind about what you are?"

"How's that?"

"I mean how you're gonna vote . . . and whether you're gonna sell the ranch?"

"That's two reasons why I'm here, and I'm getting closer on both."

"I'll still make you the best offer . . . about the ranch, I mean."

"I'm glad to hear that and looking forward to that meeting . . . and your speech."

"It's always good to look forward, and I . . ."

"Excuse me," the young lobby boy cautiously said, "Mr. Deegan . . . I know you are, aren't you?"

"I are, and what else do you know?"

"There's a long-distance phone call. You can take it in the lobby, booth one."

"Thank you, son."

Deegan rose.

"It's been nice conversing with you, Mrs. Layton . . . and you, too, Mr. Bergin."

■ ■ ■ ■

"No, that's all right, they paged me in the breakfast room, go ahead and tell me more. That's good news."

"And Dad, Black — that's what we call him — Black's getting stronger already."

"Jimmy . . ."

". . . but Ben says he's not going to ride him, says some horses weren't meant to be ridden . . ."

"Jimmy, it looks like I can wrap things up here tomorrow. I'll be home tomorrow night or early the next day and we'll spend the rest of the summer together. How does that sound?"

"Neat."

"Yeah, I think so, too."

"Maybe you could come over to Ben's and . . ."

"I thought we'd go fishing up to the lake. What do you think about that?"

"Can Ben come, too?"

"Ben's busy. Anyhow, I think it would be better if just you and I went."

Silence.

"We'll have a lot of fun. Did you get your medicine?"

"Sure."

"All right, son. I'll see you soon, now let me talk to Pepper again."

Jimmy handed the phone to Pepper and walked out of the room. Pepper looked after him a beat, then brought up the phone.

"Howdy, Mr. D."

"Is Jimmy still there?"

"Nope. I think he went out to see Pinto, took Rover with him."

"Are you two doing anything besides spending all your time with that rodeo rider?"

"Well, Mr. D . . ."

"Never mind. Just keep him home."

"Already promised the boy we'd go back and see the horse."

"You did?"

"You want me to call him back so you can tell him different?"

"No, don't do that. I'll be back soon as I can. I guess one more time won't do any harm."

"Anything you say, Mr. D. So long."

After Amanda came back to the Little Brawny, the Krantz brothers were ready to leave.

She was in the barn with Black, and Ben and the brothers were at the barn door.

"I'm beholden to you, fellas."

"Did you get your chore done, Ben?" Claud asked.

"Thanks to the both of you."

"Anytime," Clem said. "We'll be around."

"Thanks again."

"All in a day's day," both the Krantz brothers said, and walked toward the truck.

Ben walked back inside.

Amanda came out of the stall, closing her medical bag.

"Progress," she said.

"He ate good."

"That vitamin shot'll help."

"Yeah."

"Ben, what're you going to do with him?"

"I don't know. But he doesn't want to stay in some stall or corral."

"He'd better stay somewhere until Norkey and his crew move away."

As Ben and Amanda came out of the open door, a car drove up and stopped. The side panel on the door was marked SHERIFF.

"Hello, Tom," Amanda greeted.

Tom Granger nodded.

"Mr. Smith, I've followed you on the circuit for years. We sure are glad to have you back in these parts."

"Thanks, Sheriff, 'preciate you coming out here to visit."

"Well, I did want to do that, too, but . . .

273

there's something else . . ."

The sheriff looked at Amanda.

"I guess I'd better . . ."

"It's all right. Go ahead, Sheriff. Is this an official visit?"

"No. Not exactly, but I thought I'd better let you know . . . I got a call . . ."

"From Norkey?"

The sheriff nodded.

"Said there was some unpleasantness out at the Big Brawny today."

Amanda looked at Ben, who was still looking at Granger.

"Seemed pleasant enough to me," he smiled.

"Not to Weegin, said you struck him."

Ben nodded. Amanda smiled.

"Said you were trespassing."

"That's not exactly true. And he was crowding me."

"I figured it was something like that. That Weegin's a troublemaker."

"You gonna arrest me?"

"Said they wasn't going to file a complaint . . . this time . . . just wanted to warn you."

"All right, Sheriff. I consider myself warned."

The sheriff nodded, then smiled.

"I guess that takes care of that." He moved

toward the car.

"Stop by again, Sheriff . . . for a visit."

Tom Granger was in the car.

"I'll do that. How's the stallion doing, Amanda?"

"Doing fine."

"Good."

The sheriff drove away.

Amanda turned to Ben and smiled.

"What's so funny?"

"I was wondering."

"About what?"

"That bruise on your knuckles."

"Oh . . . that was a pacifier. Say, would you like a cool drink of something?"

"No, but there is something I would like."

"What's that?"

"I'd like to buy you dinner . . . and don't say no."

"Who's saying no?"

"Good! There's a nice quiet little place near the park, Jake's Steaks."

"Tonight? What time?"

"Tomorrow night. Tonight, I'll be miles away, got a date with a sick steer."

"Okay, you got a date tomorrow night and not with a sick steer. By the way, you think it'ud be all right if I took Black out to the corral for a little exercise?"

"I think so. Give it a try . . . get better

acquainted."

She smiled.

"With the horse?"

"That's what we were talking about, wasn't it?"

"Sure," she said, and moved toward her station wagon.

"You fellas going up again?"

Joe Higgins stood near Norkey, Weegin, and the mustang crew.

"Yeah," Norkey said, "just gassed up and goin' huntin'."

"Don't you think it'ud be better to wait till Mr. Deegan gets back and talk things over?"

"Already did the talkin' . . . and, Mr. Higgins . . . something else . . ."

"What?"

"You stick to your business, and we'll stick to ours. You're good at it and so are we."

Joe Higgins turned and walked away.

Ben Smith was inside the corral, leading Black with a loose lariat.

The horse seemed calm enough, breathing the fresh air and taking a few steps alongside.

Ben removed the rope, allowing Black to move freely inside the corral.

Pepper, with Jimmy, pulled up in the pickup, both smiling, opened both doors and moved toward the corral.

Sunlight gleamed across Black's body, and the horse shimmered in the glow.

Ben moved closer to the fence of the corral.

"Howdy, neighbors," pointed toward Black, "how about that?"

"He looks beautiful!" Jimmy beamed.

"Almost good as new," Pepper remarked.

"Not yet, but he's getting there — needs a little more care and he'll get it."

"Ben."

"Yes, Jimmy."

"I talked to Dad. He says he's coming back home, maybe tomorrow."

"That's great."

Jimmy's attitude was not exactly great.

"Says he wants to go fishing."

"That sounds . . ."

But there was another sound — then sounds.

First, the sound and sight of running mustangs. Black's herd, but led now by a racing Appaloosa.

Then a more ominous sound from above and increasing.

Norkey's plane was followed by the truck.

The plane swooped down across the corral.

Black reared with the memory of the plane, and gunshots that followed. Eyes blazing with fright, Black ran — bolted over the corral fence and galloped toward the ridgeline.

Norkey's plane was still on the hunt but moving toward the setting sun.

Jimmy threw his arms around Ben.

"They'll find him. They'll kill Black!"

"Maybe not. Not if he makes it to where I think he's going."

"I don't like it," Weegin yelled.

"Neither do I," Norkey yelled back.

"That goddamn engine is sputterin' like hell!"

"Shut up! I can hear it."

"We can't keep going!"

"We're not. We're going back till it gets fixed tomorrow."

"Maybe I can fix it."

"Well, somebody can. Now, shut the hell up."

Norkey banked the plane.

Ben, Jimmy, and Pepper watched the plane retreat, followed by the truck heading back toward the Big Brawny.

"Getting too dark to track Black now,"

Pepper said.

"Ben," Jimmy ventured, "Black was going . . ."

"Jimmy! Remember you spit. I'll be out at first light."

"Well, Jim, they weren't just grumbling out there anymore, some of 'em were damn near gyrating. I had to give a definite time for that meeting tomorrow."

"High noon? That's the time for most shoot-outs, isn't it?"

"Not quite in this case. They want to start earlier, grab a fast lunch and go that-away . . . home. The fireworks start at eleven a.m."

"Well, hell, then we've got almost twenty-four hours, haven't we?"

Drury nodded after he looked at his wristwatch.

"According to my brand-new Bulova, it's near seven now. I've got a dinner date with four swing votes . . . how'd you do?"

"Ditto. Four possibles."

"A majority of those should wrap it up."

"Yeah, pardner . . . but easier said than done."

"Not for us two musketeers . . . huh, pardner?"

"Tom, here I thought you were a worrier."

"Not with you around. We'll dazzle 'em with footwork. We can compare notes and numbers later on tonight. Okay?"

"Okay, but not too much later."

Fifteen minutes later, James Deegan was moving across the lobby and she was with all her glamour, looking as if she were on the lookout for somebody.

Somebody in particular.

She saw him.

She wasted no time.

"Good evening, Mr. Deegan."

"Good evening, Mrs. Layton, and as always, you look splendid."

"Then would you care to join me . . . for dinner?"

"Already got a date with four . . ."

"Voters?"

"Friends. Would you care to join us?"

"Two's company, six is a crowd. Looks like it's durable Dave Bergin again . . . see you around . . . here or there."

Laura Layton about-faced and walked away — walked like James Deegan was missing something.

"Pepper, I want to call my dad and tell him what happened."

"Jimmy lad, your dad's got important business up there, and there's nothing,

nothing, he can do to help us tonight. Isn't that right?"

"I guess."

"Then, get to sleep. You heard what he said."

"Who?"

"Ben. He'll be out at first light."

CHAPTER TWENTY

Sundown, day's done. First light, day is on its way.

So was Ben on Betsey.

Along the base of the mountain wall, approaching a narrow channel visible only from the immediate vicinity, threshold to the hidden canyon.

Horse and rider turned into the slim pathway that led to higher terrain, made their way into a ravine then still upward to a sizable tabletop, large enough for a plentiful herd of mustangs.

In front of the herd, the young, stalwart Appaloosa that led the mustangs away from Norkey's pursuit. Alongside the Appaloosa, a beautiful palomino, and just ahead of the two, the object of Ben Smith's quest.

Black.

Tall and proud.

Shimmering in the sun.

And there was something else.

Black's stance and structure were undeniably evident in the young Appaloosa.

From a distance, Ben smiled and waved, started to turn but came to a halt when he heard, then saw Black whinny and nod.

Ben reached and ruffled Betsey's mane.

"Well, Betsey," he said just above a whisper, "looks like a family reunion."

The first thing Ben wanted to do when he got back to the Little Brawny was to call Jimmy with the news.

"Pepper, how's Jimmy doing?"

"Okay, he's still asleep."

"Well, don't wake him up now. But I've got some good news. When he wakes up tell him I saw Black. Tell him Black's at our spit-place and . . ."

"Did you say 'spit-place'?"

"That's what I said, amigo, spit-place, and Black says hello."

"The horse says hello?"

"Right again."

"That is good news — and I've got some news for you."

"Fire away. Good news or bad news?"

"You decide. I got this from Joe Higgins who got it from Norkey. Norkey's plane got engine trouble on their last chase, they got the plane to the mechanic over at that small regional airport on Sylvania Road."

"Yeah, yeah, Pepper, I know the place. Go on."

"Don't know how long it'll take to fix it, but when it's ready, Norkey and company are fixin' to go up mustangin' again . . ."

"Is that the good or the bad part?"

"Well, the bad part is that the plane didn't crash with them in it."

"What's the good part?"

"Haven't figured that one out yet."

"Well, while you're figuring, I think I'll make a little visit."

"I figured you might."

James Deegan and Tom Drury walked down a hallway in the Grandview Hotel.

Drury glanced at his wristwatch.

"Well, Jim, according to . . ."

"Yeah, I know, your brand-new Bulova . . ."

"We've got just about a half hour to get ready. Are you?"

"I was born ready."

"From comparing our notes and numbers, I'd say we're looking pretty good."

"Yep, barring any last-minute bombshells."

"Just before I picked you up I got a call from dear ol' Birthistle. Said since it was an informal meeting would it be all right if he made a few short remarks before you spoke. I said I'd let him know. Any objection?"

"Just the opposite. Bigmouth Birthistle'll probably give me some ammunition."

Coincidentally or not, the door to one of the elegant suites that was ajar opened wide, revealing Mrs. Laura Layton in still another change of costume, daytime cosmopolitan.

"Did I hear some talk about ammunition?"

"I don't know," Drury shrugged, "did you?"

"Just wanted to inquire, are you going to search me before getting into that meeting?"

"Right," Deegan said, "and if you don't have a weapon, we'll give you a gun."

"Just one?"

"It's a tommy gun."

" 'Tommy' — I knew him well back during Prohibition. See you in the voting booth, and remember, boys . . . 'always keep your powder dry.' "

Laura Layton performed a semi-curtsy and closed the door.

"She's got a ready voice," Drury noted.

"It's functional," Deegan smiled.

"So are other parts, I'd wager."

"Well, pal, you can't say she conceals all her weapons."

■ ■ ■ ■

Inside the hangar, the mechanic Dick Bakalyan was still inspecting the light plane.
Another aircraft, a small two-seater, also
rested in the repair shop.

Norkey and Weegin stood a few feet away.
Both impatient.

Norkey lit a cigar, took a couple puffs,
then stepped toward Bakalyan.

"Well, for one thing, she's got a leak in
the fuel line," Bakalyan noted.

"That's what I said." Weegin came closer.

"Never mind what you said," Norkey
grunted, then turned back to Bakalyan.
"Okay, that's one thing. Anything else?"

"Well, I don't know, pal, not yet. Got to
finish my inspection and . . ."

"And what?"

Bakalyan pointed to the two-seater.

"That little sweetheart's got troubles, too,
and she comes first."

"Why?"

"Because that's the way I do business . . .
and first come, first . . ."

"Yeah, yeah, I know, but when can I get
my plane back?"

"Truth be told, I don't exactly know,
maybe this afternoon, or I'll have to work

late tonight, and you'll get her early in the morning. If I work late it'll cost you extra, but she'll be ready to take off. By the way, I don't take checks."

"Do you take cash?"

"With a smile."

With the cigar still stuck in his mouth, Norkey reached into the left pocket of his pants, pulled out a roll of bills, and peeled off a hundred-dollar bill.

"Here's something in advance to keep you smiling." He nodded toward his plane. "If she's ready to fly tomorrow morning and if you need more, you'll get it . . . in cash."

"She'll be ready, Mr. Norkey."

"So will we."

Mr. Norkey stuffed the roll of bills back into his pocket.

As they walked out of the entrance they heard a voice.

"Norkey!"

They both turned and faced Ben Smith. Norkey took the cigar from his mouth.

"Something troubling you . . . Mr. Smith?"

"You," Mr. Smith pointed to the hangar, "and that plane."

"First, there's something you oughta know."

"I'm listening."

"Just this. You might own the Little Brawny, Mr. Smith, but you don't own the sky above it. That plane's going up tomorrow."

"I didn't say it wasn't."

"We're going to round up mustangs on the Big Brawny."

"I guess you can round up all the mustangs you want . . ."

"You guess right."

". . . except one."

"I work for Mr. Deegan. He said . . ."

"I don't care what he said, but you go after that black again . . . you touch him . . . and I'm not going to see Deegan, or anybody else. I'm coming to see you."

"Is that a threat?"

"It's a fact."

Ben Smith walked toward his pickup. Weegin watched, then turned to Norkey.

"I still owe that bastard, and I'm gonna . . ."

"I don't want to know what you're 'gonna' — what you do when you're off the clock," Norkey stuck the cigar back into his mouth, "is none of my business."

Vice Chairman James Deegan sat next to Chairman Tom Drury at the large table in the front of the room. Drury rapped on the table with his gavel, signaling that the meeting was coming to session.

Beside Deegan and Drury, the other attendees consisted of forty-four males of assorted ages and sizes, plus, in the front row, one female prominently displaying a pair of lovely, seemingly endless legs crossed.

"All right . . . lady and gentlemen, before we get to the final business on the proposition of our cattlemen's association's dissolvement that Mr. Birthistle is going to propose, there are a few things you all ought to know if that resolution passes. The fact that I think it won't pass . . . and I hope it won't. Now, this is an informal session and no press or nonmembers have been admitted . . ."

"Mr. Chairman," Samuel Ogdon Birthistle, all three hundred pounds of him, rose, "before this ad hoc shindig or campfire caboodle, or whatever you want to call it, commences, I want to say that I disagree with your biased opinion of the outcome of the vote, and just in case we do dissolve, what the hell do we care what happens then? Why lose time even talking about it?"

"Because, Mr. Birthistle, we might lose a little time and gain a little sense. Dissolving the association is complicated with ramifications everyone here ought to know about. . . . Just a sample, we have a sizable fund in the bank to be disposed of. How and to whom will that be done? There's more, much more on the agenda. So kindly sit down. You'll have a chance to speak after Mr. Deegan does, then to make your resolution, and we'll vote."

Samuel Ogdon Birthistle, all three hundred pounds of him, thumped down on his chair.

NO PARKING
Sheriff Cars Only

Prominently posted near the curb in front of the sheriff's part of the building.

The sheriff's car was parked just to the left of the sign. The rest of the curb area, vacant.

Ben's pickup drove past the no-parking zone, around the corner, and picked a place to pull up. He left the pickup and headed around the corner to the entrance.

One of the cars moving along the street slowed down, and Weegin, at the wheel, watched long enough to see Ben enter, then accelerated.

Fifteen minutes later, Ben was still listening as Sheriff Tom Granger shrugged and lowered an official document.

Ben stroked his chin, disappointment in his eyes.

"I just wanted to find out what exactly the law says."

"I'm sorry, Ben. That is the law." The sheriff tapped at a spot near the center of a page, "Quote . . . 'the use of aircraft or motor vehicles to hunt certain wild horses or burros on public land is prohibited' . . . unquote."

"Yeah."

Granger glanced at the paper, then looked back at Ben.

"The operative words are 'public land' . . . at least so far. There's nothing to prevent Norkey or anybody else from doing what he's doing on private property so long as he's got permission of the Big Brawny's owner; that's the law."

"Some law. Does it allow Norkey to maim and torture those mustangs?"

"Sure, Norkey stretches the law and even breaks it, so do a lot of the other mustangers, but hell, we can't patrol everything that goes on on millions of acres of private property. He knows that, and you know it."

"Yep."

"And if he does get caught, what's the fine? Five hundred dollars. We need stronger laws, and they're working on it, but it takes time."

"Those mustangs out there haven't got time."

"You know that and so do I, but try telling it to the politicians."

"No, I'm not going to try to do that. But maybe there's something else I can do."

Ben turned and started to walk out. But the sheriff wasn't finished.

"Ben, my friend . . . don't do anything dumb. Those boys play rough."

Ben Smith headed toward the door.

CHAPTER TWENTY-ONE

Chairman Tom Drury rapped the gavel on the table a mite harder than before.

There was a mixed murmur from the ranchers.

"I've had my say for now. I hope you understand just some of the consequences of dissolvement before we even consider it."

More murmurs.

"But Mr. Birthistle wanted to say a few words before Mr. Deegan does. Then we vote. Go ahead, Mr. B."

Samuel Ogdon Birthistle took his time about getting to his feet.

"Just this, in a few words. This country and the West weren't won with words. It was all won with guns and rifles and guts. And not by a bunch of flannelmouth jaw-boners. It all got done by individuals who were independent, independent enough to get it done, who stood on their own two feet.

"Well, I'm independent, and so are all of you, or you wouldn't own your own ranch, like I do. We don't need to waste time and money paying dues to some 'association' or 'authoritarian' when times are hard as they are. When something needs to be done we do it ourselves without hypothesizing about it . . . and listening to some part-time rancher like the fellow who's going to talk next. But go ahead and talk, part-timer."

James Deegan rose, calm and confident.

"Thank you, Mr. B. Mr. Birthistle's pretty slick in his phraseology, in the use of phrases and words such as 'part-timer' and 'independent.'

"Well, I'm not so shy when it comes to using the word 'independent,' and I'm a part-timer, myself.

"First off, long before Mr. Birthistle and most of you other ranchers owned a cow and a bull, the Deegans were already here. The Deegans have owned the Big Brawny for over a hundred years, and long after I'm gone, the Deegans will still own it.

"Let me remind him and you of some part-timers and independents he and you might've heard of — just a few of the part-timers and independents, such as John Hancock, merchant, statesman — Sam Adams, farmer, businessman, brewer —

294

Thomas Jefferson, farmer, foreign affairs consultant, lawyer, and later president — Benjamin Franklin, printer, inventor.

"Were they part-timers? You bet your boots they were!

"And were they independent? Damn well told!

"So were the other signers of something called the Declaration of Independence.

"There were some other people involved, people like George Washington, Patrick Henry, and Tom Paine, who had part-time occupations besides patriotism.

"But they got things done by getting together and creating and fighting for the greatest country on God's earth.

"Sam Birthistle referred to me as a part-time rancher because I'm not always here playing poker, raising hell, or on my knees praying for rain. Well, praying for rain might help, but there's some other things we can do to help.

"You've heard of something called the Dust Bowl — it displaced and damn near destroyed thousands of our neighbors.

"We were lucky that time. The drought hit us but not nearly as bad. The next time we may not be so lucky.

"If we're ever hit like Oklahoma was, most of the ranchers in this room, and in this state, can say good-bye to tomorrow. In fact, when it comes to our rainfall, to our grassy range, most of us, even now, are in need of more water to save and expand our cattle business.

"We've got to be prepared to do something about it.

"You ever hear of Boulder Dam? It's practically finished in the driest state in the union, and hundreds, maybe thousands of people are working to provide water — enough water to nourish three states. Deserts will bloom; new farms will grow enough crops to fill a million freight cars and hungry bellies."

"So, what?" shouted Samuel Ogdon Birthistle.

"So, this! Right now, the government's looking for projects like that. And right now, a part-time rancher and some of his associates back East, between trips from New York to Washington, have introduced a bill, the TR Bill, in Congress on behalf of the cattlemen's association, to build a dam, a much smaller dam than Boulder, but to do just what I've been talking about and working for — when I'm not part-time ranching.

"TR stands for 'Theodore Roosevelt' — and the dam will be called the Theodore Roosevelt Dam, and you'll be able to see it," James Deegan pointed up and out of the window.

"You'll be able to see it right out of that window.

"What chance do you think that the TR Bill and the Theodore Roosevelt Dam have if they hear back East that we've dissolved the cattlemen's association and we no longer speak with one voice?

"About as much chance as a wax cat in hell.

"We've always prided ourselves in being independent. So did our founding fathers who got together and created a new nation with the Declaration of Independence.

"As ol' Ben Franklin said, 'We must all hang together, or we shall all hang separately.'

"I think ol' Ben Franklin summed it all up in one sentence. We don't need any more speechifying. So let's quit the gab and get to the business of voting to keep the association and get the Theodore Roosevelt Dam built," James Deegan pointed to the huge arched window with a clear view of the Sierra Loma Mountains, "so we can see it from right here through that window!"

Without hesitation Samuel Ogdon Birthistle, all three hundred pounds of him, did his best to leap to his feet.

"Mr. Chairman, I rise to a point of order, and if you don't know what that means — it means that it takes precedence at a meeting — look it up in *Robert's Rules of Order* written in 1876.

"I still am just as independent as I was when I walked through that door. But, brothers . . . and sister, I know when I'm swimmin' against the tide — when the fat is in the fire — when the referee has counted to ten — when the high, low, jack, and the dame are against me — when to hold 'em and when to fold 'em.

"Mr. Deegan, I want to shake your hand . . . and someday walk to that same window and gaze at the Theodore Roosevelt Dam.

"There is no need to vote because there will be no motion to dissolve the cattlemen's association."

Gee-haws, hurrahs, and applause as Tom Drury pounded his gavel on the table, smiled at James Deegan, and proclaimed over the celebration, "This here meeting of the Osage County Cattlemen's Association is hereby concluded. See you all at our next meeting."

James Deegan had packed early that morning and was in a hurry to get in the Chrysler and drive back to the Big Brawny.

But on his way through the lobby, he couldn't help but be intercepted by a bevy of sober and not-so-sober cattlemen — and one lone woman.

Tom Drury — sober: "Well, ol' cock, congratulations. You pulled a couple of aces out of your sleeve."

James Deegan: "Yeah, ol' pardner, now all we've got to do is get the damn dam built."

Cattleman Johnny D. Boggs — not so sober: "James, ol' saddle snatcher, I'll winter with you anytime and want to invite you to speak at our Rotary meeting sometime."

James Deegan: "Johnny D. Boggs, invitation accepted. I'll be there . . . sometime."

Mrs. Laura Layton — maybe two highballs, in high-tone latest Victoria driving attire: "Not exactly a fireside chat, but the butcher sure as hell knows his customer. Congratulations."

James Deegan: "Thank you, ma'am, but would you mind telling me how you would have voted?"

Mrs. Layton: "Don't you remember what I said I always, always, pick the winning side."

CHAPTER TWENTY-TWO

Most of the beer and free lunch customers had left. But not all. The Krantz brothers sat on their usual stools at the bar and so did Kit Carson up front near the cash register.

There was a poker game in progress at one of the tables, but the card players might as well have been in another room, or for that matter, in another world. The only thing each was interested in was what was in his hand.

Skinny Dugan walked in, as usual in a hurry.

"Not much free lunch left, Skinny," Kit Carson smiled, "just a few sandwiches."

"You know by now I never eat lunch. Just came in for my midafternoon beer."

Baldy was already drawing a beer as Skinny sat in his usual stool near what was left on one of the free-lunch platters.

"Afternoon, Claud, Clem, I see you're on

the job as usual."

"Just like you, Mr. Dugan," Claud smiled.

"Mine's just a beer and a short respite."

"What's that last word mean?" Clem asked.

"It means you are uneducated. So mind your own business. By the way, Miz Carson, how is business?"

"Same as yesterday, same as tomorrow . . . same ol' same."

"Well, my sources of news have sort of dried up. Anything around here happen worth printing?"

"Nothing you could print," Kit said.

Skinny took a swallow from his glass then smacked his lips.

"Baldy, you been waterin' your beer as well as your whiskey? This tastes mighty lightweight."

"I'll throw a lead weight in the next one."

"You know I only have one . . . in the afternoon."

Skinny reached for one of the sandwiches left in the free-lunch platter. Took a considerable bite and washed it down with another swallow of brew.

"Say, this tastes better than usual. What's between the bread today?"

"Something different," Kit Carson said. "Bunny."

301

"Bunny? Never heard of it. What kind of meat is that?"

"Bunny," replied Kit, "is a baby rabbit."

Skinny Dugan spat out half a mouthful.

"Clem and me went a-huntin' this mornin' an kilt us a whole litter of 'em."

"You two aren't hunters, you're baby murderers."

"You said it tasted good," Clem grinned.

"I didn't know I was eating babies."

Skinny Dugan finished his beer, hurried toward the door, and slapped a nickel on top of the cash register.

"Next time," Kit Carson said, "I'll put a sign on each sandwich."

"Do that. If anybody around here can read . . . or write!"

He paused just outside the door when he saw it coming and going. The Packard Victoria was breaking whatever the speed limit was in town, probably doubling it. Skinny's head swirled trying to keep the Packard in sight with Laura Layton at the wheel of the convertible.

He had shrugged and proceeded up the street toward the *Beacon* building when he saw Dave Bergin coming out the door of the Citizens Bank and moving in the direction of his parked car.

"Hey, Dave, just a minute!"

"What is it, Skinny? I'm in a hurry right now."

"This'll just take a minute. Heard you were up to Grandview with that Layton lady for the meeting. Anything happen I can print?"

Bergin swung open the door of his car.

"You can print this. I've been on a merry-go-round without a brass ring, but with the madwoman of the West, and I'm going home to recuperate by having a good old-fashioned fight with my wife."

James Deegan's Chrysler was parked in front of the Big Brawny headquarters.

They had been in the study for more than a half hour, Deegan, Jimmy, and Pepper.

Pepper still sat silent, listening to his boss doing his best to generate excitement about the fishing trip to the lake tomorrow. But his son stood stolid and continued to change the subject.

"Dad, please . . . you can't let him do it. You can't let him kill Black and the rest of those horses."

"Son, sit down. Let me explain."

"But, Dad . . ."

"Just sit down, Jimmy, and listen to me for a minute."

Jimmy sat on the edge of a chair.

"Now, I know how you feel, but this is business. Part of running a modern ranch . . ."

"Killing horses?"

"It's a matter of survival, either the cattle or those mustangs. We've had a drought, a bad drought. There isn't enough grass for both. Left alone, those mustangs multiply, scare off the cattle, and take what grass and water is available."

Jimmy just shook his head and said nothing.

"We make our living off cattle. They're the lifeblood of this ranch. I've told you, someday it'll be your ranch, son."

"I don't want it!"

"Then sell it when I'm gone. But in the meanwhile, I've got to run it the way I know best . . . and besides, the Big Brawny means jobs, work, and pay for Pepper, Higgins, and a lot of other people who depend on it."

Silence.

Then James Deegan glanced at Pepper . . . and back to Jimmy with a softer tone.

"Jimmy, things'll look different to you someday; maybe it'll start to look different when we get back from the lake. Then we'll catch up on things around here. It'll all be over by then. Norkey will be gone by then."

"So will the mustangs."

For once Deegan didn't have the proper answer. He walked to where Jimmy was sitting.

"Pepper's got the number at the lodge where we're staying so he can keep in touch in case we need to know about what's going on. He'll help you pack and get ready. I know a great little spot to fish up there, don't I, Pepper?"

"You sure do, Mr. D . . . and I know how to cook 'em. Come along, Jimmy boy."

Deegan led the way to the door and opened it. "I'll call your mom and tell her about our fishing expedition."

Norkey was in the adjacent room, waiting.

Pepper, then Jimmy, walked by. Jimmy's eyes were moist. Norkey started to say something . . . but didn't.

Deegan did. To Norkey.

"Come on in here."

Norkey followed Deegan into the study. Deegan's manner was serious, in fact, severe.

"I want you to get this mustang business over . . . quick as you can."

"Sure, but, Mr. Deegan, that cowboy's been . . ."

"Never mind about Mr. Smith. You're working for me."

"Sure thing, I said that to him."

"I'm going away for a few days with my son. Round up all you can before we get back."

Norkey nodded.

"Got a little engine trouble. I'll have it fixed up before tomorrow morning and we'll get started then."

"Good. That's when we're leaving. By the time we get back I want those mustangs and you gone."

Upstairs, Jimmy sat on the bed listening to an earnest Pepper.

"Jimmy, m'boy, I've been part of this family longer, much longer, than you have, and I'm not ashamed to say I love all of you . . . your father and mother and you. Son, right now your dad's got problems and so has your mom, trying to work things out. You do understand that, don't you?"

Jimmy nodded.

"Good boy. And you're growing up fast, maybe too fast for some, but not for you. You've got to help both of them. It's tough, but you can handle it if they can. You've got to help them. It won't be easy for any of you, but you can do your part starting up at the lake with your dad. Things have got to change. They usually change for the better.

That's what he wants to do. Will you help him?"

"I'll try . . . but Black . . ."

"Don't sell Black short. When it comes to a showdown between Norkey and Black, Black'll come out all right."

"You think so, Pepper?"

"I think so."

Pepper didn't really, but for the time being, he thought it best to say so.

"Things came out okay, Liz. We've still got the cattlemen's association. But I wanted to tell you that the mustang roundup has upset Jimmy, so I thought it best to take him up to the lake and do a little fishing together till things settle down. We'll stay at the lodge. You've got the number, haven't you?"

"I've got it. If I call this time, will that Laura Layton answer?"

"Liz, you know better than that!"

"You mean because Jimmy will be there?"

"Come on, Liz, that's not you, my old flame, talking."

"I was out of line. Your old flame apologizes. But you think it would help if I dropped everything and came out? I think I could manage to . . ."

"I'd love it, but you've got a business to run. Let's see what happens when we get back from the lake."

"Isn't there a song called 'It Only Happens When I Dance with You'? We haven't danced for a long time."

"It didn't only happen when we danced."

"Mr. Deegan, you've got a naughty mind . . . I'm happy to say."

"I'd better quit while I'm ahead, if I am ahead."

"Say good night, Jimbo."

"Good night, Stranger."

"Yes, this is Skinny Dugan. Who's this?"

"This is Laura Layton, Mr. Dugan. Say, what is your given name? It certainly isn't 'Skinny.' "

"Is that why you called, to find out my given name? You're not gonna. Besides, I'm busy puttin' out tomorrow's edition."

"No, that's not the reason I called, I was just trying to be polite."

"No need to be polite. Then, why are you calling, to complain that I didn't print that bogus interview you gave me?"

"I'm calling to inquire if you protect your sources."

"What do you mean by 'protect'?"

"If a source wants to remain anonymous will you respect that and refuse to reveal his or her name?"

"That's the code of the free press, ma'am, has been in this country since there's been a free press . . . that's why they call it freedom of the press. I'll go to jail or hell before I reveal a source. Now, we've gone the long way around to clarify that point. So, let's get to the shortcut if you've got something that ain't bogus."

"This 'ain't' bogus, but it's exclusive, no press was allowed, and I was there."

"Where's there?"

"Cattlemen's association special meeting at Grandview. What happened, how it happened, who made it happen, and about the new dam. How would you like to print that?"

"I'd like it fine . . . Ty-Roan! Tear out the front page. We're gonna work late tonight. Get out an EXTRA! EXCLUSIVE! *You hear me, Ty-roan?*"

"I hear you, Mr. Skinny. I've heard you before . . . for eighteen years."

"Go ahead, Mrs. Layton."

"You ready to take notes?"

"Don't take notes . . . haven't got a photographic body, but I got a photographic mind."

"Well, I've got both."

"Fire away!"

"Well, as the Krantz brothers would say, 'It's all in a day's day.' "

"All that, while I went out to see a sick steer."

"Did the patient recover?"

"The patient recovered, but the doctor could use a cool martini and a hot shower."

"Well, I can't join you in the shower, but if you can wait till tonight . . . by the way, is our date at Jake's Steaks still on?"

"Unless you've had a better offer."

"Im-possible."

"Then it's on and make that martini a double. And, Ben, how's Jimmy taking all this . . . about the mustangs and Black?"

"Not so good. Still vexed about the roundup and what's going to happen to Black."

"I'm not surprised."

"But Pepper called and said his dad's taking him up to the lake fishing, so he'll be away during the roundup."

"That helps, but what happens to Black?"

"I talked to Mr. Norkey about Black."

"With your usual friendly persuasion?"

"Not quite usual, and not quite friendly."

"Ben . . ."

"Please don't say, 'Be careful.' "

"Who me? Never."

"Then what were you going to say?"

"Uh . . . I forget. I'll make reservations for eight o'clock, know a nice cozy corner table."

"I'll pick you up."

"No. Meet you there. I'll drive myself, that way I know I'll drive home, not sleep in the barn."

"Was that so bad?"

"Nope. Just tempting. Meet you at Jake's."

"Are you ready, Ty-Roan?"

"Ready, willing, and disabled, Mr. Skinny."

"Then print it in the usual format with EXTRA! EXCLUSIVE! — Headline: JAMES DEEGAN BY A DAM SITE — Banner: Special Meeting, Grandview. Will Cattlemen's Assoc. Be Dissolved?"

The informal meeting began with "windy" Samuel Ogdon Birthistle, who weighs as much as a cement statue of him would, remarked about himself, how independent he was, and no need for the cattlemen's association, "a waste of time and money." Birthistle called Deegan a part-time rancher. Big B looked forward to the vote on his resolution to dissolve the association after the part-timer said his piece.

Mr. Deegan shot back with both barrels, saying, "Mr. Birthistle is pretty slick in his phraseology with such words as 'part-timer' and 'independent.' Well, I'm not so shy about using those words, myself. Independent. Deegans have owned the Big Brawny for over a hundred years."

Then Deegan gave Birthistle a lesson in U.S. history. "The Declaration of Independence was framed by a bunch of independents and part-timers such as John Hancock, Sam Adams, John Adams, and Ben Franklin, who all had other occupations, as did George Washington, Patrick Henry, and Tom Paine. All independents, but got things done by getting together and creating the greatest country on earth."

Yes, Deegan is a part-timer, too, he said, and spoke of how close to being part of the Dust Bowl that devastated our neighbors in Oklahoma. We came close, and next time we may not be so lucky, and how during the time he is away, he's spearheading a movement for Congress to create a dam, not nearly as mammoth as Boulder, but big enough to nourish hundreds of our ranches and townships in this part of the state. A dam located in the high country above Grandview and to be called the Theodore Roosevelt Dam.

"What chance," James Deegan asked, "has the Theodore Roosevelt Dam to be built if Congress hears that the cattlemen's association has been dissolved and we no longer speak with one united voice?"

His answer?

"About as much chance as a wax cat in hell."

Then Deegan repeated Ben Franklin's admonition, "We must all hang together, or we will all hang separately."

That drove the last nail into Birthistle's dissolution coffin. Even with his dim vision, Samuel Ogdon Birthistle saw the light and withdrew his dim-witted resolution.

Bravo, James Deegan!!!

Kit Carson's emporium was astir. Nine of the dozen tables were occupied by card players, six of the nine stools at the bar were seated by regulars, including the Krantz brothers, who were matching pennies and drinking beer. Kit, herself, waited on customers between punching the cash register.

The maestro was at the piano, fingering a medley of songs familiar to customers of places like Kit Carson's and some of the oldies — "Sweet Adeline," "Alexander's

Ragtime Band," "April Showers," "Wait
'Till the Sun Shines, Nellie."

At the front edge of the bar, Anson, Baker, Crane, Dorn, and Estes drank beer with their heads leaning toward the front entrance in anticipation.

Skinny Dugan hurried in. That's not what they were anticipating.

"Evening, horse killers," Skinny greeted the mustangers.

Anson cursed, but under his breath as he noticed Kit Carson approaching, and she didn't allow cursing in her presence although she, herself, would go at it on occasion, like a Saturday-night sailor.

"Salutations, Skinny," Kit smiled. "Why aren't you working on tomorrow's *Beacon*?"

"That's just what I'm doin', and takin' a beer break, if you can call that toilet water Baldy serves beer . . ."

Baldy had already set a foaming glass on a vacant spot at the bar.

Skinny took a deep swill, then turned to the twins.

"Well, well, what a surprise, the Krantz duo at the bar. How are you boys? What-da-ya-hear? What-da-ya-say?"

"Hear no evil," Claud said.

"Speak no evil," Clem added.

"Deef and dumb, huh? As usual."

314

From the street outside, a horn honked. Once, twice, three times.

The mustangers rose together like puppets on a string, each one plunked a coin on Kit's cash register, and then nearly stumbled over one another getting out the door.

"Say, them horse killers seemed in a powerful hurry — likely they was headin' for Candy Carr's hen coop."

"Likely," Kit nodded.

Skinny Dugan dropped a nickel in Kit's open palm.

"Keep the change. You ought to charge two and a half cents. It's half-beer and half–canal water."

"See you tomorrow, Skinny."

She rang up the nickel.

Ben came around the corner from where he had parked his pickup and walked toward the entrance of Jake's Steaks.

A man and woman came out the door. The woman wore a loose blouse and tight jeans. The man dressed western with a Stetson on his head and a toothpick in his mouth.

Ben was wardrobed a mite more modern western than usual. He looked at his watch then looked up as the car parked in front of

Jake's pulled out from the curb and Amanda's station wagon pulled into the now-vacant space.

She got out of the wagon and walked toward the entrance.

"Wow!" said Ben.

"Meaning me, big boy?"

"I've never seen you so dressed up."

"You look pretty spiffy, yourself."

"My tuxedo-type western sport coat and rodeo Stetson . . . and, lady, are you the lucky one."

"I know . . . to have such a tall, handsome escort."

"No, I mean I had to park around the corner by the alley and you . . . right in front of Grauman's Chinese Theatre."

"Have you been waiting long?"

"Seems like hours . . . about thirty seconds."

Ben extended his left elbow.

"I've got what I was waiting for."

"Then, shall we dine?"

"The sign says 'Jake's Steaks.' "

"First the martini."

"A double — you favor gin or that vodka stuff?"

"Gordon's gin."

"I thought you looked like a gin man, sister."

" 'Lay on, Macduff . . . and damned be him who first cries, *Hold, enough!*' "

As they went in, a car parked across the street with a driver and its passengers pulled out into the street and made a U-turn.

The interior of Jake's Steaks, not too plain, not too fancy. Sawdust on the floor, fans on the ceiling. Tables and booths, about half-full.

A waitress, Glenda LeMay, experienced, with a commanding presence, carrying a pot of coffee, trod her way toward a corner booth where half a dozen cowboys and a couple of ladies obscured the occupants.

"Come on, folks," Glenda grunted, "let me through. Gangway!"

Some of the standees turned or backed away, revealing Ben and Amanda trying to finish their steaks while the interlopers were trying to talk rodeo to, and with, Ben.

"Which of the events is your favorite?"

"When did you win your first championship?"

"Which bronc was the meanest, roughest?"

"Is bulldoggin' as perilous as it looks?"

"Did you ever meet Tom Mix?"

"How about Fay Wray?"

"Who's the up-and-comer in the circuit?"

Ben tried to be polite when he got a chance to answer.

"Young fella named Casey Tibbs, no doubt about it."

"Fella, you're going to get a potful of hot java down your groin," Glenda warned, "if you don't move."

The fella moved.

"Why don't you people let these two finish their supper in peace? Skedaddle! Amscray!"

The crowd commenced to disperse amid parting pronouncements.

"See you later, ol' Ben."

"Nice visitin' with you, pard."

"Welcome back, Ben."

"Ay-di-os, amigo."

Glenda LeMay shook her head and poured coffee into the cups.

"How were the steaks?"

"Crowded," Amanda smiled.

"Sorry," Glenda shrugged, "we don't get many celebrities. Tex Ritter was the last one. You ever meet him?"

Ben nodded.

"Nice fella?"

"Very nice."

"Too bad Jake's not here tonight, told . . ."

"Yeah," Amanda said, "we miss him."

"Well, some other time." She started to

walk away. "Maybe he'll show up later."

Neither seemed particularly pleased at the prospect, especially Amanda. She looked at Ben.

"Sorry."

Ben shrugged and drank some coffee.

"Is this what it's like to be a champion?"

"No. Mostly, it's hotel rooms, horses, bumps, and broken bones . . ."

"Sounds dangerous."

"There's worse ways to make a living."

". . . And lonely?"

"Well, you do make friends, but you've got to keep moving."

"No family? Wife . . . kids?"

"Married to the rodeo . . . but not anymore."

"Ben, no details, but what about the girl you talked about at the pool? What was her name?"

"Called her 'Wisp.' "

"You said she's gone . . ."

"Died in an automobile accident."

"That's enough. Ben, I didn't . . ."

A cowboy approached with paper and pencil. Hesitated.

"Mr. Smith, would you sign this, please? Sure would appreciate it. To Dan Packer."

"Glad to."

Ben signed the paper, handed it back with

the pencil.

"Like I said, sure do appreciate it. Thank you, sir."

"You're welcome, Dan."

Dan Packer moved away, looking at the paper.

Amanda smiled.

"You seemed like you *were* glad to do it."

"Well, he seemed like a nice young fella."

"Let's take a walk in the park . . . before Jake shows up."

"Good idea."

"Well, serenity at last," Amanda smiled while they walked through the park. "The birds and the bees, and the jacaranda trees, who could ask for anything more?"

"Are those trees really jacarandas?"

"I don't know. It just came out."

"What about the 'anything more' part?"

"Well, you came along."

"How far along?"

"As far as Jake's . . . and the park."

"Back at Jake's, you asked me . . . 'No family? Wife . . . kids?' So, what about you?"

"I'm a veterinarian. You might have noticed."

"I noticed. What's it like to be a female veterinarian?"

"It's very satisfying, once you get used to

it. And the animals don't seem to object . . . unlike my husband."

Ben stopped walking. So did Amanda.

"Greg's a lawyer. Nice proper one. Successful, but he didn't like my making barn calls at all hours."

She started to walk. So did Ben.

"And coming home with bloody blouses, smelling of manure."

"Oh?"

"He preferred lace and perfume and high society. Found it in Denver. So, I'm not married anymore."

"Poor fella. Didn't he ever see you like you look tonight?"

"Maybe it's the jacarandas, maybe it's the company. Ben . . ."

"Yeah?"

"Maybe it's time we got back."

"Yeah."

Jake's Steaks was closed. Ben and Amanda stood close to her station wagon near a lamppost.

"Ma'am. That walk in the park. It was good."

"So was the dinner, but you didn't let me pay for it."

"Wouldn't look right."

He walked her to the driver's side of the

station wagon and opened the door. She got in.

"Looking right. That's important to you, isn't it?"

Ben shrugged. She started the engine.

"Next time, I'll fix something at my place . . . I don't care how it looks. Good night, Gallant Man."

Ben watched the station wagon disappear into the dark street then walked around the corner where his pickup was parked just past the alley.

He reacted to a sound, sounds, turned, and was hit a glancing blow with a heavy board. Men out of the dark. Fists into Ben's face and body, he almost dropped, but was braced to his feet by one of the attackers. Another swung the board again with a better connection this time, still, Ben did his best to fight back but finally fell. One of the assailants kicked Ben hard in the chest and was about to do more damage but a car screeched to a stop with headlights beaming.

The assailants ran toward their car parked in the alley as Sheriff Tom Granger sprang out of his cruiser, gun at the ready, stopped at the prone body as the screeching car caromed through and out of the far side of the alley.

It was either give chase or tend to the fallen victim.

CHAPTER TWENTY-THREE

At the sheriff's office, Ben was on the couch, conscious, still dazed, head and chest bandaged, and Doc ABC was finishing up.

Tom Granger and a deputy stood by.

"Steady, son," the doctor said.

The sheriff took a step closer.

"How bad, Doc?"

"Couple cracked ribs, bruises, slight concussion, maybe, he's a tough nut to crack."

The door swung open, and Amanda rushed in, moved toward Ben, who managed to sit up.

"Ben . . ."

"You're not going to ask if I'm all right, are you?"

"I'm not. Not now."

"How'd you hear about it?"

"Everybody's heard about it."

Through the open door the Krantz brothers scurried in followed by Skinny Dugan, who managed to push both brothers aside.

"Great thunderin' hallelujah!" Dugan waved an arm. "What happened? Who done it? Where did you get waylaid? How many . . ."

"Half dozen came out of a dark alley and jumped him," Granger said. "I was cruising on the night rounds and spotted the melee. It was either go after the bushwhackers or see to him, even though I didn't know who the him was. He looked pretty bad off at the time. Recognized Ben, wanted to take him to Doc's. He wouldn't go. So, I brought him here and called Doc."

"His pickup's right outside," Clem said.

"How'd it get here?" Claud asked.

"I went over and brought it," Deputy Shad Ingester answered.

"Doc," Amanda turned to Doc ABC, "all those bandages, tell me . . ."

"Easy, Amanda, I've taken worse falls."

"I don't think so."

"Tom," Skinny faced the sheriff, "I presume you didn't get their license number."

"License number? Hell, pardon me, Amanda, it was so dark I couldn't even tell the make of the car. It was a sedan."

"Too bad it didn't happen last night. I coulda got it in tomorrow's edition."

"Skinny, I don't want it in any edition. I'll

see to this."

"Ben," Amanda came closer. "You know who they are, don't you?"

"If he does, he won't say," Granger shook his head. "Don't you think I asked him? But I got a pretty good idea. Ben, I told you they play rough."

"So can I."

"He wants a rematch," Claud grinned.

"I'll bet on Ben," Clem grinned broader.

"You people can either stand around and talk to him all night or let him go home and get some rest."

"Thanks, Doc. I'd rather go home. Where's my keys?"

"I've got 'em right here." Deputy Ingester held the keys out in his palm.

"You're not gonna drive tonight," Doc ABC said. "Doctor's order."

"I'll drive him in my car, and that's another doctor's order."

"I'll follow you, make sure everything's okay," Claud volunteered.

"And I'll drive his pickup back," Clem added, "so it'll be there when he needs it."

"Ben, listen to me," Skinny leaned closer.

"I'm listening."

"If you change your mind about me printing what happened tonight, just let me know."

"Wait till your next edition, Skinny, maybe you'll have a better story."

Ben sat on the edge of his bunk. Amanda adjusted the bandage on his head.

The Krantz brothers stood in the middle of the cabin.

"I put the pickup keys over there on the table," Clem pointed.

Ben nodded.

"Anything else we can do?" Claud asked.

Ben shook his head.

Amanda's head indicated the door.

"We'll be around," Claud assured.

"Thanks, fellas."

"All in a day's day," both piped, then left Ben and Amanda in the cabin.

Silence.

"And I thought we already said good night," Ben smiled.

"With you, I never know, kiddo."

"Neither do I."

"Ben . . ."

"Yes, ma'am?"

"You know who they were, don't you?"

Ben looked straight ahead.

"Listen, I'm going to talk to Jim Deegan. He's a decent man. He'll . . . are you listening to me?"

His head turned toward her.

"I've been doing a lot of . . . listening."

"A lot of us have been working, trying to get some legislation . . ."

"Amanda."

"Yes?"

"You do that . . . and I'll do what I've got to do. Thank you, and . . . good night again."

"I'll come by tomorrow," she sighed. "You stay in bed."

Ben nodded.

"Do you think the sonofabitch recognized any of us?" Weegin rubbed at the pouch turning dark under his left eye.

Anson took a drink from the bottle of rye on the bunkhouse table.

"If he did he's got eyes like an owl."

"I'll tell you one thing," Dorn crowed, "I kicked the wind outta him. Must've busted up his rib cage."

Crane shook his head.

"If we had a few more minutes with him . . ."

"Yeah," Weegin went to the bottle again, "if the South had a few more cannonballs, they woulda won the war. But he's outta the way for a good long stretch. Let's get some Z's; we got a lotta work to do tomorrow."

■ ■ ■ ■

The summer sun was up early. So was the squad of delivery personnel with the *Beacon.*

The front page full of James Deegan and his speech at the cattlemen's association conference in Grandview, just as Laura Layton had dictated it to Skinny Dugan, with the addition of a few of the publisher's quixotic quips . . . and of course, no mention of the previous night's encounter.

The Chrysler, loaded with fishing gear and other necessities for the occasion, drove along the two-lane road with James Deegan at the wheel and a silent Jimmy beside him.

"Jimmy, you were pretty young, but do you remember the times you, your mom, and I went up to the lake a couple of times?"

"That was before we knew about my diabetes, wasn't it?"

"Yes, the last time was just before."

"I sorta remember, but I wish she was with us this time, too."

"Well, so do I, son, but you know she's back East with her work."

"I know."

"But you can call her from the lake or when we get back and tell her all about it.

And I brought a camera. We'll have some-body take pictures of both of us to send her."

"Dad . . ."

"Yes, Jimmy?"

"Will the three of us ever be together again?"

"Oh, sure, son. Lots of times."

"That's not what I mean."

"I know what you mean. But let's have some fun this time, okay?"

He waited for a response.

It came after a pause.

"Okay."

"Yes, this is Skinny Dugan, you know damn well it is. I recognized your voice, Miz Layton. Did you get that copy I had sent over to you by special early-morning mes-senger or is something else on your unpre-dictable mind?"

"My goodness, you astonish me."

"Why?"

"Because I always thought newspaper reporters wrote and spoke in short sen-tences."

"Not to fascinating women."

"Why, Skinny Dugan, coming from a tall, handsome man, I'm flattered."

"Don't be. I've been a liar all my life . . .

until now. What did you think of our story, if that's what you were calling about."

"It's not. Your special early-morning messenger told me what happened to Ben Smith last night. How did it happen?"

"It happened when some craven bastards jumped him from behind in the dark with baseball bats or reasonable facsimiles thereof."

"Sounds awful."

"It wasn't pretty."

"Is he in a hospital?"

"Anybody else would be, but he's tough, double tough. He's home."

"Do you think it would be all right to call him and . . ."

"I think it's best to let him be for the time being."

"Okay. Thanks for the update. I've taken up enough of your precious time."

"My time's not all that precious . . . So long, Miz Layton."

Glistening in the sunlight, the light plane, anchored by guy-wires, rested on the open flatland.

The truck, loaded with heavy tires and ropes on its bed, left a wake of dust as it rumbled toward the plane.

When the truck came to a stop, Norkey

and Weegin, carrying his shotgun, got out. They walked to the plane and began to detach the wires as the rest of the crew poured coffee into mugs from a large container and went about the business of preparing for the roundup.

They were all still sluggish from the aftermath of last night's encounter with Ben Smith and the bottle of rye. The pouch under Weegin's left eye had turned black, but not a word about what happened last night had been said to Norkey, nor did he ask any questions.

In the midst of Norkey's efforts, he heard something and looked up. Then Weegin and the crew did the same.

In the distance, Betsey with Ben, still bruised, in the saddle, several lariats around the saddle horn and a Winchester in the sheath.

"Damn!" Norkey growled, "I thought you . . ."

He didn't finish.

Riding like he rose from hell with his hair on fire — a ghost out of the past — a galloping revenger — Ben Smith burned the breeze — spurring at full speed toward his target.

For a time Norkey and the rest stood frozen, but not for long. Without slowing down, Ben let the reins drop over the saddle horn, pulled the Winchester out of its boot, leveled, and fired. Once, twice, three times.

One of the plane's tires sank flat — then the other.

Ben charged close, too close to Norkey and Weegin, who dropped the shotgun. Norkey found his feet, ran toward the truck, followed by Weegin.

Ben wheeled Betsey without slowing down.

Norkey, Weegin, and the rest jumped onto the bed of the truck. Anson revved the engine, jammed the stick in low, and roared away.

Ben gave pursuit to the racing truck with pounding hoofbeats against the grinding gears.

The distance started to widen. Ben cocked and fired the Winchester — three rapid-fire shots.

One shot hit the target.

A rear tire of the truck exploded. Anson fought for control, but the truck slammed into a huge rock and the hood sprang open as if to signal surrender.

Norkey jumped from the immobilized truck, staggered, and started to run.

He didn't get far.

Still on horseback, Ben circled the lariat

over his head, then the rope flew forward, dropping over Norkey's head and tightening around his knees, sending him hard to the ground.

Ben's Winchester was now leveled at the other men, who stood dazed as Anson wavered out of the truck.

Norkey made it to his feet, looked to Ben, and held up both hands.

"Listen," Norkey pleaded.

"I'm through listening. Just shut up," he aimed the rifle, "or I'll knock the knees off you."

But then Ben Smith paused and looked toward the fast oncoming truck, recognizing it . . . with a smile.

It didn't take but a few seconds for the truck to pull up and both Krantz brothers to jump out.

"Mornin', Ben," Claud greeted.

"See you've recovered," Clem nodded at the mustangers.

"Mornin', fellas. What are you doing way out here?"

"Just happened to pass by," Claud lied.

"You mean trespass," Norkey shouted.

"I told you to shut up," Ben pointed the rifle. "None of you say a word."

"We been around," Clem said.

"Thought we'd stop by and help you . . ."

"Tie things up?" Ben questioned.

"If that's what you got in mind," Claud said.

"What I've got in mind is to give 'em a dose of their own medicine."

CHAPTER TWENTY-FOUR

There hadn't been as much hoopla on the main street of Sheridan since the last Fourth of July parade.

Word had spread from the outskirts of town that another kind of parade was on its way.

No drums, trumpets, or trombones. No high-stepping majorettes or baton twirlers, or fireworks but a procession the likes of which the people of Sheridan, or anyplace else, had ever seen before.

They stood in doorways, sidewalks, and some in the streets, some on the body of pickups or on fenders of automobiles.

Kit Carson and Baldy. Dr. Amanda Reese in front of Mary's Cafe, Doc ABC, Walt and Tommy Swicegood from Walt's Hardware, Clay Sykes, Randy Rawlins, Gotch Tompkins, Dave Bergin, Skinny Dugan, Ty-Roan, Deputy Ingester, and Sheriff Tom Granger. Familiar and unfamiliar faces. Young boys and girls. Even a smattering of ladies from Candy Carr's Cat House.

A truck horn blared in the distance, heralding the entrance of what the spectators were waiting for, although they didn't quite know what they were about to see.

The Krantz brothers' truck advanced slowly down the middle of Main Street.

Gasps, squeals, and exclamations from both sides of the street when the spectators realized what they were witnessing.

Al Norkey, tied with a rope, breathless, haggard, hollow-eyed, trudged behind the truck, with the rest of the mustangers in the same shape, all bound, and each man dragging a rope tied to a hundred-pound tire.

Ben Smith on Betsey, close behind, the look on his face that of a man with just a trace of satisfaction after finishing a piece of work.

A smattering of remarks from faces in the crowd.

KIT CARSON: "Baldy, bring me a drink. Make it a double."

CLAY SYKES: "Who do I call first, *New York Times* or *Daily Variety*?"

WALT SWICEGOOD: "He's tough as nails!"

GOTCH TOMPKINS: "Shoulda asked

three-fifty for Betsey, maybe even more."

DOC ABC: "That man's a medical miracle."

RANDY RAWLINS: "I was first to welcome Ben back to Sheridan."

DAVE BERGIN: "This isn't a quiet little western town. It's a three-ring circus."

BLENDA (of Candy's Cat House): "Why can't I find a man like that?"

HORTENSE (same): " 'Cause there ain't enough to go around."

SKINNY DUGAN: "Told me the next edition'd be better."

SHERIFF GRANGER: "He said he could play rough, too."

Dr. Amanda Reese stood silent with moist eyes.

The crowd closed in as the parade came to a stop near the sheriff's office.

"Goddammit! Cut us loose, Sheriff . . . the sonofabitch tried to kill us!"

"I'll cut you loose, but I don't think he tried to kill you or you wouldn't be here."

"Ty-Roan! Go inside and grab a camera!" Skinny Dugan shoved his associate.

"Got one with me, Mr. Skinny."

"I don't give a damn what you think, Sheriff. We'll see what the judge thinks."

338

Norkey turned his face toward Ben Smith. "And you, you sonofabitch, I'll see you in court and in jail."

Ty Roan was clicking away with a camera.

Dr. Amanda Reese stood next to Betsey and looked up at Ben.

"I went out to see you this morning, but you were gone and so was Betsey. I should've known better . . . and so should you . . . you crazy lovable . . . Gallant Man."

"What is it, Pepper? There was a message at the desk to call you when we came back from fishing."

"A little good news, Mr. D, the rest not so good. How do you want it?"

"Start off easy."

"The article about you at the cattlemen's meeting in the *Beacon* was first-rate . . ."

"Okay, what about the 'not so good'?"

"Last night Ben Smith got jumped in the dark by a gang, got beat up pretty bad, real bad, Sheriff got there just in time, but they got away . . ."

"That is bad."

"It gets worse."

"How worse?"

"Seems he recognized the bushwhackers as Norkey's mustangers."

"Damn!"

"And that ain't the finish . . ."

"Go ahead . . . How's Smith? Is he . . ."

"Bad off as he was when he rode off this morning, shot up Norkey's plane and truck, rounded 'em all up including Norkey, tied 'em up draggin' hundred-pound tires, and made 'em march all the way into town and through Main Street."

"Jesus!"

"Norkey, what's left of him, threw a fit — from what I'm told, cursed a blue streak and made all kind of threats. Hated to bother you, but thought you'd want to know."

"You did right, Pepper."

"What're you gonna do?"

"Get back right away."

"Thought you might want to. How was the fishin'?"

"Lousy."

Deegan hung up and looked down at Jimmy.

"Sorry, son, but it seems we've got to get back to the Brawny. There's some trouble . . ."

"I heard you say something about Ben. Is he . . ."

"Ben got hurt some, but he's all right."

"I want to see him."

"You will, and we've got to tend to some

other things. Maybe we can come back later, so let's get ready to go."

"I'm ready, Dad."

The vast majority of citizens in Sheridan and the surrounding area already had seen or heard about Ben Smith's real-life roundup of mustangers and muggers that played like a heroic drama out of an action-packed western movie.

But these citizens of Sheridan and environs were the first to read about it on paper, thanks to the concerted effort to print the detailed story in the *Beacon*.

Excerpts from that front page:

MUSTANGS — TO BE OR NOT TO BE?
Cowboy Ben Smith Rides Again To Save Mustangs and Avenge Attack

Three time All-'Round Champion Cowboy Ben Smith, after a cowardly night attack by a gang of bushwhackers with heavy wooden weapons, fighting back while bleeding from head wounds and suffering broken ribs, patched-up by Dr. Andrew Baines Carter, also known as Doc ABC — refused to go to a hospital and next morning mounted his horse and armed with his trusty Winchester rifle rode out with two avowed intentions: save mustangs and avenge the dastardly attack on himself.

Ben Smith accomplished both endeavors. He single-handedly via Winchester disabled the mustangers' chase plane and pursuit truck, roped and tied the varmints to heavy tires, like they do to mustangs, and marched them through Main Street for all the good citizens to see and cheer.

The leader of the craven gang ranted and raved and promised court action.

It is our opinion that justice has been and will be served.

The names of those mustangers and muggers are not worthy to appear here.

The story was picked up by newspapers and broadcasts and spread like wildfire across a grassy plain on a windy day. Other headlines and lead stories in other places:

Hollywood, California — *Daily Variety:*
**COWBOY CRUSADER BEN SMITH
VS MUSTANG SLAUGHTER**

Dallas, Texas — *Herald Examiner:*
RODEO RIDER RESCUES MUSTANGS

Abilene, Kansas — *Plain Dealer:*
COWBOY CAVALIER ON HORSEBACK

Toledo, Ohio — *Toledo Blade:*
COWBOY TAKES DEAD AIM
ON MUSTANGERS

New York City — *New York Examiner:*
CHAMPION COWBOY
CHAMPION OF MUSTANGS

Saint Louis, Missouri — *Morning News:*
BEN SMITH CHARGED
WITH MURDER ATTEMPT

"Call for Ben Smith from Mr. Will Rogers, California."

"This is Smith."

"Ben, ol' roustabout, what'd you do, hire a publicity agent?"

"My friend, that kind of publicity I don't need."

"I know that, but it's for a good cause, and I'm all for it and you."

"Thanks."

"Same goes for Tom and Buck, the Gower Gulch Gang rides again, but we can't make it there, Tom's out with his circus, and Buck's on location. Soon as I'm done with this picture, I'm flying to Alaska on an expedition with Wiley."

"I wish I could be with you."

"So do I. First off, do you need any dinero?"

343

"No, thanks, I'm okay."

"Second, you got a good lawyer?"

"Skinny Dugan, you know him, don't you?"

"We go back to hard times together."

"He's talking about a fella named Sam Elko."

"Couldn't do better, an old Oklahoma law wrangler, knows the territory. I'll call him. Got an idea."

"Will, I just want to . . ."

"Hey, never mind, they're callin' me back to the fake cabin here on Stage 17. So long, you ol' sourdough."

"So long, Will."

James Deegan and Al Norkey were in Deegan's study, but Norkey's posture was not the same.

"Just tell me one thing, Norkey, was it your crew that beat up Ben Smith?"

"Look, all I got to say is that what they do, or don't do, on their own time is none of my business."

"In this case, I think it is."

"Well, I don't . . . you know what that sonofabitch done to us."

"I said I'd pay for the damage on the plane and your truck."

"That's not enough. I'm talking about

what he done to *us*. I talked to the prosecuting attorney, and I might end up with the Little Brawny."

"You're dreaming."

"Yeah, well, this dream might come true. You and me might end up being neighbors."

"That's not the way it'll end up."

"We'll see. I was just doin' what you paid and instructed me to do, and he was trespassin' and shooting us up."

"That's one version . . ."

"It's my version, and I'm stickin' to it!"

"Okay. I tried to talk sense to you."

"I'm talking dollars and cents and a lot more."

"Norkey, you're finished around here."

"Maybe around here but not in court. You'll be subpoenaed . . . as a witness for the prosecution . . . *Mr.* Deegan."

As Norkey slammed the door, the phone rang.

"Hello."

"Mr. Deegan, this is your neighbor Mrs. Layton."

"Laura, I'm in no mood. If you're calling for me to thank you for that story you leaked to Skinny Dugan . . ."

"How do you know it was I?"

"Sherlock Holmes's deductive reasoning. Elementary, Watson, ol' girl."

"Go ahead, ol' boy."

"You're the only one here who was there and knows Skinny Dugan."

"What about Dave Bergin?"

"Never in a million years."

"You're so right."

"Now, if you want to talk about selling the Layton Ranch . . ."

"Not in the mood you're in."

"Then I'll take a rain check."

"Makes sense. See you at the trial. After that, we'll see who sells what, or anything. So long, Sherlock."

Laura Layton hung up.

Jimmy, followed by Pepper, walked in through the open door.

"Noon meal's on the table, Mr. D."

"Dad, when can I see Ben? You said . . ."

"I know, son, but he's still recuperating, and with the trial coming up . . ."

"I want to see him before that."

"You will, I promise. But you've got to eat and take your medicine, and I've got to call your mother and bring her up to date about all this. Okay?"

"I guess."

Laura Layton pulled the Packard to a stop in front of the cabin door and honked the horn.

346

Ben came out and so did Dr. Reese.

"Howdy, Mrs. Layton."

"Sorry to interrupt your little tête-à-tête."

"Come on in."

"No, thanks. I was just on my way to see Dave Bergin, thought I'd stop by for a minute and see how you are doing."

"Doing fine."

"Also, thought you might want to know something."

"What?"

"Word is Norkey's making noises about taking over the Little Brawny after the trial."

"Over my dead body."

"I figured you might say something like that. By the way, need a little loan? No interest. No due date."

"Nope. But thanks."

"So long . . . and, Doctor, take care of your patient. He's a good man."

"He is, and I will, Mrs. Layton."

The Packard drove away.

"What the hell's going on out there, a replay of the gunfight at the O.K. Corral?"

"Liz . . ."

"Or maybe Custer's Last Stand?"

"Liz . . ."

"I tried to reach you up at the lake, and they said you left hours ago. I've been in a

347

meeting since then."

"I was just going to call you . . ."

"When? After dark? Well, it's getting pretty damn dark back here already . . . let me talk to Jimmy."

"Jimmy's asleep."

"So early?"

"It's been a long day. We got up early to go fishing, drove back here, then there's that business with Norkey and that cowboy . . . he was pretty tired, so . . ."

"So, has he taken his shot?"

"Yes, ma'am. Look, he was just a little tired, to tell the truth, so am I . . ."

"And so am I, tired of this whole mess. I think Jimmy ought to come home."

"This is his home, too."

"Some home!"

"Liz, I asked him about going back, but he wants to stay, part of it is that he wants to be here when that cowboy goes to trial."

"Then maybe I should come out there, so we can be together."

"I think that would be good, the three of us together."

"I meant Jimmy and me."

There was silence.

"All this publicity, it's not good for any of us, newspapers, radio . . . Winchell just closed his broadcast, even mentioned your name, said something like, 'The shoot-out took place over the slaughter of mustangs at a ranch called the Big Brawny owned by a gadfly rancher named James Deegan who spends some of his time killing mustangs and the rest of his time at various places back East involved in a string of enterprises while separated from his industrious wife, who runs a successful design business' . . . and then as usual, Winchell closed with: 'Lotions of love.' Now, I tell you . . . this has got to stop, period."

"I'll do my best, exclamation mark."

"So will I. Good night, Jimbo."

"Good night."

She hung up.

After the commercial, the newscaster continued.

"Three time All-'Round Rodeo Champion Cowboy, Ben Smith, took to the saddle with his Winchester and wreaked havoc on a gang of men who were rounding up wild horses. Mustangs whose destiny was to be made into pet food. By the way, are you enjoying your dinner tonight? Well, so is your pet dog as a result of the brutal pursuit and slaughter of these legendary steeds by these so-called mustangers. Ben Smith rounded up the gang and tied them to heavy truck tires as mus-

tangers do to the horses. Worn and weary, the men finally made their way back to . . . prefer charges, including attempted homicide, against rodeo champion Ben Smith.

"This is Edward R. Murrow saying good night, and good luck."

Sheriff Tom Granger reached down and snapped off the radio in the jury room of the old building that housed the courthouse, sheriff's office, and jail. Granger turned and faced the people in the room.

"Right . . . and good luck to you, Mr. Smith."

Beside Ben, the rest included Amanda Reese, Skinny Dugan, Doc ABC, and the Krantz brothers.

"They've thrown the book at you, Ben," the sheriff went on. "Assault and battery — destruction of property — intent to commit murder . . ."

"Is that all?" Ben smiled.

"No, that's not all; you're going to stand trial for that and a lot more."

"Then I'll stand trial."

"Where's that lawyer you got us here to see, Skinny?" Granger wanted to know.

"He should be here by now. Ty-Roan drove out to the airport to bring him. Ol' Sam Elko said he wanted to talk to you folks for a few minutes."

"How well do you know ol' Sam Elko?" Doc ABC asked.

"Well enough, ever since July 1st, 1898. So does Will Rogers."

Amanda leaned forward in her chair.

"Has he handled cases anything like Ben's?"

"All kinds of cases . . . he's represented everybody from bank robbers to bank presidents, from poachers to preachers . . . walks with a cane . . . got shot by one of his clients."

"That's not a very strong recommendation," Amanda noted.

"Got that client free on a plea of insanity."

The door opened.

Ty Roan took a step in and pointed the way in for Sam Elko.

"Howdy, folks, sorry to keep you all waitin'. Skinny, Will sends his howdys."

Elko was not a young man, but not as old as Skinny Dugan. With a briefcase in the right hand and cane in the left, Elko moved into the room. From his speech, vintage vested suit, and manner, it was evident that he was a man of the West.

"Evenin', Elk," Skinny Dugan rose. "I was just about to tell these folks how we met."

"I know of no power on earth or sky that

could ever stop you, so go ahead while I torch up a cigar, but make it brief this time."

"Us Rough Riders were from every state and territory west of the Mississippi. We had taken our share of losses, but we knew if we made the charge to the top of San Juan Hill the day would be ours and so would the war. I was a lieutenant then, in charge of our brigade. About to give the command, and this young fella rides up to me.

" 'You Lieutenant Dugan?' he asks.

" 'No, you dumb shavetail, these gold bars on my shoulder denote a member in good standing of the Elks club. And who the hell are you?'

" 'Elko, Corporal Sam Elko.'

" 'Are you trying to be comical?'

" 'No, sir, Sam Elko, replacement for one of the wounded . . . afraid I'd be late for the charge.'

" 'Yeah? Well, I'm afraid you're just in time. Now, when I give the order we charge up that rise, guns ablaze, and you ride right behind me.'

" 'No, sir . . .'

" 'What?! Why, I . . .'

" 'I'll be right beside you.'

"Well, it was one hallelujah of a set-to, but we won the day and the war . . . to the cry of 'Remember the *Maine*.'

"And that's how we met, right, ol' Elk?"

"Well, that's one version. Your associate, Mr. Roan," Elko pointed to his briefcase on the table, "gave me your articles on Mr. Smith. You still write like a graduate of newspaper school."

"I never did graduate."

"I meant backwoods newspaper school, but let's get on with the reason I wanted to talk, just for a few minutes, about your court appearances; from what I gather, you'll all be called, even the sheriff here, which isn't all that usual on behalf of one of my clients."

"Mr. Elko," Sheriff Granger smiled, "sounds like you don't have too much use for officers of the law."

"On the contrary, some of my favorite clients have been officers of the law. But what I wanted to emphasize is this, when you get to the stand don't say too much, don't try to debate; just try to answer 'yes' or 'no,' or something deleterious to Ben here might slip out. In other words, don't give the opposition any ammunition. From what I've been able to calculate, they've got plenty of ammunition already."

"Mr. Elko," Ben smiled a wistful smile, "you don't appear to be exactly positive about this case."

"Mr. Smith, I'll be exactly positive when we win this case."

"Mr. Elko," Dr. Amanda Reese arched an eyebrow, "do you mean 'when' or 'if'?"

"Dr. Reese, I always mean what I say, particularly to a beautiful young lady. Just a minute, I've got to retorch this cigar."

He did, took a puff, then pointed to the Krantz brothers, who sat silent during the conference.

"As for the two of you Krantzes, which one is Clem?"

"I'm Clem."

"I'm Claud."

"Well, Claud and Clem, I've got to compliment both of you."

"Why?" both of them together.

"Because at this powwow you didn't say a word, and sometimes silence is golden," Elko semicircled his cigar at the rest of the people. "Remember that in court when it comes to the prosecutor and the judge."

"Do you know our circuit judge?" Doc ABC asked.

"Been before him before."

"How did you make out?"

"He's a fair man. Does that answer your question?"

"Not exactly."

"Well, ol' Judge Clarence Aikins likes

publicity. That's why he hurried this case before it loses steam . . . looks somewhat like that cowboy actor Harry Carey, even though Carey was born in New York."

"So was William S. Hart," Skinny Dugan added.

"Yes, thank you, Skinny."

"And I want you all to know that my friend Elk is handling this case pro bono, that means 'without fee.' "

"Oh, no, you're not, sir," Ben said. "I pay for what I get."

"Don't worry, son, I'll get paid plenty from other cases when — I repeat — *when* we win . . . That's all, folks. I'll be conferring with my client before the adjudication."

Sam Elko left the remainder of his cigar in an ashtray, picked up his briefcase, and cane and walked toward the door, then turned.

" 'Once more unto the breach, dear friends, once more.' "

CHAPTER TWENTY-FIVE

It was not a day like any other day in Sheridan.

The population had nearly doubled. They came from all parts of the state, and some from other parts of the country to see, or at least be there, during the trial of Mustangers v. Smith. Reporters, ranchers, strangers, and stragglers. Some with vested interest, others with a damn good excuse to escape from the humdrum.

There was not nearly enough space in the old courtroom, but a speaker had been set up outside of the building for the benefit of those who wanted to get away from the international news or goings-on at home and hearth.

James Deegan had arranged a brief phone call between Ben Smith and Jimmy, with a promise that his son could attend the hearing when Deegan had been subpoenaed to testify. Ben had assured the boy that he was doing fine and that "everything would come right," even though he was not so sure that it would.

Some businesses opened early and flourished with people in line to get in, places like Kit Carson's and Mary's Cafe. Other places, including Randy's Independent Gas, Walt's Hardware, Martini's Barber Shop, and Al's Emporium, didn't bother to open at all. The proprietors were among the first to assemble for the court proceedings.

Word spread warning the populace to be on the lookout for pickpockets. There was an influx of hobos and panhandlers.

Up and down Main Street walked a man on stilts, dressed in full cowboy regalia.

There were grifters and gamblers. If you were a betting man, you could lay a bet two-to-one that Ben Smith would go to jail. There were balloons and popcorn for sale on the street but prohibited inside the courtroom.

"I could use a cigarette," Amanda said.

"Thought you didn't smoke." Ben blinked.

"I don't, under ordinary circumstances, but these aren't exactly ordinary circumstances."

Sheriff Tom Granger walked across the jury room and held out an opened pack of Camels.

"No thanks," she shook her head.

"I must be hearing things," the sheriff smiled, then shrugged.

"I said I 'could,' not I 'would,' " Dr. Reese smiled.

"Now, there's a lady with discipline," Ben also smiled.

"Either that or she can't make up her mind." Granger walked back to the far side of the room near the door, allowing the two a little more togetherness while they were waiting for the trial to begin.

"Ben," she asked, "how do you do it?"

"Do what?"

"Keep so calm."

"That's on the outside. On the inside maybe it's a little different diagnosis, Doctor."

"I don't believe that, but in that case, I've got a prescription. You want to hear it?"

"Sure."

"Well, it goes . . ."

There was a knock on the door.

Granger opened it just a crack and listened, then turned and faced Ben.

"Mr. Deegan and his son would care to come in and see you for a minute."

Ben nodded and smiled.

James Deegan walked in with his hand on Jimmy's shoulder.

"Ben, Jimmy wanted to wish you luck and shake your hand. He said he couldn't do that when he talked to you on the phone."

Ben nodded and extended his arm.

"Good to see you, pardner."

Jimmy's eyes widened, and he thrust out his small hand.

"Good luck, Ben."

"Thanks, cowboy, we've had some skookum times together, and there'll be more."

"Will we go riding again and maybe see Black?"

"Just as sure as spittin' . . . you keep in shape."

"I will," Jimmy nodded.

James Deegan's arm went to his son's shoulder and they walked out the door.

Before Granger closed it, Sam Elko, cane in hand, strolled in.

"What ho, apothecaries . . . we three or four meet again. Ben, just do 'er like you did when we talked it over. It'll be . . ."

Joe Higgins walked through the open door.

"What is this, a convention?" Elko barked. "Who the hell are you?"

"Joe Higgins, foreman, Big Brawny, pardon the interruption, Mr. Elko, but Mr. Smith said one of his attackers hit him with something like a pickax handle. Happened to find this among Weegin's belongings, thought it might be used as evidence."

Higgins held up a heavy, long-handled pickax shaft.

"There are thousands of them in this whole wide world," Elko said, "but maybe I can find some use for this one. Sheriff, think you can get this one under our table without being . . . conspicuous?"

"Counselor," Granger smiled, "it's just become my walking stick."

"Then let's get a move on."

"Can you all wait outside for just a minute?" Amanda asked. "I just want to say something to Ben."

"Go right ahead, ma'am," Sam Elko said. "Women always get the last word."

Sheriff Granger opened the door.

Doc ABC, carrying his medical bag, walked in.

"That was very opportune of you, Sheriff, opening the door for me before I knocked."

"Didn't open it for you, Doc, but why the medicine bag? You doing a little advertising in court this morning?"

Doc ABC took a step inside.

"On a hot day like this I'm always prepared like a Boy Scout, in case like some summers ago, some lady faints to the floor

360

right here in court. Any of you folks care for a salt tablet or two," he held up the black bag, "as a little preventative?"

There was a unanimous negative shaking of heads.

"Well," Doc ABC shrugged, "as the saying goes, 'see you in court.' " He turned and walked into the hall.

The rest followed, leaving Ben and Amanda in the room.

"Ben, remember I said I've got a prescription?"

"I do."

"Want to know what it is?"

"Go ahead."

"It goes like this. We get married to each other . . . *pronto.*"

"After the trial I might have to go to prison."

"So what? If you can't break out, I'll break in. And no matter what happens, I'll be waiting for you at the Little Brawny . . . You like Dr. Reese's prescription?"

"You don't have to put it in writing."

The four ceiling fans in the tribunal were all spinning but to little effect against the summer sun, seated and standing human bodies crammed into too little surroundings.

The judge's bench and chair rested on a raised platform, with the clerk and bailiff, with small tables on the floor at either side.

There was a jury section, but no jurors, as the verdict would be decided by Circuit Judge Clarence Aikins.

Two larger tables faced the judge's bench.

On one side sat Ben and Sam Elko, on the other table, Al Norkey and the prosecuting attorney, a thin young man with steel-rimmed glasses — Warren LeRoy.

Press personnel were accommodated in a special section with a good view of the proceedings.

Among the spectators: Dr. Amanda Reese; Skinny Dugan; James and Jimmy Deegan; Pepper; Dave Bergin; Laura Layton; Doc ABC; Clay Sykes; the Krantz brothers; Kit Carson, who had left the saloon in care of Baldy; Weegin and the mustanger crew; and a bevy of other familiar faces.

The clerk became aware of a door opening; he stood and announced in a clerical voice.

"All rise!"

A solemn-faced Judge Aikins, in his judicial robe, walked from the door to his impressive chair, sat, adjusted the spectacles on his nubbin nose, peered briefly at the audience, and rapped his oversized gavel.

"Be seated," the clerk stated.

Those who had seats sat.

After the usual judicial overture, Judge Aikins got to the court's mission.

"How does the defendant plead?"

A swift answer shot back from Sam Elko.

"My client is innocent, Your Honor. He's been the victim of a dastardly . . ."

"A simple 'guilty' or 'not guilty' will suffice, Mr. Elko. You'll have sufficient opportunity to plead your case."

"I'll do that with vigor, Your Honor — *not guilty* — not by a busted cinch!"

"Let us proceed in an orderly fashion. Make your opening statements and make them brief, say, thirty seconds apiece. You'll have ample time to yap-a-dee-yap later as the hearing and the heat of the day progress. You first for the prosecution, Mr. LeRoy."

"Your Honor, we will prove beyond the shadow of a doubt the defendant, Benjamin Smith, is an unmitigated rogue, an inveterate provocateur, a brawler, hothead, trespasser, destroyer of private property, gunman, attempted murderer with utter disregard of the law and civilized conduct. Furthermore . . ."

"Furthermore, that's enough cabbage to chew on or we'll be here all summer. Take your seat, Mr. LeRoy, and allow the defense to confabulate . . . briefly."

Sam Elko rose, bowed courteously.

"If it please Your Honor, we will prove that Mr. Ben Smith, three time All-'Round Champion Cowboy, is good at ropin', ridin' . . . and self-defense, plus he has an abidin' compassion for defenseless horses."

Sam Elko resumed his seat.

"That'll settle the dust on the preliminaries. Mr. Prosecutor, call your first witness."

"The prosecution call Miss Kit Carson."

Kit Carson took the oath and the stand.

"Miss Carson. Is it not a fact that Ben Smith engaged in a brawl in front of your emporium?"

"The fact is that he disengaged a couple of aggressors."

"We'll see about that. That's all, Miss Carson."

"I've got more."

"That's all!"

"Do you care to cross? Mr. Elko?" the judge pointed at the defense table.

"No questions. Thank you," Elko said.

"Call your next witness."

"Claud Krantz."

Took the oath and the stand.

"Mr. Krantz, while you and your brother —"

"Twin brother."

"— twin brother are not charged as accomplices to the crime Ben Smith committed against Mr. Norkey and . . ."

Sam Elko rose.

"I object to the prosecutor's use of the word 'crime.' . . . No crime has been proved."

"Objection sustained. Mr. LeRoy, find another word . . . and not a synonym."

"Situation," LeRoy submitted.

"Proceed."

"You and your brother witnessed the 'situation' at the Big Brawny between Mr. Smith and Mr. Norkey."

"From a distance, we was just passin' through."

"You mean trespassing? Well, never mind that. You two did assist Smith in the 'situation'?"

"From where we were, he didn't need much assistance. Just tied things up, Clem and me."

" 'Tied' is the operative word."

"Operative? If you say so."

"I say so. That's all, Mr. Krantz."

"I want to cross." Elko rose.

"Proceed, Mr. Elko."

"Mr. Krantz, let's go back to Kit Carson's emporium. Did you two approach Mr. Smith and make untoward remarks about him and ladies within earshot?"

"Yes, we did, I'm sorry to say."

"How much do you weigh?"

"Two hundred twenty-five."

"And your brother?"

"Two hundred twenty."

"Let's add up. That's four hundred forty-five, I calculate. How much would you say Mr. Smith weighs?"

"About a hundred eighty."

"Would you say that's a fair fight?"

"Not when ol' Ben went to it."

"He disengaged both of you in self-defense?"

"In less time than it takes to tell."

"That's all, Mr. Krantz."

"Could I say one more thing?"

"Go ahead."

"We apologized before we went to jail."

"Both of you are consummate gentlemen. Dismissed."

There was a favorable reaction from the spectators.

Judge Aikins leveraged his gavel.

"The court will not tolerate demonstrations from any spectators on either side of the case. You may continue, Mr. LeRoy."

"I shall, Your Honor, with the most pertinent witnesses for the prosecution."

"It's about time. Fire away."

"Call Mr. Horace Weegin."

Horace Weegin took the oath and the stand.

"Mr. Weegin, isn't it true that on a prior occasion, while you and the crew were performing your duties on the Big Brawny, Ben Smith approached you in an aggressive, make that a threatening, attitude, and while the two of you were conversing in a quiet manner, he suddenly struck you without provocation, felling you to the ground?"

"That's true."

"And on another occasion, while your plane was being repaired, he came upon Mr. Norkey and you with threats against the mustanger roundup and all of you personally?"

"He sure did. And he meant it."

"Thank you, Mr. Weegin. Your witness, Mr. Elko."

"Just one query at this time. Mr. Weegin, where were you at the time the alley assault on Ben Smith took place?"

"I'll tell you where . . ."

LeRoy on his feet.

"Irrelevant, Your Honor. Mr. Weegin . . ."

"I'll tell you where I was. Me and my crew were playing poker at Kit Carson's Saloon that night."

"I repeat, irrelevant, Your Honor . . ."

"In that case," Elko interrupted, "I reserve the right to recall the witness."

"In that case, the prosecution calls Mr. Norkey, another victim of Ben Smith's assault."

Sam Elko leaped to his feet.

"Your Honor, I object strenuously to the prosecutor's unproven verbiage such as 'victim' and 'assault' when none of those inflammatory remarks has been sustained by any inkling of proof!"

"Objection sustained. Mr. Prosecutor, do try to employ kinder and gentler descriptions of the unpleasantness until such is proved."

"I'll try, Your Honor."

"You damn better," Judge Aikins muttered.

"Sir? Did you say something, Your Honor?"

"I said 'proceed.' "

Al Norkey took the oath and the stand.

"Mr. Norkey, prior to the 'situation' for which Mr. Smith appears in court, was there another 'situation' where and when he came upon you in an unneighborly manner?"

"Yes, at a hangar at the airport where and when my plane underwent repairs for a leaking line."

"Would you kindly relate the gist of his . . . comments?"

"He warned me about proceeding with the mustang roundup and mentioned one horse in particular, the black leader."

"That you shot and nearly killed!" Elko shouted. "And he took care of!"

"Your Honor," LeRoy exclaimed, "must we suffer these interruptions while questioning . . ."

"No, you must not. Mr. Elko, you will have your say when you cross."

"I defer, Your Honor."

"Go on, Mr. LeRoy."

"Smith ended up by threatening that if I proceeded he was not going to see Mr. Deegan — but he didn't call him 'mister,' just Deegan — or anybody else, he was going to see me."

"Later on, you did proceed, and he did come to see you . . . but not just to see, he came on horseback with a rifle. Isn't that true?"

"It is."

"And he fired shot after shot at you and your crew while you . . ."

Elko was on his feet again.

"My client hits what he aims at, and he wasn't aiming at you and your crew!"

"Is that an objection, Mr. Elko?" Judge Aikins smiled.

"You bet your boots!"

"Overruled. Sit down, Mr. Elko."

"After he fired at you, did he destroy your plane and truck?"

"That's right."

"And did the defendant rope and tie you to a hundred-pound tire?"

Elko jumped up again.

"All seven of you dwarfs?!"

"Sit down, Mr. Elko."

"We've already established that the Krantz brothers were there, and you lugged those tires all the way to town and through Main Street."

"That's right, till we got to the sheriff . . ."

"Then you were untied and made charges."

"Right again."

"You may cross, Mr. Elko."

"Where were you and your hired thugs when my client was jumped and beat up in a dark alley here in this peaceful village?"

LeRoy leaped up.

"Your Honor, I object. Mr. Norkey is not on trial here!"

"That's questionable, Your Honor," Elko shot back fast, "but what goes around, comes around."

"Objection sustained, and no more epigrams, Mr. Elko. Proceed."

"No more questions from the defense at this time, Your Honor."

"The prosecution calls Mr. James Deegan."

James Deegan took the oath and the stand.

"Mr. Deegan, are you the owner of the Big Brawny?"

"Yes."

"And where were you, sir, when the assault took place on the Big Brawny?"

Elko was up.

"Object! There is no proof that any assault took place anywhere except on my client!"

"Rephrase, Your Honor. When the *incident* took place on the Big Brawny?"

"I had left that morning to take my son on a fishing trip."

"And you were subpoenaed to testify today?"

"Yes."

"And was Mr. Norkey in your employment, doing his job at that time?"

"Yes."

"Under your instructions?"

"Well, not exactly under my instructions . . . yes."

"And did you find Mr. Norkey to be

thorough and diligent in the execution of his duties?"

Without rising this time, Elko blurted.

"*Execution and torture* of defenseless horses!"

"Mr. Elko," the judge pointed, "you're getting skin-close to contempt."

"Thank you, Your Honor. Mr. Deegan, was Mr. Norkey on the Big Brawny with your permission, performing a legal and necessary service in order to preserve the cattle from which you, and dozens of people who work for you, make a living?"

James Deegan paused. Jimmy was looking at him and sinking lower in his seat.

"Yes or no? Please, Mr. Deegan."

"Yes."

"Thank you. Now, before you left with your son, did Mr. Smith seek permission, or did you grant him permission, to trespass?"

Elko got up.

"I object! Trespass, my . . ."

"Rephrase. To come on your property?"

Deegan looked toward his son, then reluctantly replied, barely audible.

"No."

"Louder, please, Mr. Deegan."

"No."

Jimmy rose from his seat and ran out of the courtroom. Pepper followed him.

LeRoy persisted.

"Just a few more questions, Mr. Deegan."

Deegan turned toward the judge and rose.

"Excuse me, Your Honor, my son's not well. Diabetic. With your permission, I'll be back as soon as possible."

"Permission granted."

Deegan was on his way.

Sam Elko stood.

"We all hope everything turns out well for Mr. Deegan and his son. Until he gets back and continues to testify, may I call Dr. Carter to the stand briefly, Your Honor?"

"Mr. Prosecutor?"

"No objection."

Doc ABC walked toward the stand, staggered, wobbled, twisted, and sank, hitting his head hard on the witness chair, then collapsed to the floor.

Dr. Amanda Reese was the first to get there, Sheriff Granger right behind her.

"Get him to the jury room, on the table," Amanda ordered. "Somebody bring his medical bag."

In the hall near the entrance, Jimmy sat in a chair. His father and Pepper hovered over him.

"I'm all right, Dad. I just don't want to hear any more."

"Just sit here and take it easy for a few minutes. I'll stay with you. Then, Pepper, drive Jimmy home, give him his medicine, and let him rest in bed for a while. I'll get there soon as I can. There's a few things I want to clear up here."

"Sure thing, Mr. D."

Judge Aikins sounded his gavel.

"The court will adjourn for noon meal for an hour, make it an hour and a half. We'll resume where we left off at that time . . . I trust."

"Ben," Elko picked up his cane, "I got some business to tend to."

"Okay, Sam. I'll see how the doc is doing."

"Try to get something to eat. A man ought to eat every chance he gets."

When Ben turned, Laura Layton was standing near him.

"Ben, if there's anything I can do . . ."

"Can't think of anything right now, ma'am, but good of you to ask."

Still on the table in the jury room, Doc ABC had little more than regained consciousness after Dr. Reese had bandaged his head, applied cool compresses, and inlaid a couple salt tablets into his mouth.

"Where am I? What happened?"

Skinny Dugan took a step closer.

"Some old woman fainted to the floor."

"Go to hell, Skinny."

"Not yet."

Ben Smith had entered just in time to smile and comment.

"Well, I see everything's come back to normal."

CHAPTER TWENTY-SIX

Judge Clarence Aikins employed his gavel.

"Court is in session. Mr. Deegan, how's your son doing?"

"Much better, thank you."

"Do you care to proceed with your testimony?"

Warren LeRoy was up.

"That's not necessary, Your Honor. The prosecution hereby rests."

Elko stood.

"Well, in that case, the defense calls Mr. Deegan for cross."

James Deegan took the stand.

"Now, Mr. Deegan . . ."

"Excuse me, Counselor, before you question me, may I make a statement?"

Elko glanced at Ben, who shrugged affirmation.

Warren LeRoy stood.

"Your Honor, I want to confer with my witness."

"That won't be necessary, Mr. LeRoy, I know what I want to say, and I want to say it."

"What about it, Your Honor?" Elko waved his cane.

"It's up to the witness."

"I don't want to confer. I want to make a statement."

"You go ahead and do that, Mr. Deegan," Elko responded.

Slowly, but emphatically, Deegan proceeded.

"Mr. Smith has been welcomed to come to the Big Brawny as often as he chooses. And he has been of great assistance to my son in the ways of ranch life and in self-reliance. I am deeply grateful for such attention, wisdom, and instruction from the time my son and I first met Mr. Ben Smith, right up to now."

"No further questions." Elko bowed and said, "Thank you, Mr. Deegan."

As Deegan walked straight to his seat, Warren LeRoy glared at him all the way.

"I call Dr. Carter to the stand," Elko announced.

This time, Doc ABC took the oath and the stand.

"I hope you're fully recovered, Doctor; howsoever, I'll be brief."

"Go ahead with the inquisition. You'll see how fully recovered I am."

"Yes, indeed. Mr. Ben Smith was brought to you by Sheriff Granger in what condition after being attacked and savagely beaten by a gang of bushwhackers?"

"Your Honor!" LeRoy reared.

"Ease up on some of that lingo, Mr. Elko."

"Make it up to 'in what condition.' "

"Mr. Smith had sustained multiple bleeding bruises on body and face, a couple cracked ribs and other damage to his rib cage, a prominent welt on his back, caused by a blunt instrument, and a severe wound to his head by the same weapon, causing concussion."

"From your medical experience, further describe the weapon."

"Oh, a heavy board, or baseball bat, or an ax handle. He should've landed in a hospital but wouldn't hear of it."

"Thank you, Doctor. That'll be all, unless Mr. LeRoy . . ."

"No, thank you. I've heard quite enough."

"I recall Mr. Horace Weegin to the stand."

Weegin took the stand.

"Mr. Weegin, I remind you, you are still under oath. Now, earlier you claimed that on that evening you were in the bunkhouse playing cards with your crew."

LeRoy was up.

"I remind the court as before, that neither Mr. Norkey, nor anybody else is under trial."

"Mr. Elko, where are you going with this question?"

"Motivation, Your Honor, bear with me."

"Barely, Mr. Elko, but go on. We'll see where it leads."

"Now, Mr. Weegin, we have multiple witnesses present who will testify that earlier, I repeat, earlier, your crew was drinking at Miss Kit Carson's emporium, until a car horn honked from outside, at which time you all responded by making a hurried exit. And this took place before, I repeat, before, shortly before the dastardly attack on Mr. Smith took place."

"I don't remember, maybe I did."

"Then you were not playing poker at the time of the attack!"

"I don't know. I wasn't looking at my watch."

Elko made his way to the table with his cane, sat it on top, and from under the table, retrieved the pickax handle. He came back to the stand and held forth the handle.

"Mr. Weegin, I am hereby returning to you your pickax handle."

"Uh, I . . ."

LeRoy was up.

"How do we know this particular ax handle even belongs to Mr. Weegin?"

"Well, sir, it has smeared bloodstains and was found among Weegin's belongings . . . and I will prove that . . . if this goes any further. Motivation. Retaliation from Mr. Smith, who recognized this culprit. That's where I was going, Your Honor." Elko turned back to Weegin. "And you can have your pickax handle back after further examination of the damn thing. That's all at this time. Dismissed."

LeRoy stood, took a deep breath.

"Then may this trial proceed against Ben Smith, which is what we are here for?"

"That's smack-dab what I intend to do, Mr. LeRoy." Sam Elko turned toward the judge. "Your Honor, during the recess, I spoke to you about a sixteen-millimeter film we've just received. We're all set with the film and projector, and the screen is being set up as I speak. May I go ahead and show it?"

LeRoy was up.

"Your Honor, I haven't seen the film. This has gone too far!"

"Neither have I, and I'll decide when too far is too far. We'll start the film. If you have any objection, speak up then. But right now, sit down and clam up, Mr. LeRoy."

The film opened with an exterior shot of Will Rogers standing close to a fence post while holding a Bible, in the background a mountain landscape.

There was a startled reaction from just about everyone in the courtroom as Rogers began to talk.

"Your Honor, friends, I'm Will Rogers, and I hereby swear to tell the truth, the whole truth, and nothing but the truth, so help me God.

"I wanted to be with you there in Sheridan as a character witness for my friend Ben Smith, a man of character, strength, humanity, honesty, and independence. God-given traits that made the West, and our entire country, yes, our flag, the symbol — the envy of people all over the world — the hope for a better way of life.

"Ben Smith's life sums up what this country stands for — and I stand beside him in this case and cause that will be decided in your courtroom.

"In the past years, we have come a fair piece in the preservation of two American symbols. The eagle and the buffalo.

"But there's another symbol of America, of America that ought to be preserved in this high, wide, and sanctified country — the mustang!

"And in that cause, I walk hand in hand with Ben Smith.

"As I said, I wanted to be there with Ben and all of you. But by the time you watch this film, another friend and I will be flying on an expedition to Alaska and other line camps.

"We've just wrapped up shooting on the set of *In Old Kentucky.* So, until we meet again — adios and Godspeed — from a damn lucky cowboy, who, like Ben Smith, grew up in the great American West."

The magna-majority of people sitting and standing, in fact all except those favoring the prosecution, clapped, whistled, and yay-hooed when Will Rogers concluded. Most of the film's spectators were fans of Will Rogers and welcomed the sight and sound of the Oklahoma cowboy.

"Order! Order!" The gavel drummed, and Judge Aikins blared above it, "Order! I say. The court is still in session. When this tribunal is terminated you can beat drums, build bonfires, and parade from here to Christmas! But there will be no more demonstrations while Judge Clarence Daniel Aikins sits on this bench. Now, Mr. LeRoy, if you have any objection to the film we've just seen, you can save your breath to blow out the candle. Mr. Elko, you can go ahead with your defense."

"The defense calls Ben Smith."

Ben Smith took the oath and the stand.

"Now, Ben, my friend . . ."

LeRoy was up.

"Your Honor!"

"Well, he is my friend as well as my client. Ben's a lot of people's friend, and you ought to have more friends like him and Will Rogers . . . Mr. LeRoy."

"Elko," the judge pointed, "you've had your last shot. Now, behave yourself or it'll cost you a hundred."

"I stand contrite, Your Honor. Now, Ben, you're an All-'Round Champion Rodeo Cowboy, aren't you?"

Ben Smith had been uncomfortable throughout most of the proceedings and more so now on the stand.

"Aren't you?" Elko repeated.

"Yes, sir."

"Three times. That right?"

Ben bit his lip, took a breath, and made up his mind. He stood up and faced the judge.

"What's the matter, Ben?" Elko took a step and leaned on his cane. "You sick?"

For answer, Ben spoke faster than usual.

"I'm getting sick of all this talk, Your Honor. I want to change my plea to guilty and . . ."

The spectators and press, and prosecution and judge reacted, but not as much as Sam Elko.

"Over my corpus delicti! Your Honor, I want a recess to confer with my client, who is temporarily insane."

"This whole thing is insane," Ben slowed down to his usual tempo. "Judge, no matter what Sam Elko, my friend, says, I'm not gonna change my mind. I'm guilty . . . but can I say something?"

Amanda Reese and all the other spectators in the courtroom waited as Judge Aikins paused for just a beat.

"It's a mite irregular, Mr. Smith . . . but so's this whole shebang. Go ahead and say."

Elko threw up both his hands, including the one holding his cane, then scratched his head with the other one.

Ben, unused to making speeches, started uncertainly, but as he went on, his voice and the words got stronger.

"There's something wrong, Your Honor. Killing mustangs is wrong. Those herds . . . well, there's nothing can take their place."

He found the words because he was saying what was in his heart and everyone listened.

"I know the arguments. The mustangs are

worthless. They eat up the grass. Their time has passed. Maybe they're what you call 'obsolete.' I know something about that."

Judge Aikins smiled.

"But in their time, well, they were worth something. They did something for all of us. They helped us to settle this land. We couldn't've done it without them. They helped us when we needed help. Now they need us to quit killing 'em."

James Deegan looked at Norkey, who was not looking at anybody.

"To let 'em stay independent. They're about the last free spirit — as Will Rogers said about the eagle and buffalo — there is . . . out here."

By now, Sam Elko was smiling.

"The government sets up thousands of miles of land as what they call 'testing grounds' — where they blow up the earth and everything on it. Couldn't they set up a place for something to live?"

Amanda Reese was getting close to tears.

"We ought to have refuges for the wild horses that are still left. My place could be one of them. There's got to be other places in this creation-big country where they could live . . . and we can remember . . . how it was . . . and should be."

Amanda, Skinny Dugan, the Krantz broth-

385

ers, James Deegan, Laura Layton, Elko, Sheriff Granger, Kit Carson, Randy Rawlins, and virtually all the rest, except for Norkey and the other mustangers, were stirred in reaction to Ben Smith's poised, but impassioned plea.

"Your Honor, there's got to be a way. It can't be right to drive 'em half-crazy from airplanes — shoot 'em with shotguns — chase 'em with trucks till their lungs bust — break their legs — hobble 'em — truss 'em up suffering — and ship 'em half-dead to a cannery. There ought to be laws against that."

The press corps was getting it all down, all of what would be a hell of a story, of a series of stories.

"I think — well, there's got to be something else to feed dogs and cats besides those horses. Your Honor . . . I'm guilty of that."

Ben Smith sat down, but just about everybody in the courtroom got up, clapping and whooping — a standing ovation.

Judge Aikins banged his gavel at least a half-dozen times, each time louder.

"Order! Let's have order. Everybody quiet down or I'll clear the courtroom before rendering a verdict."

Some semblance of order was restored,

and Judge Aikins knew when and how to take a dramatic pause before he began.

But before that, Sam Elko was on his feet.

"Your Honor, I just want to make it official, speaking on behalf of my client, the defense rests gleefully."

"That's a relief, Mr. Elko. And I am declaring that on this hoedown there's been enough arguin', on both sides, so we'll dispense with the summations. I'm ready with the verdict. So, stand up, Mr. Smith."

Ben Smith stood. So did Sam Elko.

"Ben Smith, you will pay the damages to those . . . 'gentlemen' — the court sentences you to one year in prison . . ."

There were gasps and groans throughout the room, until . . .

". . . Sentence suspended."

Cheers and applause. People rushed up to shake Ben's hand. Amanda, Elko, Skinny Dugan, the sheriff, even James Dugan. Hugs and congratulations overlapped.

"Jurisprudence in its finest hour," Elko shouted. "Congratulations, my boy!"

"Ben," Amanda whispered, "Gallant Man."

James Deegan shook Ben's hand.

"I want you to know that I'm going to make some changes, Ben."

Among them was a man about forty with

an easy smile who might have been a school-teacher, but wasn't.

"Mr. Smith, my name is Charles Sutton. I'm the junior senator of our state, and I agree with you. So do a lot of other people, including my colleagues. I want to thank you for giving us some ammunition. I'd like to be consulting with you if you don't mind."

"Just try me, sir."

Norkey stepped through and faced Ben.

"Since you're going to pay damages, I'll send you my bill for damages . . ."

"Give me that bill," James Deegan said, "I'll pay."

"No, sir," Ben shook his head, "I pay my own bills, but thanks."

"Then I want to check that bill, and Nor-key, send it to me. I never want to see you on the Big Brawny again."

The press corps started to crowd in around Ben Smith with questions and shouts.

Judge Aikins banged his gavel.

"As for the gentlemen of the press, you all can hike over to the jury room. Mr. Smith'll get there when he gets around to it . . . and so will I."

"Ty-Roan!" Skinny Dugan ordered. "Back to the press-plow! Once again, the *Beacon*'s

388

scooped the whole country!"

"All in a day's day!" both Krantz brothers proclaimed.

Laura Layton pressed Ben's arm.

"Ben, congratulations and good luck."

"Thank you, ma'am."

Elizabeth Deegan and Pepper pushed their way into the room and through the crowd.

"Liz! Honey, when did you get here?"

"She called me from the airport to pick her up," Pepper said. "Jimmy was asleep, so . . ."

"I came out to hit you some good news. Instead, we got hit with this."

She handed her husband a piece of paper.

"Read it," she said.

Deegan did.

Dad — I don't like you for what you did to Ben and the mustangs. I'm going to find Black. I don't want to see you anymore.

Jimmy

Deegan turned to Tom Granger.

"Sheriff, I want you to order a search-and-rescue operation — land, air — everything! I'm offering a reward — five thousand dollars. Without his insulin, Jimmy'll die."

Deegan hadn't quite finished the last word when he caught himself and looked at his wife.

Elizabeth Deegan came as close to crying as he could remember.

Ben brushed Deegan's arm.

"Wait just a minute . . ."

"Wait for what? My son will . . ."

"There's more than one kind of medicine . . . I'll tell you on the way. Let's get a move on!"

CHAPTER TWENTY-SEVEN

Through the vast domain of landscape, the caravan raced across the flat grassland toward the ridgeline.

Amanda driving, Ben next to her — in the backseat, James and Elizabeth Deegan — followed by Pepper in the pickup — with Doc ABC, Sheriff Granger, and Deputy Ingester in the sheriff's car — an ambulance — and above them, two search planes.

Ben pointed toward the barely visible narrow-channel threshold to the escarpment.

Amanda wheeled the station wagon into the passageway and forged into the concealed canyon with the caravan following the wake of dust.

The pack of searchers was forced to slow as they climbed higher toward the escarpment near the summit cap.

"Hold it!" Ben called.

Amanda slammed the brake.

"What is it?" Deegan leaned forward. "Why'd we stop?"

Ben nodded, smiled, poked ahead and to the right.

Black stood near the summit, his head high, his mane fluttering in the wind, then nodding. Next to him Black's mare and the Appaloosa.

In front, Pinto, and beside the pony, Jimmy, weary, but wide-eyed and smiling at the sight of his mother and father together, with Ben and Amanda coming toward him.

His dad lifted Jimmy, and his mother kissed him again and again.

The rest of the caravan came to a stop.

Amanda reached for Ben's hand.

At that moment, no words were spoken. No words were necessary.

Laura Layton's Packard was parked near the front of the Big Brawny headquarters. Word had already spread about Jimmy's rescue. She and Dave Bergin stood near the first step of the porch, along with Joe Higgins and some of the ranch hands, all in good spirits.

The Deegan family, and Pepper, carrying Jimmy, got out of Deegan's Chrysler.

"I'll take Jimmy up to his room, Mr. D. Okay?"

Deegan nodded.

"We'll be right up, Jimmy."

"Neat," the boy said, his eyes half-closed.

Higgins and the wranglers smiled, waved, then walked away.

Laura Layton took a step. Looked at James and Elizabeth Deegan.

"Excuse me. This won't take long. Mr. Bergin has a piece of paper with a figure on it for the Layton Ranch. If it's agreeable to you, the ranch is yours."

Deegan reached for the paper, started to unfold it.

Laura Layton shrugged.

"The West is not for some people, and some people are not for the West. I'm leaving. Going back to greener pastures."

She pointed to the paper.

"Is the figure agreeable?"

"You've got a deal."

Laura Layton turned her radiant face to Elizabeth Deegan.

"And so have you, Mrs. Deegan. You've got a good man. Treasure him."

She turned away.

"Come on, Dave, you can work out the details later. These people have got things to talk about."

They walked toward the Packard.

■ ■ ■ ■

Pepper, near the bed, pointed.

Jimmy, his head on the pillow, nodded just a bit, blinked, smiled, and closed his already half-closed lids and was asleep.

Pepper turned and walked softly past James and Elizabeth Deegan, then through the open door.

The Deegans followed, closed the door, stood in the hallway, and looked at each other.

"Not a bad day so far," she said.

"What do you mean, 'so far'?"

"Well, Ben did all right at the trial. Jimmy's safe in bed . . . and you, executive *ranchero* that you are, made a deal for a next-door *ranchera* . . . not bad so far."

"But let's go a little farther."

"Like what?"

"Like what was the good news you came all the way out here to hit me with?"

"Oh . . . that?"

"Yeah, that."

"What do you know! I nearly forgot about that."

"Are you teasing . . . just a little bit?"

"Who? Little ol' me?"

"Yeah, little ol' you . . . like in the good

old days."

"Oh, no . . . not like that. It's just that I've severed my Gordian knot."

"Your what?"

"My deal with Liz-E-Design."

"What do you mean 'severed'?"

"Sold out."

"True?"

"For a sweet profit."

"Congratulations."

"But . . ."

"There's always a 'but.' . . . But what?"

"I still have a title . . . and a stipend."

"Uh-huh. What's the . . ."

"Stipend?"

"Title."

"We're still thinking about that. Probably 'Consultant.' "

"What's wrong with 'Executive Consultant'?"

"Nothing . . . not a damn thing," she smiled.

"I think we've come to that 'farther' part."

"What's that?"

James Deegan looked across the hall to the master bedroom.

She moved closer to him.

"Lead the way, Jimbo."

"This way, Stranger . . . no more."

■ ■ ■ ■

Ben and Amanda stood on the porch, facing the open front door of the cabin on the Little Brawny.

"Just a minute, honey."

"What is it, Ben?"

He turned and looked at the sweeping landscape, the flat, green open range, the up-sloping hillocks, and the purple peaks that touched the clouds.

"It's beautiful, Ben. Isn't that what you're thinking?"

He nodded.

"And something else . . ."

"What else?"

"About that song that says, 'You can't ever go home again.' I think you can, if you bring someone home with you . . . like I'm lucky enough to do."

"Luck, fate, destiny, kismet, call it what you will. That coin has two sides, yours and mine."

"It was good of Judge Aikins to stick around long enough to hitch us up in double harness."

"I wanted to go Dutch on the two dollars," she smiled.

"We're even. I didn't pay you for the

prescription, Dr. Reese. Besides, this cabin isn't much. Doesn't even have a bedroom. Just a bunk to sleep on."

"Sounds cozy."

"But I'm going to do some reconstruction on the Little Brawny, including our home, with a real bedroom and everything. You need a space to carry on your veterinary work."

"You want me to do that?"

"Told you I go for bloody blouses and the fragrance of manure. Now, can I carry the bride across the threshold?"

He started to do it.

"Oh, hold on. I just thought about something."

"What?"

"During the construction, where are we going to sleep?"

"Uh . . ."

"How about the barn?"

"Now why didn't I think of that first?"

"You did."

Ben lifted and carried Amanda into the cabin, then kicked the door closed.

In the distance the Krantz brothers watched from the seat of their truck, turned to each other.

"All in a day's day," they both said.

■ ■ ■ ■

Inside the Gulfstream executive jet, Senator Jimmy Deegan still sat at the small desk talking, and Patrick Merrill still sat listening without interruption.

"Well, Patrick, that's about it. Ol' Skinny Dugan got his scoop in the *Sheridan Beacon.* It was out on the street within hours. With, as I remember, an Extra that went something like this:

"Headline: MUSTANGS TO BE!

"Lead: Ben Smith, Local Hero Rides to Save Mustangs

"First paragraph: Ben Smith, falsely accused of destruction of property, assault, and attempted murder, is a free man. Smith was defended by lawyer Sam Elko — hero of San Juan Hill. Our cowboy had been bushwhacked and beaten up by a gang of marauding mustangers. The next day, Ben rode into the crew at their dirty work, with his Winchester at ready aim and went to work. Smith disabled their plane and truck. Then he roped, tied the culprits to heavy tires, and marched the mustangers through our fair community."

Deegan leaned back and recalled.

"Newspapers all over the country carried

the story on the front page above the fold.

BEN SMITH, CHAMPION COWBOY, PREVAILS — SAVES MUSTANGS

Boss of Little Brawny Has His Day in Court

WESTERN STATES ACT TO PRESERVE MUSTANGS

"Radio commentators chimed in with accounts about Ben and his heroic effort to stop the brutal roundup and slaughter for pet food of historic horses.

"Ben could've made a considerable fortune just appearing at rodeos but chose to stay on the ranch with Amanda and spread the word from there."

Patrick Merrill raised both hands and finally spoke.

"Senator, that's some story. Why didn't you let me get out a press release that you were coming to the memorial? We could get a lot of publicity. It's still not too late."

"No. This trip isn't for publicity. It's on my own time and expense. I don't want anybody at the memorial because I'm there. I want them to come because of my friend."

Neither the senator nor Merrill had noticed that the attendant, Trudy Ryan, had been standing and listening to Senator Jimmy Deegan.

"Excuse me, Senator. You might be interested to know that as we're preparing to land, we're passing over the Theodore Roosevelt Dam."

"Thank you, miss."

"You know," she smiled, "they ought to make a movie about Ben Smith."

"If they do," Patrick Merrill said, "I'd be pleased to take you to see it."

"And my fiancé?"

"Oh . . ."

She didn't wait for an answer.

The voice of the pilot came over the speaker.

"This is Bob Radisson. Buckle up, folks, we're about to start our descent. By the way, Senator, you can look out the window and to your right, catch a glimpse of the Big Brawny; so, you're practically home away from home again."

EPILOGUE

There were changes.

During the forty years from 1935 to 1975, this country staggered from FDR and the Great Depression to World War II, Harry Truman, and the atomic bomb, to Korea, the happy days of the Eisenhower years, JFK's assassination, LBJ, Vietnam, Nixon and Watergate, to President Gerald Ford.

And in motion pictures an actor went from B-minus westerns to the longest-lasting, most formidable Academy Award winner on screen — John Wayne.

And there were changes on the Little Brawny. Not so much *of* the landscape, but *on* the landscape.

Still attractive, Dr. Amanda Reese Smith stood straight and proud, with a serene gleam in her eyes looking at, and thinking about, what had been her home, her life, since Ben Smith carried her over the threshold of a little cabin four decades ago.

The cabin gone. In its place what Ben Smith had described to his bride on the porch. A real ranch headquarters, with space for her to carry on her work even to this day. Then there was a larger, more accommodating barn and corrals. And there were two other structures, a bunkhouse for the ranch hands and quarters for the regulars and volunteers to tend and arrange for mustang ponies to be adopted as ranch pets, and for young riders.

All evidence that cattle and mustangs can exist together.

And there was a temporary change for this day. The area around headquarters had been set up with platform, table, and chairs where Amanda would be seated as Senator Jimmy Deegan would speak. And the surrounding area, chairs, chairs, chairs, to be occupied by men, women, and children — and space for those who would have to stand. Some dressed in ranch attire, but among them, businessmen and -women, bankers, and those in military uniforms. Citizens from all walks of life. There was a section of seats set aside for current wranglers on the Little Brawny and for the young and older volunteers for the preservation of mustangs.

By noon, they were all on the Little

Brawny. They had come to bid farewell to the last cowboy of the Gower Gulch Gang.

WILL ROGERS — August 15, 1935
His plane, piloted by Wiley Post, on an expedition to the Soviet Union, crashed at Point Barrow, Alaska, killing Post and Rogers.

TOM MIX — October 12, 1940
While speeding in his Cord Phaeton from Tucson, Arizona, the car skidded off a broken bridge. Tom Mix did not survive.

BUCK JONES — November 30, 1942
He went into a blazing fire three times and rescued victims. The fourth time he didn't come back.

Today, those pilgrims had come to the Little Brawny in tribute to the life of another remembered buckaroo.

Ben Smith at eighty was still strong, rugged, and handsome. Then, after all those years of robust, often dangerous, living, Ben Smith, in less than a minute, was dead of an embolism.

The Little Brawny's nearest neighbors, James and Elizabeth Deegan, had been gone for three years. They passed away two days apart. First Liz, then James, after one of their adventurous travels, this one on an African safari.

And most of the old-timers were gone during those forty years.

Skinny Dugan, Tyrone Roan, Sam Elko, Doc ABC, Walt Swicegood, Gotch Tomkins, the Krantz brothers, Tom Granger, Dave Bergin, Clay Sykes.

But two of Sheridan's WWII veterans who had known Ben were present. Tommy Swicegood, survivor of Tarawa, and his family. Nearby, Randy "Lucky" Rawlins, of the "Bastards of Bastogne" in the Battle of the Bulge. Young Sergeant Rawlins stood three or four feet from the platoon's lieutenant who was torn apart by a German shell, and Randy came home without a mark on him.

Kit Carson was absent, still kicking but not as high, retired in a Palm Springs sunburnished bungalow she had purchased under her baptismal name, Irma Krompke.

Laura Layton Aldrich, hale, beautiful, haughty, and splendidly engowned as ever, sat in the front row next to her "greener pastures" real estate tycoon of San Francisco, Robert Ellis Aldrich.

Nearby, also in the front row, Patrick Merrill, and next to him, out of uniform but even more fetching in a blue summer dress,

404

Trudy Ryan. Fiancé or not, Trudy wanted to hear the rest of Senator Deegan's story, so Merrill took the opportunity of inviting her. Besides, it was a long way back to the East, and anything could happen.

Dr. Amanda Reese Smith, defying her seventy-odd years with grace and surety, sat near Senator Jimmy Deegan, who stood speaking to the assemblage.

The senator paused briefly and looked beyond the crowd toward the expanse he, as a young boy and in his later years, had ridden with Ben Smith, then he continued.

"Ben Smith never held public office. He never aspired to possess great power or wealth. He was strong and independent, but a good neighbor and husband."

The senator looked at Amanda, who nodded slightly and smiled.

"Ben Smith changed my life. And I didn't realize how many other lives until I came back here today."

Senator Jimmy Deegan pointed to the table filled with three baskets stacked to the brim.

"Hundreds and hundreds of telegrams, letters, and cards from every section of the country.

"From John Wayne, Gene Autry, Clint Eastwood, Roy and Dale Rogers, Clint

Walker, Burt Reynolds, Fess Parker, Casey Tibbs, Charles Bronson, Angie Dickinson, Barbara Stanwyck, Dale Robertson, and the governor of California, Ronald Reagan.

"From Senators Barry Goldwater and Ted Kennedy . . . and from President Gerald Ford.

"And newscasters David Brinkley, Dan Rather, Walter Cronkite, and Roger Mudd."

Senator Jimmy Deegan walked around to the front of the table.

"Because of Ben Smith a lot of things have changed. But just as important, because of Ben Smith and people like him, a lot of things haven't changed . . . not in nature's cathedral."

He took a breath.

"Please turn, listen, and take a look."

There was the far-off sound of hoofbeats, hoofbeats drumming closer . . . a galloping panorama . . . a high-headed herd of fleeting mustangs. Mustangs led by a striding stallion, swarming across the flatland toward the horizon and the distant shoulders of the Little Brawny.

The audience, led by the Little Brawny wranglers and volunteers, stood, cheered, and clapped, then sat back, turned to Senator Jimmy Deegan, who paused to remember.

"Ben Smith had the heart of a mustang. His life embodied the spirit of the West. And it's that same spirit that unites us . . . and at the same time sets us free.

"I remember so many things about Ben Smith. You all know the old adage:

" 'There never was a horse
that couldn't be rode.
There never was cowboy
that couldn't be throwed.'

"When I was a youngster, Ben told me about another legend of the West.

" 'Cowboys don't die.
They ride into the sunset
and come out to the sunrise . . .
along the Rainbow Trail.'

"So, good night, Ben . . . and good morning."

THE WISE OLD MAN OF THE WEST: PATHS OF GLORY

For
MARY FRANCES
"Walking through the path
of life with you, ma'am,
has been a very gracious thing."

It was between wars.

A somber twilight April afternoon at the Arlington National Cemetery in Virginia.

The Wise Old Man of the West stood with a solemn look. Clean-shaven except for a neatly trimmed military mustache, dressed in his usual attire, a dark gray vested suit, but now his homburg was in one hand, and in the other, his Malacca cane with the tip gently touching the faint imprint of one of the graves.

It was not his first visit.

But, inevitably, it would be his last — sometime in the future — not too soon, he hoped — in one of the narrow cells that lined the landscape.

The cemetery had been dedicated during the Civil War in 1864 on land formerly owned by General, then President, George Washington, to honor soldiers of previous and future wars of this country.

A shadow fell over the simple tombstone.

CAPTAIN THEODORE GRAY
1841–1865

The Wise Old Man turned and faced a handsome woman dressed in black whose age was not far from his own, on one side or the other.

Her voice was even younger and stronger than she appeared.

"I come to this field of yesterdays — and no tomorrows — to say good night to Ted whenever possible. And you? You must have known him, or you wouldn't be standing here."

"Yes . . . he was my commanding officer . . . and you, ma'am?"

"School-days sweethearts. We were to be married when the war was over. But for Ted . . . and me, the war was over too late."

"Yes, ma'am. Exactly thirty years ago. One day too late. April ninth, 1865. The day Generals Grant and Lee met at Appomattox, only we didn't know it at the time even though we weren't too far from Appomattox."

"But there were rumors, weren't there?"

"There are always rumors in the army . . ."

"Ted mentioned them in his last letter,

mailed to me after he died."

"Yes, ma'am, I mailed it."

"I thank you for that."

"I mailed several letters to . . ."

"I still have mine."

She gazed at the tombstone and spoke just above a whisper.

"Captain Theodore Gray . . . it's irony, or fate, or destiny . . ."

"That you and I should meet here?"

"Ted used to say, with a smile because he wasn't sure about his family origins, and Gray is a common name, that he might have been a relative of Thomas Gray, who wrote a poem called 'Elegy Written in a Country Churchyard' and this is his country's grave-yard — irony, fate, destiny. Are you familiar with the poem?"

"Somewhat. I know how it ends." The Wise Old Man spoke slowly.

"The boast of heraldry, the pomp of pow'r,
    And all that beauty, all that wealth e'er
      gave,
Awaits alike th' inevitable hour.
    The paths of glory lead but to the
      grave."

She took a step back from the grave.

415

"And this is how Ted's path of glory ended."

"Are you so sure?"

"I said it. . . . Here, there are no tomorrows."

"That depends . . ."

"On what?"

"On what you believe."

"Or what you don't believe." She looked again at the tombstone. "I don't believe that Ted can hear us now."

"Then why do you come?"

She closed her eyes then opened them.

"Because I can't be buried here. I come to be near him and think of what might have been . . . what a waste."

"Maybe not."

"What do you mean?"

"There was a not-so-young lieutenant in our regiment, never mind his name. We were all close to the edge, but he was leaning over it. He had heard those rumors that the South was doomed and would surrender within days . . . probably within hours . . . if not already.

"The lieutenant made a cardinal mistake of arguing audibly, on the brink of disobedience with a superior officer, for enough of the regiment to hear.

" 'Captain, Hill 103 won't make a speck

of difference. The war is virtually over.'

" 'Lieutenant, there's no such word as *virtually* in war.'

" 'Captain Gray, some of us have followed you for years — tired and wounded — can barely stand, much less ride and attack. This isn't Vicksburg, Gettysburg, Atlanta, or Richmond. It's a hill, a pile of dirt with a number — not even a name. If we charge up Hill 103 more of us will die . . . and *why*?'

"Ma'am, your Captain Gray removed a piece of paper from his tunic and answered so most of us could hear.

" 'This is this morning's dispatch from General Philip H. Sheridan. It reads, *Captain Gray, your regiment is ordered to attack and take Hill 103 . . .*'

"The lieutenant smirked.

" 'Suppose that dispatch, that order, never arrived — maybe the war is over — dispatches get lost — it's happened before . . . and . . .'

" 'This one didn't get lost, and one more thing you ought to know, Lieutenant — yes, we're tired, exhausted, but soldiers obey orders. My hand is not as steady as it should be, but it's steady enough that if you say one more word that even sounds like disobedience of an order, I'll pull my sidearm, aim it between your two front teeth, and squeeze the trigger. *Why?* Because soldiers live or die — but the regiment lives forever. Now, this regiment has its orders . . . We will mount up and attack.'

"We did that, ma'am . . . and took Hill 103."

"And that took Ted's life . . . and in a way, mine. For what? Glory? If so, was it worth it? Think of what he left behind."

"I do. Often."

"You can't take anything with you."

"Yes, ma'am. You can."

"What?"

"You can take glory with you."

The Wise Old Man looked around at the countless tombstones.

"They all take glory with them. Those who are buried here, and those who will be."

"I'd like to think so."

"So did another poet in another poem with a different ending. Would you care to hear it?"

"I would," she nodded.

"Sound, sound the clarion, fill the fife!
To all the sensual world proclaim,
One crowded hour of glorious life
Is worth an age without a name."

418

The Wise Old Man's gaze shifted from the tombstone to the school-days sweetheart.

"Maybe Captain Gray and all of them are still reliving that crowded hour of glory. In the regimental record, Hill 103 is now known as Captain Theodore Gray Hill."

"It is?"

"Yes, ma'am. Your captain won his last battle."

"You think he knows that?"

"I do."

"So do I. . . . Tell me, what happened to that not-too-old lieutenant?"

"He survived. Not a mark on him."

The Wise Old Man removed the watch from his vest pocket.

"It's getting late, ma'am. Soon be dark. May I walk you back to the gate?"

"No. I'd like to be with Ted for a while, until . . . the next time."

The Wise Old Man nodded and started to walk away but turned and looked back at the sound of her voice.

"Just a minute."

"Yes, ma'am?"

"Thank you . . . soldier."

The Wise Old Man of the West reached into a pocket for his meerschaum pipe.

ABOUT THE AUTHOR

Andrew J. Fenady was born in Toledo, Ohio. A veteran writer and producer in Hollywood, Fenady created and produced *The Rebel* (1959-1961) for television, starring Nick Adams. The top-rated show lasted three seasons and the Fenady-penned theme song, "Johnny Yuma," became a No. 1 hit for Johnny Cash. He wrote and produced the 1969 John Wayne hit *Chisum* and the popular TV western series *Hondo* and *Branded.* His other credits include the adaptation of Jack London's *The Sea Wolf,* with Charles Bronson and Christopher Reeve, and the western feature *Ride Beyond Vengeance,* which starred Chuck Connors. His acclaimed western novels include *Big Ike, Riders to Moon Rock, The Trespassers, The Summer of Jack London, The Range Wolf,* and *Destiny Made Them Brothers.* Fenady presently lives in Los Angeles and has been honored with The Golden Boot

Award, the Silver Spur Award, and the Owen Wister Award from the Western Writers of America for his lifetime contribution to westerns.